Hoping

for

Hemingway

a novel by

Kelsey Kingsley

D1737035

Copyright

To Ernest Hemingway—

For the inspiration to lose myself again in the craft.

A Note from the Author

Dear Reader,

Some months ago, I watched a documentary about Ernest Hemingway, and I fell madly in love with a man who loved to fall in love. It sparked such a wonderful inspiration in me, to write a story about a woman with ridiculously high standards, who connects with a mentally ill man who's otherwise perfect in every way.

So, I wrote it.

Now, I have written some books that really resonate with me. They thrive inside my head for months after writing them—sometimes, even years. *The Life We Wanted*, for example. Oh, man, that Sebastian Moore. He will forever be a character that speaks to me, long after I'm willing to listen. This book, though …

This book was different, and it was difficult and heavy. Maybe due to the subject matter, or perhaps it comes down to simply where my head has been these past couple of years. But no matter how hard it was, the love between Clara and August kept me going. I felt it too deeply to give up on it.

I hope you'll feel it, too.

Kelsey

CHAPTER ONE

The screen door opened with an agonizing groan and swung out into the torrential downpour. Yesterday, the skies had opened to drench southern Connecticut with some much-needed rain, and it hadn't stopped since. The dark, angry clouds overhead were lit from within with another bolt of silvery lightning, right before the clap of thunder sounded from not so far away. And I was standing in the middle of the storm. With eyes squinting and hair dripping, as I waited for Agnes to muster up the courage to leave the house and use the bathroom.

"You're killing me, Ag," I complained, gesturing wildly for my four-legged companion to accompany me into the wet embrace of the worst storm either of us had seen since a Nor'easter had pummeled the area a few years ago. "You asked to go outside, so come on."

The dog eyed me with stubborn refusal, her eyebrows lowered and tail still against the kitchen floorboards.

"It's not even that bad out here," I shouted, just in time for another resounding boom of thunder to raise the hairs on my arms.

Agnes turned and hurried to hide beneath the table, so with a begrudged sigh, I entered the house and allowed the screen door to slap closed within doorframe behind me.

"Suit yourself," I muttered in her direction as I returned to my chair.

I left the back door open to let the house fill with the peaceful sounds of rain and thunder, and after a few minutes, Agnes emerged from her hiding place. She took her usual place by my side, while I resumed a dinner of reheated roasted chicken and rice. It was delicious, one of my mother's best recipes, but after eating the same meal for the third night in a row, the flavors had begun to shift against my taste buds. It was now boring and uninspired, but there was still half a tray left in the fridge.

When my mother had dropped it off three days ago, I had protested, insisting there was no way I could eat that much on my own. Her response was to remind me that, if I would finally get married, there would be no such thing as "too much." So, out of spite and stubborn determination, I was going to make sure I ate every last bite, even if I had to choke it down.

Agnes lifted a paw and laid it in my lap. I rolled my eyes toward her until our gazes met. She opened her mouth in a tongue-waggling smile, and I sighed. The dog was as manipulative as they come and she knew I would never deny her.

"Fine, I'll share a little with you, too," I muttered through my smile, before scratching her behind the ears. "Just don't tell Mom. I don't need her using wasted food as a reason to set me up again."

***

The sultry beat of Peggy Lee's "Fever," combined with a flickering candlelit glow, provided the perfect atmosphere for a late-night soak in my cherished clawfoot tub. It had been one of the biggest selling points when I bought the small, two bedroom cottage a few years ago, and I made sure to enjoy it at least a few times a week.

Somewhere in the bathroom, a glass bottle was knocked over, and I rolled my eyes.

"Bumby! Knock it off!" I scolded for what felt like the thousandth time since I'd returned home from work. One of my four cats jumped from his favorite perch—a shelf above the toilet—and dashed out of the room in a flurry of clumsy limbs, leaving Peggy and me alone to enjoy the solace and relaxation of the candlelit bathroom in peace.

When the song ended, I was burdened by precisely two seconds of complete silence before the next song began. With my eyes closed, those two seconds provided an acute awareness of how alone I was in this house, despite the small zoo of animals I lived with. The dog, cats, bird, and fish generally kept me from succumbing to loneliness. But there is a very specific type of companionship that only another person can give and that was a companionship I hadn't felt in a long time. Not since my last boyfriend, who I had only been with for a summer a few years ago and before I had realized that I only enjoyed his flavor of companionship when we could be outside. While we were on the beach, with the sun touching his hair with blond highlights and a cold beer in his hand. Come the Fall, when the air was too cold to spend our nights with sand and waves, I had quickly learned that we had nothing to talk about. It was only then that I realized we had spent the summer not really talking at all.

In my entire life, I had never had a problem breaking up with a man, and I had no problem breaking up with him then. But for those two seconds, in between Peggy Lee and Perry Como, I wondered what it might have been like if I had learned to talk with him and if we'd still be together today. We might have gotten married and had a baby or two. We might have decided that a little house on the shore with a clawfoot tub was no place to raise a family, and we might have sold the cottage to buy a much bigger, more suitable home. I imagined it would've been a nice house, because I liked living in nice houses, and I smiled at the thought of having a big, flourishing garden, where my husband and I would spend our summer afternoons, while the kids played in the yard. Because we liked being outside, where the sun could touch his hair with blond highlights.

Two seconds isn't really much time at all though, and when Perry Como's voice began to flood the silence with sound and joy, I didn't feel all that lonely anymore. That boyfriend from a few years ago was probably married by now, to a wife who cared more about his conversation than his blond highlights, and I hoped he was happy. I hoped he had everything he ever wanted, and that he hadn't waited until it was too late.

For me, at forty-two, it all seemed far too late now. But I didn't mind, as I soaked in my tub, waiting for the bubbles to melt and the water to cool. I had my life, and it was good.

I just dreaded those two seconds.

***

With the windows open to welcome the songs of the storm and the Sound into my home, I curled up on the couch in my bathrobe, with a book in my hand and Agnes at my feet. I sighed at the familiar creak of the book's spine as it opened, and looked down at the comfortable words of Ernest Hemingway's *The Old Man and the Sea*. It was a story I had read so often the pages now seemed to wear the patterns of my fingertips. I knew it well, like an old friend knows the things a new friend doesn't, and it knew me.

I smiled as I began to read, the weather outside provided the perfect ambience for a night of being curled up with a book. Agnes settled in on the red Persian rug, laying her head against my feet, while Bumby cuddled with his litter mates, Patsy, Twain, and Peggy, on the loveseat. The words began to wrap around me like a warm blanket, as the characters greeted me with lines etched into my memory, and I hunkered down against the plush back of the couch for a night of comfortable perfection.

A crash of thunder rekindled the dwindling storm, and the dimly lit lamps flickered. Startled, Agnes lifted her head and I sat up straighter to calm my heart with reminders that the electricity had only blinked momentarily and that it was fine. But deep down, beneath the strength I encouraged my heart to hold onto, I wished someone else was there. Someone other than the animals. What I really wanted, was a man to make me feel safe, to assure me that he was there to protect my foolish mind from the threatening thunder and lightning. The loneliness crashed in as swiftly as the storm above, with foreign memories of kisses and cuddles, and I sighed to *The Old Man and the Sea* and the old friends within the pages. Those characters I knew so well but could never hold in my arms, and I was unsure of which I preferred.

CHAPTER TWO

My mother—Nora McKinley—had always been a fine lady, with a fondness for Gordon Lightfoot, white wine, and Old English Sheepdogs. She loved the beach, lighthouses, and a nicely cooked steak. Her love for her husband was meant for the movies and her passion for painting was romanticism at its best. But nothing, absolutely nothing, rivaled her devotion to her two little girls. Not a thing in the world could ever tear her away from them. Even when Marjorie, the younger of the two, had announced that she was pregnant at sixteen, Nora didn't reprimand or demand for drastic measures to be taken. She had simply looked at her teenaged daughter, pulled her into a reassuring hug, and told her they would do what they had to do to figure it out.

Because that's what Nora McKinley always did. She figured things out. And right now, she was once again trying to figure out a solution to my decaying love life.

"So, guess who I ran into today at the Fisch Market?"

As I reached for the bowl of scrambled eggs, I shot a glance at my mother over my sister's dining room table. Her eyes were directed at only me, her hands held to her chin in hopeful anticipation.

Groaning, I asked, "Gee, Mom, I can't imagine. Who did you run into at the Fisch Market?"

"Dave," she replied in a sing-song tone.

"Who's Dave?" Marjie asked, glancing between my mother and me.

Shrugging as I spooned a heaping serving of eggs onto my plate, I muttered, "No clue."

"Is he that guy with the, um, the …" Christy, my sister's eldest daughter, snapped her fingers with every beat of her shaking head. "Oh! Wait! He's that guy with the ugly bulldog and top hat, isn't he?"

My mother pursed her lips and pulled in an impatient sigh. "No," she groaned, shaking her head. "He's the waiter at Dick's Diner. You know, the cute one?"

"There's a cute one?" Marjorie asked, and Christy grimaced.

"You're joking, right?" I guffawed, ignoring my sister and cocking my head, as I stared at my mother with incredulity. "He's a kid!"

"How old is he?" Christy asked, and Mom said, "He has to be well into his twenties, at least."

Marjie hummed at my side, squinting one eye, and said, "Well, I don't know that I'd call that a *kid*. But he's definitely younger than you." She jabbed an elbow into my elbow.

"That's what I'm saying," I said, then gestured toward Christy with a thrust of my hand. "He's her age!"

Mom dismissed my protests with a flighty flourish of her fingers. "Nothing says a woman of your age can't have some fun with a younger man," she declared defiantly. "Your father is five years younger than me, for crying out loud."

"Five years is a whole lot different than fifteen," I muttered, rolling my eyes toward my sister, searching for corroboration.

Thankfully, Marjie took the bait and nodded in agreement. "It is. And not for nothing, but he's probably not even Clara's type."

"Oh, and what exactly is Clara's type?" Mom asked, folding her hands and pursing her lips, to wait expectantly as she dodged her eyes between my sister and me.

"Um, Cary Grant?" my sister threw in, before snorting with laughter. "Or, um, Gregory Peck? You know, someone dead and no longer on this planet."

I clapped a hand dramatically over my heart and threw my head back. "Oh, Lord! Gregory Peck!"

Mom hummed her appreciation with closed eyes and a slow nod. "Mm, I do love that man," she said, before opening her eyes and saying, "They don't make 'em like they used to."

Scooping some eggs onto my fork, I muttered, "Exactly."

One of the French doors in my sister's sunlit dining room opened, and in walked my father Martin, along with Marjorie's husband, Mark, and their twin daughters, Lydia and Leah. The nine-year-old girls kicked off their sneakers, letting them land haphazardly beside the door, and scrambled to get into their seats at the table. Mark complimented Marjie on the breakfast spread with a hug around her shoulders and a kiss on her cheek, before taking his seat next to her, while Dad sat beside Mom. The usual Sunday tradition then commenced with lively conversation, clanging utensils, and gulps of orange juice and coffee. I adored every member of my family and the role that he or she each played. We all fit together in this comfortable unit, every piece seemingly made to join with the next, and I enjoyed this time with them—I always did.

But when breakfast was over and they scattered to further enjoy each other's company in activities that no longer involved me, I was forced again into those dreaded moments of silence. To remind me of the things they had and I didn't.

***

Later, sitting on the back deck of my cottage on the shore, I closed my eyes to the crashing waves and my sister's voice. With the phone pressed to my ear and the sea touching my hair with salt, I breathed in, long and deep, before exhaling into the late Spring air as a few seagulls cackled across the sky.

"I don't know what's going on with Christy and Josh."

"Mm," I mumbled, reaching out to find Agnes's soft head.

"She came home all upset earlier," Marjie said. "She sounded like she had been crying, and ran straight up to her room."

"They probably had a fight," I replied, stating the obvious, as my fingers stroked gently over the long, silky ears in my grasp.

"You say that like it's not a big deal."

With a sigh, I opened my eyes to the setting sun, casting its heavenly glow onto the wide expanse of water, a mere fifty feet from my deck and the dog by my side.

"Because it isn't a big deal," I laughed incredulously. "People fight, Marj. It happens."

My sister groaned noisily against the phone. "I know that, but she's my baby. I don't want her to come home crying and not tell me why. She should know she can come to me about anything."

"She does," I assured her. "And if she needs you, I'm sure she will."

Marjorie hummed, a sound so heavy with thought and melancholy. "I miss when she always needed me."

An ache pained my heart then, as I thought of my sister, her daughter, and where their lives had begun. From the beginning, they'd always had us—my parents and me—but in a lot of ways, it had just been them, and it was that way for a long, long time. They had leaned on each other, and later, they had grown up together. Then, Mark entered the picture when Christy was ten, and Marjorie and her daughter went headfirst into the relationship together. There had been a wedding, another pregnancy, and a brand-new life, but even still, Christy was always the center of my sister's universe. She hardly understood a world without her oldest girl, but now, that girl was all grown up and embarking on a life of her own, and Marjie was struggling to let go, even just a little.

"You're going to be fine," I told her, as I always did.

"Yeah, I know. I'll be okay in the morning. But right now, I just feel kind of ... sad," she admitted with a forlorn sigh.

Then, clearing her throat and making the decision to perk up, she asked, "Anyway, what did you say earlier about a new patient this week?"

A gentle breeze was carried from the water to caress the windchimes hanging from the pergola overhead, and it sent its song into the night with a melody that reminded me of dandelions and hummingbirds.

"Oh, yeah, at St. Mary's," I said, recalling the phone call I'd received from the hospital on Friday night. "They don't expect him to be there for long or anything, though."

"Still, I bet Agnes will love seeing someone different," Marjie offered.

"Oh, for sure," I agreed, stroking my best friend's head. "She loves making new friends."

CHAPTER THREE

Mondays never felt quite like Mondays when I walked Agnes into St. Mary's Hospital and took the elevator to the third floor. I knew it wasn't a job many would find enjoyable, visiting psychiatric patients for varying periods of time, but I found it rewarding. My life was given meaning by comforting people and helping them find happiness and peace. It was my calling, and I answered it with an open heart and wide-spread arms.

As I stepped out of the elevator, I found Dr. Sylvie Sherman with an iPad in her hand. She greeted Agnes with an excited squeal and crouched to the ground to scrub her a hand against the smiling dog's face. Then, she regarded me with a friendly smile, her eyes twinkling with unabashed joy.

Agnes wasn't just wonderful for the patients, but for the doctors and nurses as well. She brightened their long, albeit usually rewarding days, and she gave them something to look forward to on the days in between our visits.

"How was your weekend?" I asked my friend.

"Ah, you know, the usual," Sylvie sighed, as she stood, reluctantly pulling her hand from Agnes's face. "Fought with my toddler, cleaned, dug deeper into the never-ending pile of laundry ..."

"So, just another weekend in paradise, huh?"

Rolling her eyes, she muttered, "Oh, yeah. It was lovely, but I won't bore you with the details. How was yours?"

"Relaxing," I replied, thinking about my serene view of the water and my house's private beach. "After that storm on Friday, the weather was beautiful. I spent all of Saturday and Sunday evening on my deck, just listening to the waves."

"Wow, no need to rub it in," my friend grumbled good-naturedly, the hint of a smile twitching at her lips. "Not all of us live in a gorgeous house on the water, you know."

"Hey," I said, holding up my pointer finger, "that little house wasn't always gorgeous. And I've told you a thousand times, any day you need a break, come on over. There's a lounge chair and a glass of wine with your name on it."

Sylvie closed her eyes and sighed happily, as if she were right now on that beach with that glass of wine in her hand. "Trust me," she said, opening her eyes, "as soon as my husband finds the courage to be alone with

Teddy for a couple hours, I'm taking you up on that offer."

Teddy was Sylvie's two-year-old son, and ever since he came into their life, her husband's anxiety over being left alone with him had remained a prevalent part of our conversations.

"When do you think that's going to be?"

Sylvie pursed her lips and shrugged. "When he doesn't have to wipe his butt, maybe."

Laughing, we walked away from the service elevator, and down the hall toward the nurses' station. The familiar faces at the desk beamed with eager anticipation as we approached, before they rushed to greet Agnes with kisses and gleeful words of praise. Agnes wagged her tail wildly, as they assured her that she was indeed a good girl and the best dog in the world. Meanwhile, Sylvie retrieved a few slips of paper from behind the desk and handed them to me.

"Mr. Logan was discharged last week," she informed me. "Did anybody tell you that?"

I nodded, holding onto Ag's leash, as she panted happily on the floor alongside the nurses. "Yeah," I said. "I got a phone call last Friday."

"Okay, good," Sylvie said, as she looked at the next page. "So, you're going to see Mrs. Marshall. She's been having a rough few days, so hopefully, Agnes will cheer her up. Then, Phoebe—you saw her last week, didn't you?"

"I did," I said, remembering the young girl with bandages wrapped tightly around both wrists. "How is she doing?"

"Better," Sylvie said, smiling encouragingly. "She'll be happy to see Agnes today."

She ran me through the short itinerary, until she reached the last slip of paper. Then, she addressed me with a weary sigh. "And then, there's the new guy," she went on. "August Gordon."

"Okay."

"He's …" She pursed her lips and tapped a finger to the paper, before looking to one of the nurses, still cooing over Agnes. "How would you describe Mr. Gordon?"

The nurse stood and smoothed her scrubs out, as she said, "He's a, um … he's a nice guy. Very charming. But he has a wall up that is just … *very* difficult to get over." An expression of exhaustion and defeat washed over her face.

"So, you're hoping Agnes will get him to open up?" I asked, nodding.

"You know the drill," Sylvie replied. "He's diagnosed bipolar and came in over the weekend, saying he was about to commit suicide. But when we talk to him, he doesn't seem at all suicidal."

"So, he hides it well," I muttered, nodding solemnly.

"I suspect so, yeah. Either that, or his highs and lows are really *that* fleeting. See if you can work your magic with him. I might come in after you visit for a while. Or maybe I should just let Agnes visit without me intervening." Sylvie's voice trailed off, as she weighed out her options, and I tightened my hold on the leash, anxious to begin making our rounds.

19

"We'll play it by ear," I told her, and then, I steered Ag in the direction of Mrs. Marshall's room.

***

"Good afternoon, Phoebe!" I exclaimed cheerfully, stepping into the eighteen-year-old's room, with Ag leading the way.

"Agnes!" she cheered excitedly and patted the bed with enthusiasm.

The dog wasted no time in jumping up onto the bed beside the girl and wagged her tail, as Phoebe began scratching her belly. I sat down, still holding onto the leash, as I waited for the blonde teenager to speak to me. If she even wanted to. If not, that was okay, too. This time wasn't about me—it was for her and Agnes to visit. Nothing more.

I noticed the bandages had been removed, and now, her wrists wore the mark of her sadness and the attempt she had made to end it all. Outwardly, I remained seemingly unfazed by the sight of her healing scars, but it was never easy to visit these patients and know they suffered unbearable amounts of pain. I wished I possessed the power to do more to help, and hoped that what I could do was enough, while knowing it generally wasn't. But through Agnes, I knew I provided a reprieve from their sadness and pain, and that was better than nothing. It had to be.

"I'm going home soon," Phoebe said to me after fifteen minutes of watching her interact with Agnes. "They said maybe in a couple days."

"Oh, yeah?" I asked, smiling.

"Yeah," she replied, nodding. "My mom will be happy about that. She can't wait for me to come home."

"And what about you? Are you happy?"

She shrugged. "I guess so."

This wasn't the first time Phoebe had been at the hospital, and she wasn't a stranger to me. Every time she was discharged, I hoped that she'd finally find peace within herself and live her life happily without the need for this place or us. But I also knew to not be surprised if I did see her admitted again, and I thought how that was horrible, to expect that of someone so young, whose life had barely begun.

"I'm kinda excited to see my little sister," she continued, offering a little ray of hope.

"That's great! How old is she?"

"She's fourteen," Phoebe said, stroking Ag's ears.

"I have a little sister," I told her, offering a little look into my personal life. "Marjorie. She's four years younger than me, too."

"That's cool."

"I was just at her house yesterday for breakfast," I went on, smiling.

"Taylor is *obsessed* with pancakes. Those frozen ones? She eats them all the time."

I laughed. "They're pretty good."

Phoebe's mouth twitched, but she wouldn't allow herself to frown. Instead, she remained indifferent, absentmindedly petting Agnes.

"I can't eat that stuff, though. I'd blow up and then, I'd never hear the end of it from my mom."

21

"You?" I scoffed, making a mental note of what she'd just said about her mother. "Come on, you're such a little thing."

"Yeah," she snorted, rolling her eyes. "Because I don't eat that stuff. I'd get fat and ugly if I did."

"You're fine, Phoebs," I told her, reaching out to touch her knee and pat it gently. "You're beautiful."

She smiled, bright and cheerful, as if this moment was the very first time she'd allowed the light in, then nodded. "No, I know," she said, and yet, somehow, I knew there wasn't a hint of sincerity in her tone.

***

My last stop of the day was the room of August Gordon, the floor's newest patient. As I approached, I found the door was open to the cheerful sounding "Papa Loves Mambo" by Perry Como, and I smiled at the familiar song I seldom heard outside of my home. From the sound of the music, I half-expected an older man, so imagine my surprise, when I steered Agnes into the room and found a young man, not much older than Christy. Pacing the floor and singing along, with an open book in his hand.

I stopped in the doorway and watched him, waggling his finger in the air to keep time with the song. Agnes sat at my feet and smiled at the stranger, as her tongue lolled from her mouth and her tail wagged fiercely. In a black t-shirt, grey sweatpants, and a pair of white socks, August walked the width of the room, back and forth, oblivious to our intrusion, until the track ended and we entered

22

those dreadful two seconds. But this time, I wasn't lonely. I was transfixed on him, and in that time, he looked up and saw me, granting me a better view of his face, and although I couldn't comment much on his mental state, I found there was nothing wrong with his appearance. Nothing wrong at all.

He filled the remainder of those two seconds with a grin, revealing a mouth of teeth I instantly envied. Straight, white, and perfectly fitted to his mouth. I stood straighter, as he dropped the book on the bed, and approached with hands on his hips, and I quickly coaxed my tongue to speak.

"Hi, August. I'm—"

"Clara, right?" I nodded, startled by the easy way in which he used my name. He extended a hand as he said, "Dr. Sherman told me you and Agnes were coming by today. I didn't know when, so I decided to do some reading and listen to a little music, and—"

Perry Como's buttery voice began to sing "Round and Round," one of my personal favorites, and August's grin widened, and his eyes closed.

"Sorry," he said, shaking his head and chuckling. "I just really love this song."

"So do I," I admitted. "I love Perry Como."

His eyes opened, giving me a better view of the shimmering silver flecks in his irises, and he nodded slowly with what I could only read as approval. "You have good taste, Clara," he complimented in a smooth, velvety tone that revealed every bit of depth his voice contained, and I cleared my throat, just to keep from blushing.

"So, um, Agnes and I are going to spend some time with you today, if that's okay," I said, resisting the temptation to hurry around him and into the room, in order to escape his gaze.

Thankfully, August nodded eagerly and gestured inside with a wide sweep of his arm. "Oh, sure, of course. Come on in," he said, and then, as I stepped into the room and toward the bed, he added, "It's not much to look at but, you know, I only just moved in."

I laughed easily at the jab about the drab hospital room as I sat in a chair. While most patients sat on their beds, August chose to sit in the second chair, giving our meeting less of a clinical feel. It felt like visiting a friend, and I pinched my eyes shut with a gentle reprimand that he wasn't a friend at all.

He grabbed the small radio from the mattress and lowered the volume on the music, although I wished he hadn't. I could have listened to Perry Como all day. "I wasn't sure they'd let me bring this," he said. "The last time I admitted myself, they took everything away from me, but I told them music helps, so ..."

"Music definitely has a way of healing the soul," I agreed, nodding and smiling and watching as he situated himself in the chair.

"Indeed, it does," he agreed. Then, as he folded his hands in his lap and eyed Agnes with curious intrigue, he asked, "Okay. So, how do we do this?"

"How would you greet any other dog?" I smiled, scratching her behind the ears.

August pursed his lips and seemed to consider the question, before saying, "You know, honestly, I've never had dogs and I don't make a habit of approaching ones I don't know. Always seems risky."

I cocked my head and asked, "Do you like them?"

"Dogs?" he asked, and I nodded. "Oh, yeah! Don't get me wrong, I love animals. My parents weren't into cleaning up after them, though, so we never had them when I was growing up. And now, I'm too busy working to take care of something other than myself, and I do a pretty lousy job of that as it is. So, it's probably best I don't take on the responsibility of caring for something else."

Smiling at his long-winded explanation and the speedy pace of his tone, I reached into my pocket and grabbed the plastic baggie of dog treats I carried with me. I handed it to him and asked, "Why don't you try becoming her friend first, and see where that goes?"

There was no hesitation, as he took the bag and opened it to grab one of the treats. He held his hand out and Agnes eagerly moved forward to gently take it from his fingers. He smiled at her and stroked her snout with careful fingers, and Agnes sat at his feet, tail wagging and mouth smiling.

Then, taking her face in both of his hands, he said in a soft, gentle tone, "Well, it's lovely to meet you, too, Agnes."

CHAPTER FOUR

Monday night brought with it the excitement of going out for drinks with Christy and Marjorie. As soon as I came home from the hospital, I stripped off my work clothes and got into something more suitable for a night out. Then, after choosing a red swing dress with a sweetheart neckline and a pair of black pumps, I did my eyeliner with a simple wing, slapped on a coat of red lipstick, and was ready to go.

I met my sister and niece at the bar in New Canaan. We had decided to check this one out after frequenting the old watering hole in River Canyon one too many times. A change of scenery never hurt anyone, and we entered the chic establishment with healthy anticipation before heading straight to the bar.

"I.D.'s, ladies," the bartender demanded in a gruff tone that said he meant business. Yet, I laughed and pressed a hand over my heart. "I'm flattered!" I gushed, and he surprised me with a soft chuckle, as I fished my driver's license from my purse.

After he confirmed that we were all of age to be served and drink, he set to mixing our cocktails, and we turned our backs to the bar to survey our new surroundings. It was only a Monday night, but it was also Ladies' Night. Women young and old crowded the tables, chatting with their friends and eyeing the lingering men with either disdain or interest.

"Hey ... Aunt Clara," Christy hissed, as she jabbed her elbow gently into my ribs.

"Hm?"

"You know, the bartender is pretty hot."

"Oh, come on, Chris," Marjie groaned with embarrassment. Still, she peeked over her shoulder at the man working behind the bar. Then, she looked back at me and nodded. "He actually is."

"I already saw him when we ordered," I muttered, completely disinterested and hoping this guy wasn't listening in on our conversation.

"Yeah, but did you really *look* at him?" Christy whispered. "I mean, check out his arms."

"I don't need to—"

"Just look at them," she urged through wide eyes that kept volleying from me to the oblivious bartender.

Sighing, I glanced over my shoulder to discover that the man was certainly gifted in the department of muscular prowess, and I shrugged as I looked back to my niece. "Okay. So, he has nice arms."

27

"Talk to him," she encouraged, smiling with too much hope for my taste.

Rolling my eyes, I shook my head. "You're worse than your grandmother."

"Oh, come on, he—"

"Here you go, ladies. Enjoy," the bartender interrupted, and I turned around to grab my martini and take a better look at this man my sister and niece had insisted was so attractive. And after taking in his smooth face and meticulously groomed hair, I quickly assessed that, in my opinion, they were wrong. The man wasn't unattractive by any stretch of the imagination, but he was too pretty, too thought out and pampered. I found nothing attractive about a man who very likely spent more time looking in the mirror than I did, and so, I took my drink and didn't give him a second glance.

Christy found us an empty booth adjacent to a pool table, where a cluster of college-aged men were playing a game. My niece slid onto the bench, while keeping her attention firmly on the group of guys, and my sister and I shared a pointed look.

"How are things with Josh?" I interjected gently, tearing Christy's attention away from the game.

"Oh, um, fine," she answered with forced nonchalance, as she absentmindedly stirred her Cosmo.

"Oh, yeah? Everything's okay?" I asked, and she nodded. "Good. I was just wondering. I haven't seen him around much lately."

As close as my niece was with her mother, she was nearly as close to me. It never took much persuasion to make her crack and spill the details on anything going on in her life. So, with a heavy sigh, she dropped her elbows to the table and the straw fell against the lip of the glass.

"It's just … we've been talking a lot lately. About the future and stuff."

Marjie swallowed, as she pinched the toothpick in her martini and lifted the olive to her mouth, then asked, "What kind of stuff?"

Christy shook her head, grabbing the straw again and bringing it to her lips. "You know, like kids, marriage …" She shrugged casually. "That kind of stuff."

My sister's demeanor shifted momentarily, as the admission shook her soul gently toward the reality that her little girl had, at some point, become a woman. Christy wasn't far from her twenty-third birthday and had been with Josh for over three years now. It was reasonable that she'd be having these conversations with him, and my sister was generally a reasonable person. But that didn't make this any easier for her to handle and accept.

She cleared her throat and recovered quickly, as she nodded and lifted her glass to her lips. "What does Josh think of all that?" she asked, flicking her gaze toward her daughter, and then, back at her drink.

Christy sighed and shrugged in a way that told me the prognosis wasn't good. "We broke up," she admitted easily.

Before Marjie could take a sip, her glass was lowered to the table with a loud *clink*! "*What?*"

"Are you serious?" I exclaimed, clapping a hand to my chest.

My niece's blue eyes were always so jubilant and sparkling with life, but now, they glinted with sadness and the birth of fresh tears. "Oh, honey," I said and hurried to reach for her hand, as Marjie reached for her bag, and Christy began to softly cry.

"I'm okay," she laughed through her tearful embarrassment, accepting a tissue from her mom. She dabbed at her eyes, as she continued, "We just want different things. He doesn't want kids, he doesn't want to get married, but I do. So, it is what it is."

I jolted in my seat, slightly taken aback, and shook my head. "Sweetie, you're only twenty-two—"

"Almost twenty-three," she corrected, before blowing her nose.

"Okay, you're almost twenty-three. You have plenty of time to get married and have kids. You have your whole life ahead of you."

Christy shook her head, crumpling the tissue up and clutching it in her hand. "But I don't. Not really," she protested, before taking a sip of her drink. Then, she said, "Like, let's say Josh decided to propose to me next week. I'd get married a year or two from now, and then, I'd be twenty-five. After that, we'd probably take a year or so until we decided to start trying to have a baby, and then, I'd be twenty-seven. If all went well and I happened to get pregnant right away, I'd be twenty-nine by the time I even gave birth. I'd like three kids, so if I decided to space them out by two or three years, I wouldn't be done having kids until I was, what? Thirty-six, thirty-seven? And at that point, I'd be geriatric—"

"Oh, gee, thanks!" I exclaimed, as I barked with short, cut laughter, dodging my eyes between my sister and niece.

Christy groaned and shook her head. "It's not the same," she said. "You don't want to get married or have kids. But I *do*. Everybody always thinks they have plenty of time for this stuff, but the reality is, I'm already twenty-three. If I start over now, and I meet someone new, I'll be lucky if I got married by the time I'm thirty."

"I get what you're saying, sweetheart," Marjie replied gently. "But you know, I think you'll find that, no matter what, life won't ever go exactly the way you planned it to. I mean, look at me—"

"I know, Mom," Christy interrupted gently. "But I also don't think it's a smart idea to just … wing it, either. I need a plan. Maybe I'll have to change things as I go along but it's better than not having any clue whatsoever. I mean, look at you guys."

The blow hit hard and swift, and the damage had already been done by the time she quickly muttered a hasty, "no offense." Marjorie gawked at her daughter, while I pursed my lips and turned away. My pride hadn't been hurt by the comment, and I understood what she was trying to say. It was more that it was another unintentional interpretation of the thoughts that had been crowding my mind over the last few days. The loneliness. The persistent reminder that time continues on, whether you want it to or not. The harsh bite of reality that I was, in fact, a middle-aged woman without a husband or children, and it wasn't what I had wanted for my life. Not at all.

"I love you guys," Christy went on. "I just don't want to be you or make the same choices. It's not a bad thing. It's—"

"Who says I don't want to be married?" I abruptly interjected, turning to face my niece.

"What?" she asked, taken aback.

I shrugged with exaggerated indifference and repeated, "Who says I don't want to be married? I never once recall saying that, so why does everyone always think I don't want a husband?"

Even my sister seemed to be surprised by the comment, as she turned to face me with amounting intrigue. "Wait. I didn't know you—"

"Nobody ever asked," I said. "Everybody just assumed I didn't want those things, but I do. And I could have settled on someone by now to have that life. But then, what? I'd have a husband and kids, but I'd also be miserable, in a relationship with a man who I never really wanted but settled for. Why should I do that to myself?"

Christy dropped her gaze to the glass on the table and said, "You shouldn't, but—"

"No but's. I shouldn't, simple as that. And neither should you."

The table fell silent, making room for a resounding burst of laughter from the game of pool taking place beside us. My attention was drawn, and I watched them, the young men with bright smiles and nicer arms than the bartender. They were all athletic and muscular, maybe even to a fault. Their necks were a little too thick and corded for my personal tastes, and their thighs were just a little too big. But even still, there was no denying they looked good and it would have surprised me to find any one of them had problems finding a date.

"Aunt Clara," Christy said, her voice cutting through my fixation on the men beside us.

"Hm?"

"You're staring."

I laughed, only a little embarrassed, and shook my head. "Oops."

"Go talk to them," she urged me, as Marjorie laughed.

"They're like, twenty," she hissed, amused and incredulous.

"*So?*" Christy stared at her mother with challenging disbelief. "Who cares? Nothing says she can't flirt a little."

"I don't know," I muttered, shifting in my seat. "It's weird."

"What's weird?"

I groaned and rolled my eyes. "I don't know! I just … I just always found it kind of weird when younger men get with an older woman. I mean, it's none of my business, people can do what they want, but it's just …" I cringed and made a face of disgust, like I had just put something foul in my mouth and was being forced to swallow. "It's just weird."

Christy and Marjie shared a glance, and I looked away toward the game of pool, as I began to wonder if there was truly anything particularly gross or weird about an older woman being with a younger man or if I'd always been wrong. I considered that maybe it wouldn't hurt to say hi, or even wave. Just to get a reaction, maybe a little boost to my ego. But then it occurred to me that maybe these particular men *did* find something gross or weird about it, and in which case, I had no desire to be rejected. Not to mention that persistent fact that they simply weren't my type, and I very seldom wasted my time on things and people who weren't.

But nothing said I couldn't appreciate the view.

CHAPTER FIVE

"**P**hoebs, those flowers are beautiful," I said, settling into the chair, while Agnes visited with her friend.

"Thanks," the girl replied, smoothing her hands over Ag's back and tail.

"Who sent them?"

"My dad," she answered, her tone blunt and harsh.

The daisies sat on her bedside table in full bloom, with a card peeking out from between the petals, still sealed with a silver sticker. I frowned and turned to the girl, who hadn't yet smiled. "You haven't opened the card," I commented observantly.

"Nope."

"Don't you want to know what it says?"

She pursed her lips, then shook her head. "Nope."

I studied the girl while she petted Agnes. She sat tall, her spine rigid, moving her hands in a stiff, methodical way. Agnes typically pulled a smile from her or even a hint of jubilance, but not today. Today, Phoebe was different, unhappy. She reminded me of the girl I met months ago, when she'd first entered St. Mary's. That girl was lacking in hope and the willingness to survive another day, and she seemed to be back.

I didn't like it.

"So," I started, shifting on the upholstered chair, "what—"

"They're not sending me home yet," she said, cutting me off with her bitter words. Then, when I looked at her, wide-eyed and mouth opened with surprise, she shrugged. "What? That's what you were wondering, right? You wanted to know why I'm sad?"

I offered her a small smile and lifted one shoulder. "I was curious, yeah. But you didn't have to tell me, if you didn't want to."

"Well," she muttered with an indifferent shake of her head, "I guess I didn't say exactly what I was supposed to the other day, because last night, they told me they wanna keep me for at least a few more days."

"Oh, Phoebs. I'm—"

"Whatever. It doesn't matter."

Phoebe's hands stopped moving along Agnes's back and were now folded tightly in her lap. I sat across from her, with my head cocked and my hands resting gently on the arms of the chair. I was making a conscious effort to keep my body language open, to make her feel welcome to say whatever it was she needed to say and hoping she would say *something*. But Phoebe also had a tendency to shut down. She clammed up tighter than a bank safe, and when she decided to, there was nobody that could get her to open up again. Not even Agnes. And that's exactly what was happening now.

"We'll see you on Monday," I said to her after fifteen minutes of silence at the end of our session. "Okay, Phoebs?"

She stared ahead, avoiding my gaze, and I reached out to lay a gentle hand on her shoulder, and squeezed. I took solace in the fact that she didn't pull away, while wishing she would stop me before I could leave. I wished she would tell me what she had said or done to change her doctors' minds. I wished she would tell me why she wouldn't open the card in the flowers. But she said nothing, and I still had other patients to see. So, with a final squeeze of her shoulder, I left and headed down the hall.

***

August Gordon wasn't listening to music today, but his attitude was just as warm and friendly as it had been when we'd first met. He greeted me into his room with a blinding smile, before pulling the two chairs together, to face each other, like he was welcoming me into his home.

"How do you feel about tea?" he asked me, as I took a seat and looked up at him curiously. "Oh, I was gonna run down the hall and grab a cup. I thought I'd ask if you wanted one, too."

"Oh, um," I smiled and nodded eagerly, "sure. How about we take a walk down there together?"

"That sounds good to me," he replied, offering a smile that shouldn't have made my heart flutter ... but it did.

Just as soon as I'd been seated, I was standing again. I offered August the leash, inviting him to walk Agnes down the hall, and he gratefully accepted, taking to it like a pro. Together, we left his room. I noted the way August walked beside me, not one step behind or ahead, and I found that nice. That told me he was thoughtful, a seemingly rare quality in people today, and I appreciated it.

"So, is this all you do?" he asked, regarding me with curiosity and genuine intrigue.

"For a living?" He nodded and I replied, "Yeah, this is it."

"You just visit the looney bin with your dog? That's it?" He raised a brow with the playful jab.

I sniffed an awkward, hesitant laugh. "We don't call it the looney bin."

"Sorry," he said with a warm, throaty chuckle. "I'm not a strong advocate of political correctness. I can't keep track of what everybody is offended by. The list is never-ending."

"Well, what you *can* keep track of here is, we don't call it the looney bin—"

"What about the nut house?"

I laughed at that and the teasing expression on his face, as I shook my head. "No, definitely not that either."

"Hm," he mumbled, nodding. "Fine. I'll just call it ... this *place*."

"That's safe," I laughed, as we turned into the rec room and walked toward the electric kettle.

August nodded by way of greeting toward the single orderly, keeping watch beside the room's coffee station. He then grabbed two paper cups and tea bags and poured water into both. I watched without interruption, as he steeped the bags in the boiling water, and appreciated his attention to detail, when he wiped up a dab of splashed water from the countertop.

"Do you like sugar?" he asked over his shoulder, taking a packet from the small canister.

"No, I prefer just straight black tea. No milk or sugar."

"Well, then," he said, handing me the cup, "you're all set."

"Thank you very much," I replied gratefully, accepting it and taking a sip.

August shook the packet and tore it open, sprinkling the sugar into his tea, then stirred with a plastic spoon. He took a sip and smacked his lips, before nodding thoughtfully.

"Good?" I asked.

"Nope," he said, casually tossing the spoon into a trash can. "But it'll have to do."

The rec room was nearly empty, except for the orderly and a passing janitor. The television on the wall was tuned in to a home improvement show, and the couch in front of it was unoccupied. I thought perhaps we could sit there with Agnes, instead of going back to August's room, and I began to walk in that direction.

But August had different plans.

"So, Clara, do you and Agnes play Chess?"

"Um, not very well, but I know how. I can't say the same for Agnes." I laughed, as he headed toward a table, where a Chess board sat, all set up and waiting for someone to play with it.

He sat on one side of the table and extended a hand, beckoning Agnes. She happily went to him, her tail swishing, then took a seat at his side. I pulled out the chair across from him, and without any grand declaration, we began to play.

"So, August, what do you do?" I asked, moving a pawn.

"Well," he said, sliding his pawn to stand before mine, "when I'm not living in the lap of luxury in *this place*, I write."

Taking another pawn, I moved it to stand diagonal to his. "What do you write?"

"Books."

His pawn moved, taking mine out. He smirked as he dropped my piece to the side of the board. "First casualty," he said triumphantly.

"To be honest, you're probably going to win," I told him, laughing. "I don't think I've ever won a game of Chess in my life."

Another pawn moved, as I then asked, "What kind of books do you write?"

"All different kinds. I don't like to limit myself to one genre," he replied, taking another of my pawns.

His hand worked tirelessly at Agnes's fur, stroking gently and massaging her ears, as he watched my next move and then, the next. Something in his studious eyes told me he was a little more skilled in the game than he had initially let on, and I laughed when he declared the game was finished after only ten minutes of playing.

"Are you kidding me?!" I exclaimed, staring at the board in complete disbelief.

"I took your Queen out with a pawn," he said, shaking his head. "That's just sad."

I stared at that rogue pawn through narrowed, suspicious eyes. "That's unbelievable," I muttered. Then, I looked up to point at him, and said, "You didn't tell me you were *that* good."

"I'm really not," he said, chuckling as he put the pieces back to their rightful spaces. "You're just *that* bad."

August leaned back in his seat, sipping his tea and petting Agnes. I didn't make a habit of gawking at people, especially ones I was seeing professionally. But when his eyes closed to savor a moment of quiet, I gave myself a sliver of permission to take in the sight of him. I had already decided, during our first meeting, that he was an attractive man, and that was still true. But now, with his hand brushing a curly lock of hair from his forehead, I further decided that he was also beautiful. He reminded me of Michelangelo's David. Not a single one of his features stood out from the rest, and if looked at individually, you might find that his lips weren't the fullest or that his nose wasn't the most structurally perfect. But when put together and taken in as a whole, you would then find that the grey in his eyes played perfectly with the subtle reddish tones in his hair and that the angular shape of his nose suited the rounded curve of his lips and that the point of his chin gave balance to the roundness in his cheekbones and that there was no disputing that this man was, in a very unconventional way, beautiful.

He opened his eyes and lowered the cup of tea to the table. Then, he asked, "What made you want to get into the dog therapy business?"

I pushed all thoughts of his beauty from my mind and reverted to my usual air of professionalism, as I replied, "I love to help people."

"That's such a generic answer," he snickered, shaking his head.

"Well, it's the truth," I said, slightly miffed by the gentle insult.

He shook his head. "No. I think it's what you say to people to avoid telling them the deeper truth."

I took a sip of my tea, now cold and unsatisfactory, and said, "But it *is* the truth. I love helping people and getting through to them. I—"

"Okay. Fair enough. Maybe that's why you do it *now*. But what was that moment in your life that made you think to yourself, I'm going to go to the looney bin and talk to some nuts while they pet my dog?"

My interactions with August up until that point had been, for the most part, comfortable and pleasant. I had liked him from the moment I met him, and I knew that, when he was released from St. Mary's, I would miss him fondly the way I always miss the good ones. But now, I sat across from him, unable to meet his steely gaze and wanting so badly to run away.

"Augu—"

"Why does that question make you uncomfortable?"

"It doesn't—"

"But it does, though. The second I asked, you looked at me differently. Your posture changed. You're bothered by it," he accurately assessed, and I met his gaze then, just to prove him wrong, and he smiled. "You're the first person without a lab coat to come and see me since I admitted myself last weekend, and I'm just trying to make conversation. If you don't want to answer the question, that's fine, I understand. But if you want to tell someone, I am genuinely curious."

I shifted my stare to the orderly and found that he was still busying himself with whatever was on his phone, and the janitor had long left the room. For all intents and purposes, I was alone with August, and there was only the dog to hear my confession. And she already knew.

"When I was in my twenties, I didn't know what to do with my life," I told him, a stranger. "I had no direction and no real prospect for a future. After spending eight years in college, getting a degree that didn't matter and racking up an obscene amount of student loans, I was working a crappy retail job I hated and still had no clue what to do. I was so overwhelmed and stressed, that I became depressed. I decided one night that I didn't want to live anymore, and I was ready to …" I hesitated. The sensible part of my brain knew that mentioning suicide to a suicidal patient was the equivalent of waving cocaine in the face of a coke addict, and the last thing I wanted to do was add to this man's suffering and temptation.

"You can say it," he said, as if reading my mind. "I'm not gonna hang myself with the sheets after you leave, I promise."

He smiled, but I didn't. "That's not funny," I said, and he asked, "Who's laughing?"

I dropped my gaze and swallowed, before continuing against my better judgment. "When I was about to ... do it, my old dog scratched at my bedroom door, telling me she wanted to be let out. And I started to think, if I was gone, who would take care of her?" I swallowed again at the mounting wave of emotion. One that felt as fresh now as it was then. "And realistically, I knew that someone would have come along and taken her in, my mom or my sister probably, but it wouldn't have been me. She would have spent God knows how long waiting for me to come back, and then, who knows how much longer she would have spent wondering what she did wrong to make me leave."

August's demeanor changed from subtle cockiness to empathic understanding, as he said, "So, she saved you."

I faltered in my nod, as I replied, "Yes."

"And so, because your dog saved you, you have now devoted your life to the hope that this dog will save someone else."

There was nothing more that I could say. So, I simply nodded and swallowed at my emotional past.

"Well, Clara," he said gently, running his hand along the crown of Agnes's head, "it's a little early to be sure, but I'm feeling pretty hopeful."

44

CHAPTER SIX

I *probably shouldn't be back here*, I told myself, as I headed down the hallway to August's room, after a frustratingly unsuccessful visit with Phoebe.

She had remained completely shut down since my last visit on Friday. Her eyes stayed fixed to the window, even as Agnes whimpered at her feet, begging for attention. It left me worried, and I promptly had a conversation with Dr. Sherman. It felt like tattling, and I didn't know if it was beneficial or not, or if it would only serve to hurt my relationship with the girl. It was the right thing to do though, even as I wondered if the right thing even mattered to me anymore.

After divulging far too much information last week, going back to August's room didn't feel at all like the right thing. I told myself that we had left the conversation on a high note, and that maybe, by letting him in a little, it would give him the willingness to let me in as well.

But I couldn't shake the feeling that I had told him too much, and I tensed as Agnes and I approached his perpetually open doorway.

Perry Como greeted my ears, as August, wearing a white t-shirt and sweatpants, greeted my eyes.

"I was afraid you wouldn't come back," he admitted, as I entered the room.

Agnes went right to him, bumping her flank against his knee, and he responded by crouching down to pet her.

"Why wouldn't I come back?" I asked, dropping my bag into the chair.

"Because I have this habit of unintentionally chasing people away," he replied, looking up at me and wearing a good-natured smile.

"I don't scare easily," I replied, sitting and watching as he allowed Agnes to take the lead.

Her tail resembled a motorboat's propeller, winding up excitedly, as she licked his checks and the scruff blanketing his chin. He laughed with eyes squeezed shut, before pulling his face from her reach.

"I love your kisses, Ag, but I don't need your tongue in my mouth, thanks." Then, opening his eyes and turning to me, he said, "She's not really my type."

Laughing airily, I nodded. "Don't worry. I doubt she's offended."

He stood up and came to sit beside me, crossing one leg over the other. He reached onto the bed and grabbed the book I had seen him reading the first time we came. Then, he handed it to me.

"What's this?" I asked, turning it over to take a look at the cover.

"What does it look like?"

The paperback was a matte, deep red in color, with **MUSINGS OF MURDER & MAYHEM** written in a bold, white typewriter-style font on the cover. My eyes drifted to the bottom, where August's name was printed. I looked back to him, impressed and thoroughly intrigued.

"It's my latest published novel," he explained, smoothing his hand over Agnes's head.

"What is it about?"

August cocked his head and slumped into his chair, before sighing with excruciating depth. "Uh, well, it's basically about the thoughts and temptations of a serial killer," he said, rubbing at his upper lip. "I put myself into the killer's mind and told the entire story from his point of view. It ... it's an accurate depiction of what it's like to be stuck in the head of a psychopathic murderer and gives the reader a taste of what it would feel like to be driven to do things that society as a whole finds horrific."

Turning the book over again in my hand, to read the synopsis, I nodded. "Wow," I said. "It sounds interesting."

"No, it doesn't. It's garbage."

I looked back to him, surprised by the harsh bite in his tone. "I'm sure it's not—"

"No, trust me," he chuckled bitterly, shaking his head. "It's complete trash."

"How do you know that?"

August blew out an angry breath, before standing from the chair and heading toward one of three windows in the room. He held his hands to the frame, his arms

47

spread wide and his head bowed toward the pane. Then, after a moment of thoughtful staring toward Connecticut's busiest highway, he turned back to me, shoulders loose and arms hanging at his sides.

"Because it is," he answered simply.

He came back to the chair then, but appeared restless, with legs jouncing and hands fidgeting with the hem of his shirt. Agnes seemed to be in tune to his mounting anxiety, as she sat and rested her head on his leg. He exhaled deeply, laying a hand on her back, and working his tireless fingers into the scruff at the back of her neck.

"It's funny," he said in a low, hoarse voice. "When you tell most people that you're an author, they think you have this amazingly whimsical job, and they envy you. Like it's so cool to be trapped inside your own head with a thousand voices all battling to speak at once."

"That doesn't sound cool at all," I replied. "Sounds pretty awful, actually."

He looked at me, seemingly startled, and nodded. "It is. And that's not even the worst part."

Realizing that I was on the brink of a breakthrough, I asked, "What is?"

Pursing his lips and tipping his head back to stare at the bright florescent lights and boring, beige tiles, he said, "Mm, that's a tough call. Struggling to tell the story exactly the way it's meant to be told and having to balance the world in your head with the real life you have to lead … both of those are a bitch. But honestly, I think the worst part is being a nutcase on top of it all and the

48

pills they want me to take to," he raised his fingers in quotation marks, "manage it."

Somewhere not so far away, I could hear the door to August's heart creak open, and I dared myself to step ever so carefully over the threshold. "Don't you want to feel better?" I asked, keeping my gaze pinned on him and judging his reaction to my inquisition.

He didn't flinch, as he replied, "Well, I guess that depends on what your definition of what feeling better is, wouldn't it?"

My forehead crumpled with curiosity. "What do you mean?"

"Feeling better in here," he said, tapping his temple, "also means stifling the voices."

Allowing the pieces to come together, I slowly nodded and held up the book. "And this ..." I left the sentence open, with a welcome sign tacked to the end, in the hopes that August would finish it for me, and he did.

"That," he said, pointing to the book in my hand, "is what happens when I'm on my meds. Every sentence was a battle, and even still, it isn't right. But my publisher needed *something* from me, so ..." He thrust his hand again toward it and said, "There it is."

"So, when you're not on your meds ..."

"My work thrives. But I don't."

I narrowed my eyes, knowing they were filled with what was probably unwanted sympathy. I had no idea what it was to have a passion, to be touched by a gift and be driven by it. But I liked to believe I could try and put myself in his metaphorical shoes, and if it was as I imagined it, it was awful. What torture it must be, to feel the constant necessity to do something, while this other foreign substance prevents that need from coming to fruition. Like a fat cork in an overflowing bottle, threatening to explode at any moment. But what can you do, when removing that foreign substance could be catastrophic?

"Can't they adjust your meds? Or put you on something different?"

He shrugged. "I guess they *could*, but I'd rather not be on them at all."

"But you need them," I stated, and he nodded flippantly.

"Sure," he replied sardonically, and I raised my brows. August laughed easily and waved a hand, as if to brush away my nagging insistence that he take care of himself. "Relax. I know. I'll be a good boy and take my medicine."

Our visit from that point on was filled with casual commentary about music and the saddening truth that it just isn't what it used to be. He spent the rest of the half hour with his hands in Agnes's fur, his arms around her neck, and his lips spread into a wide smile that I found too contagious to resist. I caught myself wishing that more patients were this easy to be with and talk to, but as the session too rapidly neared its end, I finally came to terms with the fact that August wasn't just another patient. We had clicked, and we had bonded. We spoke like peers and laughed like friends, and as I stood up from my chair, I found I couldn't wait to see him again. And neither could my heart.

"So, we'll see you on—"

"Oh," he said, standing to walk Agnes and me to the door. "Actually, I'm being discharged tomorrow."

I was immediately ashamed of my suppressed disappointment, as I turned to him and said, "Oh, well, that's great!"

He nodded, meeting my gaze. "If I'm ever back here, I'll look forward to seeing you again."

Laughing through a touch of melancholy, I glared at him and said, "Then, I hope I never see you again."

"Forgive me for hoping the opposite," August laughed and winked, sending an unwanted shiver down my spine.

The corners of his eyes wrinkled with mirth, and I hoped he would hold onto that when he was once again out of the doctors' care. I wanted him to always be that jovial, while understanding how hard that could be, while also battling the demons that plagued his mind.

"Oh!" I exclaimed, picking his book up from the chair I had occupied. "Here's your—"

"You keep it."

I glanced at him, with the paperback in hand, and asked, "What? Are you sure?"

He nodded. "Yeah, I have a ton of them. Let's just call it a souvenir."

Smiling gratefully, I tucked it inside my bag and held tight to the leash. I extended a hand toward August, and when he accepted, we shook somberly, knowing this would be the last time.

"Be well, August. And thank you for the book."

"You, too, Clara. And thank *you* for everything else."

CHAPTER SEVEN

On Tuesdays and Thursdays, I found myself walking the halls of a children's hospital, visiting sick kids and their families. Every day, on our drive to The Lucas Wilson Hospital for Children, there was a part of me that feared the place, where children are forced to face the things even adults are terrified of. I hated the thought of becoming too attached to those I knew were terminal. Once I was there though, witnessing the fleeting moments of happiness I could bring them by simply being Agnes's escort, I was no longer afraid. We laughed, hugged, and talked about the things they liked and hoped to do. But then, the moment I left, I hunkered down into that fear again, wondering if I was strong enough to handle the pain of losing one of them and knowing I never could be.

Mom called me that Thursday and asked how my day had gone.

"It was good," I said, turning onto my sandy street. "A little sad but good."

"Children's hospital day?"

"Every Tuesday and Thursday," I reminded her, as I pulled into the driveway of my little white cottage.

"I don't know how you do it," she said, as she always did.

"It's not easy, but I just think about how hard it is for them and their families to live that reality every single day. The least I can do is bring them a little happiness for a few minutes."

"You're a Saint."

I laughed and shook my head, as I turned off the car. "I don't know about that."

"Well, I do," Mom declared affirmatively.

Agnes and I traveled the flagstone walkway together, up the steps, and onto the small porch. I opened the door and was greeted immediately by a welcoming call from the caged bird and four tentacle-like tails, twisting around my ankles and meowing at my feet.

"Hey, guys," I said, closing the door behind me and letting Agnes off the leash. "I'll feed you all in a second, okay?"

"Are you coming by Marjie's place on Sunday?" Mom asked.

"Don't I always?" I replied, as I walked through the living room and into the eat-in kitchen.

Years ago, when I had bought the little house, I knew the kitchen would be the first thing I'd renovate, and that's exactly what I did. My dad and I had taken the 1960's time capsule and spruced it up, replacing the floral wallpaper with white beadboard and swapping out the plank cabinet doors for solid oak. It had been a big project, one that set my bank account back more than I would have liked. But I never had a single regret about it. It was now one of my favorite rooms in the house, especially at this time of day. When through the arched window above the sink, the sun could be seen setting over the Long Island Sound, streaking the sky in burnt orange and gold. When the whole world became a canvas, and all of the chaos and sadness I'd witnessed at the hospital became a part of a bigger, much more beautiful picture. Then, as if by magic, it all made sense. Every part of it. And I could feel calm, knowing it was all as it should be, even for just a few minutes.

"Did you hear Christy broke up with Josh?" Mom asked.

"Yeah," I replied, staring through the window, and breathing deeply for the first time since I'd left the house that morning. "She told me last week."

"I liked him," she said with a forlorn sigh. "I was hoping they'd get married."

"They would've been cute together," I agreed, as the sun disappeared beneath the Sound. "But she's gotta do what's best for her."

"Yeah," she replied, in that tone she used when she was about to play the devil's advocate. "But I'm wondering if she's just acting on emotion."

"As opposed to what?"

"I'm just saying, maybe she should've thought it through instead of making such a big decision so quickly. If I only ever acted on emotion alone, I would've gotten divorced years ago. Hell, I probably wouldn't have gotten married in the first place."

Tearing my gaze from the window to open a cabinet, I muttered, "Well, sometimes thinking things through too much gets you into trouble."

"Are you saying I shouldn't have gotten married?"

Laughing boisterously, I grabbed two cans of cat food and began to peel back the lids, as I replied, "Yes, Mom. That's exactly what I'm saying. Go ahead and divorce Daddy now before it's too late."

"Wiseass," she laughed with a snort. "Anyway, I'm just saying, I'm going to miss Josh. He was a nice guy."

"I know," I agreed, dumping the food into the communal dishes. "I'll miss him, too."

"So, I'll see you on Sunday."

"Always," I replied with a smile, as I watched the four felines come together to enjoy their dinner. "Have a good night, Mom."

"You, too, baby."

With the call over, I succumbed to the silent nothingness of living alone. I took in a deep breath and glanced out the window, to watch the Sound, rippling beneath the familiar glow of the day's last bit of sunlight. I considered going out there and sitting on the rocks with my toes in the salty water. The water was never quiet and without the quiet, I was never lonely. But instead, I decided to open the windows, to welcome the shore inside my home, and ran a bath.

Before I could fully submerge my body in the bubbly water, I remembered the new loofah I had bought earlier and tucked into my tote bag. Cursing under my breath, I stepped out of the tub and hurried, naked, through the house to the living room, where my bag waited by the door. I grabbed the loofah and was about to run back to the tub, when I spotted a flash of muddy red. August came rushing back to my mind, and I decided to do some reading in the tub.

***

The woman on the other side of the room looked at me. Her eyes just met mine and I just smiled. I turn away and that relentless nagging in my stupid stupid stupid fucking brain tells me to look at her again. So, I do, and she's not looking at me anymore, but fuck she's pretty and now I'm staring. I can't even help it. She has a long neck and it's the exact same type of neck that I love on a woman. Thin and bony, easy to wrap my hands around and crack like one of them bones you rip apart from a chicken. Wishbone. That's what those things are called. I want her to look at me and see me. If she looks, I'll go over there, but only if she looks, and then, I'd give her a name but not mine. She doesn't need mine, because it doesn't matter. She just needs a name to give her friend there and that'll make her feel better about coming with me. But she shouldn't feel better. Nah, she should be scared, terrified, horrified of me but I don't like them scared from the get-go. I like to watch the fear come to be, like watching the birth of a baby. And then I like to watch it build into something big and powerful and impossible to fight until they can't do anything but scream.

I smile and think about what she sounds like when she screams. I bet she looks real pretty when she screams.

F U C K

I'm hard, and she's walking away. She's leaving me. Fuck her for leaving.

I'm going going going going going. I'm going to stop her. I have to. I can't let her leave, I can't give her that chance. Her friend will have excuses but fuck her too.

You know what that's what I'm gonna do.

I'm gonna fuck em both.

Why the hell not?

I always like a challenge.

***

I lowered the book to my lap and checked the clock at my side. It was after two in the morning, and I had to get up in just a few hours to see Phoebe and the others at St. Mary's. This book, *Musings of Murder & Mayhem*, had completely captured my attention and I had allowed my ears to deafen to the ticking clock. But I needed to stop now and get to bed. God, it was good though, and I didn't want to stop reading.

August had given me this book, after telling me what a pile of garbage it was, yet I was entirely captivated by the twisted power of his imagination. If this was his garbage, I quivered with excitement at the thought of what his masterpiece might be.

I decided then to grab my phone from beside me on the bed and type his name into a web search. There, I was greeted by his face, captured in a professional photograph. The guy was the real deal. Seven years ago, at twenty-one, he was published by S&S Publications, making him the publishing house's youngest signed author at the time. He had since released four books, with *Murder & Mayhem* being his most recent, published seven months ago, just days after his twenty-eighth birthday.

Disregarding the time and my need for sleep, I slipped willingly down a dark, winding rabbit hole of information, as I uncovered the truth about August's traumatic childhood. When he was only nine, his father had taken his own life due to a fifty-one-year long battle with mental illness. Then, at the age of fifteen, August lost his mother to breast cancer. As an only child, he had found himself orphaned and alone, and was sent to live with his grandmother in Connecticut, who showered him with the love of two parents and then some. But no amount of love could combat the bipolar disorder he had inherited from his late father.

By the time I had finished reading his biography, it was three-thirty, and I cursed under my breath at allowing my brain to become so distracted by this man I'd never see again. And then, I was sad, as my eyes fell to the plain, red book. I hated that my time with him had been so fleeting, and I hated that I had allowed my heart to like him so much. The man was twenty-eight years old, for crying out loud. Twenty-eight! He was only a few years older than my eldest niece, and I was fourteen years his senior. Something about those niggling little facts left my skin crawling with disgust, and yet, I couldn't fight the truth.

I liked him. I was taken by his appearance, appreciative of his taste in music and literature, and fascinated by his undeniable talent.

But I was never going to see him again, none of it mattered, and that made me so, so sad.

CHAPTER EIGHT

Connecticut was trapped beneath another rain cloud that Friday, and when I entered the hospital, the woman at the front desk looked up from her book and smiled sympathetically at the sight of my drenched hair and soggy companion.

"Gross day, huh?"

"Not for me," I said, smiling and heading toward the elevator. "This is my favorite kind of day. It makes you appreciate the sun that much more."

She scoffed and thrust a hand into the air. "You can have your rain. I don't need it to appreciate a nice, sunny day, thank you very much."

I laughed, pushing the buttons to head up to the third floor. "Well, I hope you have a good day, anyway. Maybe the weekend will bring some sun."

"We can only hope," she grumbled, before returning to her reading.

Inside the elevator, Agnes decided to shake herself out, spraying my legs with rain water and the scent of wet dog. I sighed as we arrived at Floor Number Three, and the doors whooshed open. Sylvie Sherman was waiting for me at the nurse's station and at the first sight of me, she laughed, sympathy heavy in her eyes.

"Ag got you good," she noted, nodding toward my soaked pants. "She looks pretty proud of herself, too."

Agnes sat at my feet, wagging her tail happily, and I laughed. "I'll get her back later, when I hose her down in the bath," I replied mischievously, waggling my brows and grinning.

Agnes cocked her head and her ears fell back at the word *bath*, bringing both Sylvie and me to laugh at the poor dog's expense. One of the nurses handed me a towel to dry her off, while Sylvie explained that I only had one patient to see today, and that was Phoebe. I asked what had happened to an elderly woman I had been seeing, and Sylvie sighed mournfully.

"She passed away Wednesday night," she told me, as I rubbed the towel along Ag's back and legs. "I thought someone might've called, otherwise I would have done it myself. I'm sorry."

"Oh, that's too bad," I said, remembering the old woman who had been living with debilitating anxiety since the sudden death of her husband. Then, I hesitantly began to ask, "Did she ..."

Sylvie shook her head quickly. "No, no, no. She died in her sleep."

"Thank God," I muttered, grateful for that and glad she was finally with her late husband again.

After Agnes was as dry as she was going to be, I headed in the direction of Phoebe's room and found her laying on her bed, reading a paperback and kicking her legs in the air. It was such a dramatic change from the catatonic girl I'd seen just a few days ago, and I smiled at the sight of her.

"Miss Phoebe!" I exclaimed, entering the room, and letting Agnes off her leash.

The dog jumped onto the bed, and I immediately grimaced, knowing she was still damp. Phoebe didn't seem to mind though, as she grinned and laughed at Ag's wagging tail and excited, puppy-like pouncing.

"Okay, Agnes, okay," she said, tucking the bookmark away and closing the book, to give the insistent dog her full attention. Then, she turned to me and smiled, bright as the sun. "Hi, Clara."

"Whatcha readin'?" I asked, dropping my tote bag onto a chair.

"Um," she held the book up and showed me the cover, "*The Phantom Tollbooth.*"

"Ah." I nodded, smiling at the old, familiar illustration of a boy and a dog with a clock in its belly. "That's an old favorite of mine."

Phoebe rolled on the bed with Agnes, digging her fingers into the dog's fur and laughing as Agnes tried desperately to lick her face. I took a seat at the edge of the bed and took note of the daisies still on the bedside table, now a little drier than they'd been on Monday, and I noticed the note, laying open to the side of the vase. I wanted to ask what it said and what had made her finally decide to read it, but I wouldn't pry. Not unless she told me herself.

"Guess what?" Phoebe asked, sitting upright and gently luring Agnes into her lap.

"Phoebs," I groaned playfully, "I am no good at guessing games and you know it."

"No, no, no, come on. Guess."

I groaned, throwing my head back. "Why do you hate me?"

She laughed and rested her temple against my shoulder. Phoebe only ever showed affection toward me when she was in a very good mood, when she had overcome her lowest of lows and was riding an incredible high, and I smiled.

"Come on, Clara. Please?"

"Okay, okay," I sighed, feigning aggravation. "You … had the best scrambled eggs of your life this morning for breakfast."

"Ew, no. They have no idea how to cook here. Guess again."

"You said I only had to guess once!"

Phoebe laughed and nodded. "Okay, fine. They're sending me home, but this time, I'm going to my mom's place instead of my dad's. She lives in Florida and has a house on the beach, and I am *totally* going to get my tan on."

"You prefer it at your mom's house?" I asked, remembering that the flowers had been sent by her father.

Phoebe nodded eagerly. "I love my mom."

"Don't you love your dad, too?"

Her petting of Agnes slowed at the mention of her father, but she otherwise didn't react to the question. I didn't need to be Sherlock Holmes to know there was something going on between this girl and her father, and I made a mental note to mention it to Dr. Sherman.

"I live on the beach," I said, quickly changing the subject.

Phoebe lifted her head, eyes full of intrigue. "Really? I didn't know that."

I nodded. "I do, in River Canyon."

"That's so cool. I *love* the beach."

"Me, too. I love the sound of the waves at night," I told her, smiling at the thought of my quaint cottage. "I have this totally amazing clawfoot tub, so what I like to do is, open all of the windows, light some candles, and take a bath by candlelight, just listening to the waves. It's one of my favorite things ever."

Phoebe was silent and when I looked at her, I saw a look of whimsical melancholy in her eyes. Surprised by her reaction to my attempt at conversation, I reached out and laid a hand on her arm.

"Hey, Phoebs, are you okay?"

As if to snap herself out of it, she gave her head a rapid shake and then smiled. "O-oh, yeah, I'm fine," she said, smiling reassuringly. "That just sounds really nice."

"It is," I agreed hesitantly, afraid to say anything more and unsettle the balance she had found.

"Maybe I can have that one day," she replied, then laughed and lifted her shoulders in a heavy shrug. "I mean, I doubt it, but it's really nice to think about."

***

Sylvie handed me a cup of awful coffee and we toasted to the weekend. I took a tiny sip of the bitter brew and swallowed against the urge to spit it out into the cup, and she laughed.

"It's terrible, I know. I keep telling them to get some new stuff, but they just keep buying this crap."

"It's better than nothing, I guess," I offered weakly, while I begged the taste to erase itself from my tastebuds.

She put her cup down on one of the break room tables before leaning her back against the wall. Then, she asked, "Did Phoebe tell you she's leaving next week?"

"She did," I said, nodding. "She told me she's going to Florida to stay with her mom."

Sylvie narrowed her eyes and shook her head. "Uh, no. She's not."

"What? She said—"

"She did call her mom earlier in the week and asked if she could go down to Florida, but her mother said no."

"Then, why—"

"Phoebe has been deflecting her unhappiness onto her father. I don't know if she's mentioned anything to you, but she's blaming him for why she's depressed, when really, it's just … how it is, for lack of a better explanation."

I nodded slowly. "But then, why lie about going to her mother's place?"

Sylvie looked utterly downtrodden and defeated as she shrugged with her whole body and slapped her thighs with her hands. "I don't know. I guess … because it's

66

what she thinks would make her happy? Maybe pretending is how she's choosing to cope? I don't know. I wish I could keep her longer if I'm being honest. I'm worried about her. But her father's insurance needs a more valid reason to keep paying for her to stay here, and he doesn't have the money to pay out of pocket. So, I have no choice but to release her."

A sickening feeling filled my stomach and left me bloated as I glanced out the door, as if I could peer down the hall from here and into Phoebe's room.

"You don't think she's going to—"

"I don't know," she replied, cutting me off before I could finish the dreaded question. "I don't know what's going to happen. But I am worried, and I don't like to release a patient when I feel this way."

I nodded empathically, thinking about my young friend and her troubled mind, and said, "Neither do I."

***

On the way home, to take my mind off Phoebe and the questions I had about her relationship with her father, and a persistent feeling of dread, I pulled into the parking lot of a small, hole-in-the-wall bookstore. I cracked a window for Agnes and headed inside, where a clerk asked if he could help me find anything. There were few things I enjoyed more than wandering the aisles of a bookstore without any particular destination in mind, but that was only when I didn't have my four-legged companion waiting for me in the car.

So, not wanting to make her wait any longer than was necessary, I nodded eagerly at the man and said, "Yes, you can. What do you have by August Gordon?"

His eyes took on a quixotic look and he pursed his lips, before hurrying off to his computer. "Let's see here," he muttered to himself. "That was August—"

"August Gordon," I repeated, nodding.

He typed quickly and clicked around with his computer mouse. "August, August, August ... yes, hmm, okay, it looks like we have two, no, wait, three books written by August Gordon. So, if you will just follow me ... over ... here ..."

The man moved like a buzzing bee, weaving in and out between the heavy, wooden shelves, and hurrying around displays of books and magazines. He was making me dizzy, as I tried to follow him through the crammed little store, and I began to think I would have been better off finding the books myself. But then, he stopped at a shelf in the store's expansive Fiction section and used his finger to scan the rows of colorful spines.

"And here you go," he said, swiftly pulling the three books from the shelf.

They were the only books of August's they had in the store, each one of them looking as though it'd been tossed around a bit and neglected, but they were the three I didn't have. So, I told the man I would buy them all, and he rang me up with a smile on his face. Then, as I left with my completed collection of August Gordon novels, I wondered which one was his favorite, which one he thought was less like garbage, and I hated that I would never be able to ask.

CHAPTER NINE

We ate breakfast quietly, avoiding the topics of Christy's ex-boyfriend and recently found venture into the world of being single. Instead, we focused our collective attention on the twins, their third grade graduation, and the excitement of summer plans. My sister and her family had decided they were going to take a few trips this year, one to Disney World, another to Long Island's Montauk Point, and the last, a two-week long journey to Boston, to visit my brother-in-law's family. I was envious. Getting away and seeing different scenery sounded lovely, but when I mentioned as much, Marjorie groaned with a roll of her eyes toward her husband.

"This coming from the woman whose backyard is the freakin' beach," she muttered begrudgingly.

"Hey!" I exclaimed, laughing. "It's not a vacation when it's my everyday life."

Christy tapped my ankle with the tip of her big toe. "You should totally do one of those staycations," she said. "Order a crapload of food, get a ton of wine, and just spend the whole weekend relaxing in your house with the phone turned off."

"There is absolutely nothing relaxing about taking care of four cats, a bird, a bunch of fish, and one big dog," I grumbled through a smile. "But hey, if you wanna pet sit, I'd be glad to vacay in my house for a whole damn week."

"I'd take Agnes," Christy laughed, "but there's no way I'd take the rest of them. Especially Bumby."

The jab at my mischief-prone cat pulled another laugh from my lips. She wasn't wrong. Bumby had spent his first few years on this planet breaking every vase I brought into the house and keeping me on my toes.

With a declaration that I was finished eating, I excused myself, cleaned my plate, and headed into my sister's sunlit covered porch, where I sat down on a wicker couch and pulled *Musings of Murder & Mayhem* from my tote bag.

Ever since I was a little girl, the best way I knew to spend time was to hide my nose between the pages of a book. The words always played out as a movie in my head, and in most cases, the books that kept me company were better than any movie I could've spent my time with instead. I read everything from romance to horror, and there were very few books I found I couldn't at the very least tolerate to the end. This one wasn't any exception, and since that first night I'd started reading it, I had purposely taken my time to make it last. I didn't want it to end just yet, no matter how badly I wanted to fly through the pages. It was a work of expertly crafted prose, one that had thrust me head-first into the dark mind of a killer, and I was completely and utterly obsessed.

"What book is that?"

Immediately frustrated, my eyes slammed shut at the intrusive sound of my sister's voice. "Do you not see that I'm reading?"

"No, I know," she said, walking onto the porch and sitting beside me. "I'm just—"

"And so, you keep talking," I muttered before groaning impatiently.

"Huh?"

Ever since Marjie and I were kids, she had held tight to the annoying habit of disturbing me while I was reading. She didn't share the same love I had for the literary word and could never understand why I didn't like being interrupted. So, I sighed and slipped the bookmark back into place and closed the book, knowing I wouldn't be getting anymore reading done until I got home.

I handed the red book over to my sister and she took it from me. "*Musings of Murder & Mayhem*," she read, before turning it over to read the back blurb. "What is this? I've never heard of it."

"There's lots of books you don't know, Marj," I muttered dryly.

"Obviously," she groaned, rolling her eyes. "Where did you hear about it?"

"One of the patients at the hospital gave it to me," I said, and swallowed at the thought of actually telling her about August.

"Oh," Marjorie replied. She hesitated, she always did whenever the topic of my job came up, as if she didn't know how to proceed or if she even should. Then, she finally said, "Well, it looks interesting."

"It's very good," I agreed, taking it back. Then, before I knew what I was saying, I offered, "He wrote it."

"Who did?"

"The patient," I said. "Well, he's not a patient anymore. He was discharged. But he gave this to me before he left."

"Oh, cool," she said, taking it from me again to read the author's name. "August Gordon. Is that a pen name, or …"

"No, that's his name."

She nodded, like she was impressed. "Good name for an author."

"Yeah, it is. We really clicked, actually," I told her needlessly, as she passed the book back to my hands and I clutched it in my lap. "He was really into classic literature and old music, and one time, he talked me into playing Chess and seriously kicked my—"

"Wait a second," she said, holding up her hands and halting my words. Then, she declared, "You *liked* this guy."

I swallowed again. "Well, yeah, I mean—"

"No, no, no. You had a *thing* for him." Then, she held out one finger and poked my cheek, as she said in

73

her annoying little sister tone, "Or maybe ... you *still* have a thing for him ..."

Brushing her hand away, I rolled my eyes. "Oh, get out of here," I grumbled, knowing my cheeks had been set on fire and it had nothing to do with the sun, beating down on the little screened-in porch.

"You're blushing!" Marjorie squealed, grabbing my arm with too much excitement. "God, when was the last time you actually *liked* a guy? This is crazy!"

"It's not," I said, before hastily adding, "And I don't *like* him. Even if I did, there's absolutely nothing I'd be able to do about it. I have no way of finding him—"

"Clara, there are probably a thousand ways to find a person. You have a smartphone, for crying out loud. Pull up the White Pages and look him up."

I sighed and dropped my gaze to the book in my hands. "I can't do that," I insisted, shaking my head. "How creepy would that be? And in any case, the guy is twenty-eight years old. I'm not ... like that."

Marjorie scoffed. "Like what?"

"Into younger men!" I exclaimed, drawing the attention of my niece and mother.

"Who's into younger men?" Mom asked, wandering onto the porch with Christy following closely behind.

"Nobody," I groaned, rolling my eyes toward my infuriating sister.

"Clara likes this guy who happens to be in his twenties," she tattled in a matter-of-fact tone.

Christy gasped, a broad grin forming quickly on her lips, as she dropped into a chair. "*What*? Who is he?"

74

I had been blessed with a close-knit family and I was usually glad for it. Very few times in my life had I ever cursed them for being too nosy, but right now was one of those times, and I struggled to think of a way to get out of the conversation.

"I met a patient a couple weeks ago and I enjoyed his company, that's all," I said, hoping that would satisfy them enough and cursing myself for even bringing it up in the first place. I had known I shouldn't—why hadn't I listened?

"And now, Clara's reading his book and wishing she had the guts to find him," Marjie added, and I jabbed her swiftly in the ribs with an elbow.

Mom studied my stern, stony face for a moment, not saying anything as my sister and niece continued to tease and prod. In a fleeting glance, I met Mom's eyes, to see if I could tell what might have been going on in that head of hers, only to quickly look away and stare ahead at the door. Wondering if I could make a fast getaway.

Then, Mom declared with finality, "Leave Clara alone. If she doesn't want to talk about it, then don't make her. If she wants to find this man, she will, and if she doesn't, she won't."

Marjorie and Christy were disappointed, but there was an unspoken rule in our family that my mother always had the last word. With lead-filled shoes, they left the porch to carry on with their day, leaving Mom lingering at my side. I didn't say anything, as I took a deep breath and slipped the book back into my bag. I stood, with every intention of wishing my mother a good

Sunday before leaving, when she stopped me with a hand to my cheek.

"Things always have a way of working out, honey," she said, smiling with a knowing little glint in her eye. "Even when you're convinced they won't."

"I don't know about that," I muttered, allowing myself the briefest moment to bare my soul. "Nothing's ever really worked out for me before."

"Hm," she hummed contemplatively, still smiling. "Then, I think it's about time something *did*, don't you?"

CHAPTER TEN

The children's hospital left my shoulders sagging and my body weary, as I pulled into my driveway wearing a frown. One of the little girls Agnes was seeing lost her battle to leukemia just hours before we'd arrived that day, and I felt like a failure. Like I had let her down by not visiting sooner, as if I could've done anything to stop the inevitable from happening. I knew it was foolish, but when has grief ever been known to make a person think clearly?

My phone rang just as Agnes and I walked into the house, and I answered.

"Hey, Marjie," I said, knowing who it was without checking.

"Hey, are you ready to go?"

Over the weekend my sister, niece, and I had made plans to go to the movies tonight, but that was before I had lost someone I'd cared about. Now, I sighed at the thought of doing anything other than eating my weight in ice cream and crying to the tune of sad songs sung by crooners of the past.

"I don't know," I moaned, sighing again. "I just got in the door and I'm really not sure I feel like going."

"What? Why?" Marjie exclaimed.

"I didn't have a great day."

"But it's *Rear Window*! You love *Rear Window*!"

She was right; I did love *Rear Window*. I loved anything starring Jimmy Stewart, especially when Hitchcock was involved. But I wasn't so sure good ol' Jimmy or Hitchcock could make me smile on a day like this, and I answered with another groan, while wandering down the hall to the tranquility of my bedroom.

"I don't know," I muttered hesitantly. "A little girl Agnes and I were seeing died today."

"Oh, no," Marjie replied, an instant injection of sadness flooding her tone. "I'm so sorry."

"Yeah, so I think I just want to stay home and—"

"No. Come on, Clara," she said with defiance. "Staying home is only going to make you feel worse. Sometimes, the best thing you can do is have some fun, if for nothing else but to distract yourself for a little while."

When Marjie and I were kids, our last grandparent had died in his sleep. Martin McKinley the First was old, and it hadn't been unexpected. But he was one of the most influential people in my life, being the one to introduce me to the classic singers, books, and movies I adored. When he passed away, the amount of love I'd held for him had nowhere else to go, now that he was no longer in the world. My sister and I had spent that first day without him in tears, unable to look at each other or our parents without breaking down. But the next day, our father had suggested we spend more time smiling than crying, and we found that, sometimes, smiling was as beneficial as crying to the grieving process.

So, I agreed to go out that night to see Jimmy Stewart on the big screen, as long as she didn't mind I wear a comfortable pair of sweats and an old, worn t-shirt.

"I'm just glad you're coming out," she said, and I hung up to throw on my coziest clothes.

***

A few hours later, I left the theater with a soft smile on my face, thankful for that time Jimmy Stewart and Grace Kelly filmed a movie together, and wishing to live in that era. I missed it, as if I had lived in those years myself, when men wore fedoras and held doors without being asked or told. I was all for the womens' movement and fighting for our rights to be treated as equals, but I wished that with it, there wasn't also a loss of a man's desire to treat a woman like a lady and hold a door open for her.

I headed down the sidewalk with my sister and niece, talking about our love for a man in a good hat, when we came upon a coffee shop on our way to the parking lot. Christy's hand was already on the door handle when she asked if we'd mind her stopping in to grab something heavily caffeinated.

"It's already ten o'clock," Marjie commented in a motherly tone with a raise of her brows.

"I know," Christy said, diverting her eyes from Marjie's gaze and pulling the door open. "But I have some stuff to do, and I need something to keep me awake for a while."

With another grumbled protest from my sister, we stepped inside to find the coffee shop empty of customers, while a young woman mopped the floor and stacked chairs on tables. She was obviously in the process of closing and Christy stopped abruptly on her way to the register.

"Oh, sorry," she said. "I didn't realize you weren't open."

The woman stopped mopping and shook her head, wearing a tired smile. "Oh, you're fine. We don't close for another half hour. Hold on a second." Then, gripping the mop in both hands, she turned her head and asked a man behind the counter if he could help us out.

"Oh, of course," he said, turning around to ring us up.

I am a believer in Fate, and I believe that everything in our lives is somehow perfectly aligned to happen exactly the way it is meant to. Now, whether it's all designed by a higher power or the zodiacs or something else entirely, I couldn't exactly say for sure, but I believed in *something*. At that moment, on a Tuesday night, in a little hole in the wall coffee shop, I believed Fate had put August Gordon back in my life for a reason. And if that reason was for my brain to lose all sense of cognizance, then I was absolutely making Fate proud.

"What can I get for you?" he asked Christy as she approached the counter without any clue of who he was or why my tongue was suddenly tied up in knots.

"Can I just get a medium Americano?"

"Absolutely," he said, punching in the order. Then, lifting his head, he asked, "And for you—"

His words were abruptly halted when his eyes landed on me. We shared a moment of silent stammering, our mouths flapping like the lips of guppies in a stream and our eyes locked on each other, unblinking. A pinkish color rose from the collar of his blue polo shirt to wash his cheeks, and I realized then that he was embarrassed to be seen by me. I wondered if I should leave. If I should turn around and pretend this moment never happened, like I never saw him in his black Beanery cap with his curls peeking from beneath the brim. Running away seemed like the best option, since talking didn't seem feasible at the moment, and just as I was about to scoop my pride up off the floor and turn around, he spoke.

"Clara?"

He looked at me as if I were a ghost and he said my name as if it were a question. The desire to run away had still continued to build, but I couldn't leave now, knowing that he had recognized me, and so, I chose to own it.

"Hey, August," I said, stepping toward the counter on unsteady legs. "I had no idea you worked here."

He hesitated before smiling and shrugged. "Yeah, well, it helps to pay the bills," he explained, as if he had to explain anything at all.

The world around us had, for a moment, stopped, and in the blink of an eye, it all started up again with the strength of my sister's hand, grabbing onto my arm. "*This* is August?" she asked in a voice too loud to be suitable. I looked at her, wide eyed and angry, and she swallowed. "Sorry."

But it was too late. August had heard her, and his blushing cheeks deepened in their pinkish hue, as he asked, "So, can I get you ladies anything or is it just the one drink?"

"Um," Christy turned to glance at my sister and then at me, "just the one."

August rang her up and went to brew her coffee, as she came to stand beside her mother and me. She nudged me in the ribs and gave me a look that said I should be saying something to him instead of standing awkwardly on this side of the counter. I knew she was right, but my tongue was tangled up, and words wouldn't form. Seeing him in this capacity felt different than before. At the hospital, I was in my element, and he was vulnerable, dressed only in a t-shirt and sweatpants. But here, in a setting where we were peers, and he looked more like himself and less like a patient, he possessed an even stranger power over me that left me both terrified and excited.

"How's Agnes?" he finally asked, as the espresso machine worked its magic.

I smiled, grateful his tongue was working better than mine, and said, "She's, um … she's good."

"I miss her. Been thinking about getting a dog, actually, but I don't think my grandmother would appreciate it."

"You never know," I replied. "She might like it."

"Hmm," he said with a nod. "Maybe. I'll have to ask her."

"You live with her?" I asked, grasping at things to talk about, while he poured Christy's coffee.

He nodded. "I've been with her since I was fifteen. Can't abandon her now."

Then, he popped a lid onto the cup and handed it to my niece. But he was looking at me, his lips soft and his eyes full of confidence and determination. Marjorie and Christy had already begun to head back toward the door, giving me a little privacy and space, while my legs remained frozen to the ground and my mouth begged to speak the words wrapped inside my tongue.

"It's crazy you walked in here tonight," he said.

I nodded, biting my lip, before saying, "I know. It really is."

"You have no idea how much I've been thinking about you," he went on. "Just before you came in, I was wondering if I should find you, and then, there you were. You found me instead."

The air felt tight, trapped inside my lungs, as I smiled. "I've thought about finding you, but I didn't know if I should."

Then, he asked, "Can I take you out?" Just like that. No hesitation, no stammer of his words.

"*Out?*" I echoed stupidly. "Um … I don't know. I have to—"

"Don't think about it," he interrupted gently. "There *is* a reason why you walked in here tonight, and I'm not letting you leave until you agree to going out with me."

With a quick glance over my shoulder, I saw my annoying sister and even more annoying niece, waiting by the door and watching with more hope than I could begin to feel in a moment where my stomach threatened to expel the popcorn I'd just eaten. I knew what I wanted to say to him and I knew how I wanted to say it, but letting the words out seemed impossible when the issues that had bothered me before still bothered me now.

He had been a patient in a hospital I worked in, and he was so young.

"August, I want to," I said. "But—"

"Why does there have to be a but?"

"Because you were a patient," I said. "And I've worked with you."

"But I'm not anymore," he countered with a mischievous grin.

"Okay, but that doesn't change the fact that you are so much younger—"

"Clara," he cut me off. "Let's pretend it's gentlemanly of me to ask how old you are."

"I'm forty-two," I said firmly, as if to prove a point.

"Does that bother you?"

"My age?"

He nodded, as his lips began to curl in a slow, sultry smile. "Yes."

"No, but—"

"It doesn't bother me, either. So, if it doesn't bother me and it doesn't bother you, then what does it matter?"

My hands twisted tiredly around themselves as my stomach tied into knots. "I don't know, August. I just—"

"It has been a long time since I've enjoyed spending my time with someone as much as I enjoyed spending time with you, and I knew I could've loved you. Letting you walk away from me was one of the hardest things I've had to do recently. And here I've been given a second chance at making sure I don't let you walk away again without at least getting your number," he said, speaking with confidence and grandeur, and not caring that his coworker was still there, cleaning and getting ready to leave for the night. "So, what do you think? Will you give me the chance to fall in love with you?"

I raised a hand to my forehead, certain I was sweating, and groaned, as my nerves swam in a bottomless pit of nausea at all of this mention of love and going out. "God, I don't—"

"Clara, for Christ's sake, just say yes," Marjorie hissed loudly from behind me.

August laughed and pointed in her direction. "See, your friend knows what's best for you. Thank you, friend."

"You're welcome," she answered quietly, then giggled girlishly with her daughter.

"She's my sister," I corrected unnecessarily, before dropping my hand and saying, "Fine. I'll go out with you. But only once to see what happens."

August's grin rivaled the brilliance of the moon, reminding me of a kid on Christmas morning. His happiness was contagious and flattering, knowing I had put it there, and I smiled along with him, my cheeks burning hot and bright with the thrill of being asked out by this man I liked more than I should.

Then, he said, "All I ever wanted was to be given a chance."

I gave him my number and the promise that, when he called, I would answer. Then, before I could talk myself out of the undeniable feelings I had for him, I left with my sister and niece in tow and a smile so wide my cheeks threatened to quit. Because my bad day had taken a turn for the better, and I could easily see myself falling in love with August Gordon.

CHAPTER ELEVEN

I walked into St. Mary's with the strangest blend of emotions fighting for my attention. On one hand, I was jittering with excitement and nerves for my phone call and eventual date with August. But on the other, I was weighed down by the sadness of knowing this would be my last day with Phoebe. It was hard to remember that I had already been through other "last days" with her, but every time was still just as hard as the last.

Agnes ran into Phoebe's room and jumped onto her bed. Her tail swished wildly from side to side, as she lapped at the squealing girl's face, and I laughed as I dropped my bag into the chair.

"She's happy to see you," I commented, grinning with adoration.

Phoebe looked at me over Agnes's head, squinting to avoid catching a tongue to the eye, and said, "I know. I just wish she could say it in a less nasty way."

Still laughing, I commanded for Agnes to calm down, and she did, settling into our young friend's lap with a smile on her face. Phoebe wrapped her arms around the dog's neck and kissed the top of her head.

"I'm going to miss you guys so much," she said, a touch of melancholy in her tone.

"We'll miss you, too," I replied, encouraging my smile to hang on tight, while my own sadness threatened to take it away.

"I don't know what I'm gonna do without you."

The statement brought pause, as I wondered how she would handle her next stint outside of the hospital. There was hope that she would be fine and that her life would finally bring her enough joy to keep her demons at bay. I wanted that for her, she deserved it, and so, I grasped her gaze and smiled.

"You're going to be just fine," I assured her, hoping she'd believe it. Hoping it was true.

She met my gaze with a somber expression, and asked, "Do you think that, um, I could have your number?"

It was the second time in less than twenty-four hours that someone had asked for my number, but this time seemed more out of necessity than August's desire to take me on a date. "Of course, you can," I said. "You can talk to me whenever you want."

"I don't even know if I'll ever need it or anything, but I just ... I don't know. I guess I'll feel better to have it this time. You know?"

"Phoebs, you don't need to have a reason. You can call me every day, if you want, or you can never call me. But if you think you need it for whatever reason, then I want you to have it."

She diverted her gaze to the top of Agnes's white-blonde head and nodded. The last time I had seen her, she had exhibited an excitement in being released, but today, she was nervous. Almost like she didn't know if she could trust herself outside of these walls.

"Are you excited to go home?" I asked, gently prying.

Phoebe shrugged. "I guess. I mean, it'll be nice to see my sister, and of course, my mom. I haven't seen her in so long, so that's cool. But ..." She shrugged again. "I'm just gonna miss you. And Dr. Sylvie."

"You're going to be just fine," I repeated, reaching out to gently clip my knuckles against her knee.

"And what if I'm not?" she asked, lowering her brows and biting her bottom lip.

"Then, we'll be right here," I promised, hoping she'd remember that when times inevitably got hard.

***

"I'm worried about her," I admitted to Sylvie over another cup of bad coffee. "She just seems so ... uncomfortable about leaving. And she mentioned her mom again."

"I know. And it's hard to tell if she's just nervous to be on her own after being here for a while, or if she's genuinely scared. Maybe it's both. I don't know."

"She asked for my number, and I gave it to her," I said. "I feel a little better knowing she has it."

Sylvie nodded and took a sip from her paper cup. "She has mine, too. Maybe next time she needs some help, she'll be in the frame of mind to call one of us instead of hurting herself."

"I hope so."

"Me, too."

A lull in the conversation fell over us, and my mind took the opportunity to wander. I chewed my lip, as I thought about August and when he would call and if I was doing the right thing by going out with him. I glanced toward Sylvie, as she typed on her phone, and made the split decision to mention it to her. I wanted to gage her reaction and get her opinion, while also bracing myself for the possible backlash.

"So," I began, circling my coffee cup with the tip of my finger. "I was out last night with Marjie and Christy, and I bumped into August."

"August ... Gordon?" Sylvie lowered her phone and cocked her head.

I nodded. "Yeah. We stopped into a little coffee shop in Hartford—The Beanery, I think it's called—and he was working there."

"Wow," she said, leaning back in her chair. "Small world."

"Seriously." I cleared my throat and fidgeted with a pen I had laid on the table. "Um, he kinda asked me out."

Her casual demeanor quickly snapped and became more startled and urgent. "August? He asked you out?"

I swallowed against the never-ending collection of nerves, plucking endlessly at my heart, and nodded. "Yeah. He asked me for my number and was really persistent about me giving him a chance, so …" I shrugged. "I gave it to him, and I guess we'll see what happens. But …"

"But?"

"What do you think?" I asked cautiously.

She barked with an abrupt laugh. "What do *I* think?"

"Yeah," I said, nodding. "Do you think I should go?"

Sylvie laughed uncomfortably and shrugged. "Clara, I can't tell you what to do in this situation."

"Well, what would *you* do?"

"*Me*?" She pressed her hand over her white-coated heart. "I wouldn't be in this situation at all. August is my patient and—"

"No, I know that," I said, nodding. "But if you were in my position, what would you do?"

She leaned back in her chair and considered the question with a contemplative crumple of her brow. Then, she said, "If I were you, and I really liked him, I think I would go."

I hadn't expected that answer. "You would?"

"Yeah. I mean, you're not seeing him in a professional capacity at this point, so ethically, I don't see anything wrong with it," Sylvie replied with another shrug. She then pursed her lips, like she had something else to add, but gave her head a little shake and reached for her coffee instead.

"Was there anything else?" I pressed, my curiosity running away with me.

"No," she said, shaking her head before taking a sip.

I narrowed my eyes. "Are you sure?"

Sylvie sighed then and lowered the paper cup to the table. "Clara, you know that saying anything would be a violation of HIPAA."

Of course, I knew that, and I felt ashamed for even asking. "I know," I said, laying a hand against my forehead. "I shouldn't have said anything, I'm sorry."

She waved a dismissive hand and smiled. "It's okay. And while I can't say anything about *him*, I will, as your friend, tell you to just be careful."

"Careful?" I parroted, narrowing my eyes with surprise. "Why do you say that?"

"You know," she shrugged again, looking for the words inside her cup of bad coffee, "men can be real assholes. And sometimes, when you get a guy who's so much younger—*or* older—they're not always looking for a lasting thing. They're just out there, looking for a thrill, and I just don't want you to get hurt."

Slowly nodding, I allowed her words to settle inside my brain, while my heart demanded that I protest and defend a man I barely knew. There was no reason to dispute the things she was saying, though. What did I know? Maybe he really was a sleaze, just looking for a roll in the sand with a woman nearly old enough to be his mother.

Outside the window, the sun, framed by happy, fluffy clouds, was burning bright in the sky. Summer was just around the corner, my favorite time of the year, and I recalled the months I'd spent in the arms of the last man I was with. I had been infatuated with him for a summer, a few months of shared companionship on the beach and in my bed. But come the fall, I had released him easily without any bad feelings between us. I considered the possibility of something similar occurring between August and me. If he was what Sylvie described, an asshole just looking for an experience with an older woman, and I was forever hesitant to be tied to a man nearly half my age, then maybe one summer of fun was all we were meant to have. And I hoped that maybe I could eventually convince my heart that was fine.

CHAPTER TWELVE

I had given August my phone number on Tuesday
night, so by Wednesday evening, I began to wonder
if he was ever going to call at all. It irked me, the
way I kept checking my phone for messages, like I was
an eager teenager waiting for the attention of the cute
boy in class. This wasn't who I was and never had been.
But no matter how many times I scolded myself with the
reminder that I was a sensible, middle-aged woman, I
couldn't help the impatient giddiness that filled me up at
the thought of hearing his voice again.

"Maybe he's not gonna call tonight," I said to
Bumby, the mischievous little bastard, as he crossed my
path on his way to the living room, while batting at a
little, jingling ball.

He had nothing to say and instead disappeared
behind the couch with his toy. I sighed and sprinkled a
bit of fish food into the tank for the second time that

night, before heading into the kitchen to wipe down the counter. It was unnecessary busywork, but I needed something to do and something to focus on, until it was time to curl up in bed to do it all over again the next day. Then, just as I was about to add a little more food to my cockatiel's dish, the phone rang from inside my sweatshirt, and I nearly dropped the birdseed on my way to answer it.

"Hello?" I answered hurriedly, while rushing to put the food away.

"Hello, Clarice."

It wasn't the first time in my life someone had used the iconic *Hannibal* line on me, and my typical response was to groan and roll my eyes. This time hit differently though, as my usual groan was replaced by a girly giggle I wasn't proud of, and I dropped to the couch, curling my body around a quilted throw pillow.

"Hi, August."

"Okay, now I've gotta ask," he said. "Is your name actually Clarice, or is it just Clara?"

"No, it's … it's actually Clarabell," I answered and chewed on my bottom lip, waiting for him to laugh. Everybody usually teases and makes livestock jokes when hearing what my given name is. But August didn't laugh.

"Clarabell," he repeated in a way I'd never heard my full name spoken before. Low and whispered. Sensual, even. "I like that. It's uncommon."

Goosebumps sprinkled over my arms and a shiver trickled down my spine, to settle low in my belly, but I quickly pulled myself together with a deep breath, before replying, "My parents decided to name their kids after their respective mothers. So, I'm named after my father's mom, and my sister is named after my mother's mom."

"What is her name?"

"Marjorie."

He hummed reflectively, and I thought about sex. "I like that, too. Not as much as Clarabell, but I might be a little biased," he said. "I like unusual names, the ones you don't hear all the time nowadays."

"I like a lot of stuff that's not popular these days," I snorted, laughing in spite of myself.

"Like Perry Como."

"Yes," I replied with a nod. "And Peggy Lee ... and Sinatra ... and Nat King Cole ... and—"

"Etta James?"

"Of course."

He sniffed a soft chuckle and said, "You're a rare breed, Clarabell."

"It's a problem," I groused, laughing again and wrapping my fingers in the tassels hanging from a blanket.

"It is," he agreed. "I haven't found a whole lot of women who meet my standards."

"I haven't found a whole lot of *men* who meet mine," I admitted, while remembering what Sylvie had said. The possibility that he could just be looking for an uncommitted fling.

"So, then I'm going to guess you've never been married."

I licked my lips and shook my head. "Nope. Never found someone worthy enough," I replied, only half-joking.

"Should I be embarrassed then, to tell you I've been married and divorced twice?"

"Twice?" I squeaked, eyes widening to stare at the cat by my side. "You're only twenty-eight, and you've been divorced twice," I repeated, disbelieving and wondering if that should be a red flag.

He choked on a laugh and coughed into the phone. "I guess this is where I confess that I fall fast and act on impulse a lot of the time," he admitted.

"And then, what?" I asked, hardening my tone and quickly guarding my heart, as I remembered the words Sylvie had said. Could it be that there was more truth to them than I'd realized? "You fall out just as quickly? Or do you just get bored?"

"Actually, neither. Not really," he replied. "My first wife left me after she realized I'm not the most attentive when I'm deep into my writing, and the second just got bored," he said, enunciating those last three words in a mocking tone that scorched my cheeks and left me embarrassed for so quickly jumping to conclusions.

"I'm sorry," I said, feeling it was necessary.

"Don't be. I'm not the first man to end up in a couple of shitty marriages." Then, he laughed. "But I guess a lot of them can't say they're still under thirty."

"How old were you when you got married the first time?" I pried.

"Twenty," he answered without hesitation. "We met when I was nineteen, got married a year later, and then

97

divorced two years after that. The second time, we met when I was twenty-four, got married six months later, and she was out of my life by the time I was twenty-seven."

"And you've also published four novels in that time," I mentioned, inadvertently divulging that I had looked him up.

"I see you've been doing your research," he said in that same low voice, encouraging my toes to curl a little against the couch.

The statement left a door open, and I made the decision to climb on in. "Well, after you gave me that book, I couldn't just *not* look you up," I laughed, dangerously close to giddy. "You probably had no idea that I love reading."

"No, I didn't," he replied, a smile in his voice. "But I can't say I'm surprised."

"Well, now you know. I read more than I do just about anything else. I rarely turn on my TV, and when I do, it's mostly for background noise. You should see the shelves in my living room. I have so many classics, it's not even funny. I collect them."

"You'll have to show me one day."

My stomach growled, reminding me that I hadn't eaten that night, and I got up from the couch to hurry into the kitchen with the phone pressed firmly to my ear.

"Who's your favorite author?" I asked him, as I threw the refrigerator door open.

"Hemingway," he answered without a moment's consideration.

Warmth balled up inside my belly and made itself at home as I stared at a container of leftover ziti, courtesy of my mother and her need to make sure that I was fed, and replied breathlessly, "Mine, too."

CHAPTER THIRTEEN

Heavy rain pelted noisily against the roof as the sun quickly retreated behind the cover of ominous, black clouds. Agnes and the cats slept, all cuddled up on my bed, while I hurried into the bathroom to shower before my date with August. He had given me strict instructions to dress nicely, no jeans or sweatpants allowed, and the elated anticipation had me belting out Sinatra's "Fly Me to the Moon" beneath the shower's heated spray.

When I got out, I stood before the mirror and wiped away the fog. With wet hair and a naked face, I studied the shadows beneath my eyes, lined with deepening creases I hadn't paid much attention to in months. It seemed the creams and elixirs I'd been investing in weren't doing their job, regardless of how much money I spent on them. I gnawed at my bottom lip, keeping my eyes on that woman, who looked a little like someone I used to know, and wondered when it was she had started to look so old.

Pulling a deep breath in, I collected my arsenal of beauty products and began to do my makeup. Self-consciousness grabbed a hold of me, as I slathered the stuff on and watched the spots and wrinkles disappear. As if someone had waved a magic wand, my face was transformed into a gorgeous woman without sallow, splotchy skin. It made me worry that, if August ever got a good look at me without all of this stuff on my face, he wouldn't want me anymore. The fear of being rejected was then suddenly alive and thriving in my gut, along with a helpless anger toward the cruelties of time. How dare it allow me to get old without asking my permission first.

After doing my hair in a braid suited for fairytale princesses and drugstore paperbacks, I walked back to my room, to get dressed, when my phone rang.

"Hey, Mom," I answered, putting her on speakerphone. "I can't talk for long."

"Ah, right. Marjorie told me you had a date tonight." She said it as though she'd misplaced the information somewhere, but I knew better. She had called to pry, and I smiled at my reflection in the full-length mirror, knowing I would let her.

"Yeah, I'm meeting August at a bookstore tonight," I said. "There's a nice Italian restaurant next door and a park down the street, if we decide to go for a little walk after dinner."

"Well, that sounds lovely," she replied.

"Right?"

101

I stepped into my dress and pulled the straps up and over my shoulders, then reached around to secure the zipper and clasp. Standing back to study my reflection, I smoothed the long, flowing skirt out, then adjusted the sweetheart neckline. The pretty, white dress with small, pink roses filled me with hope and happiness, as it offered promises of a wonderful summer on the beach, and I smiled with approval, before stepping into a pair of strappy, white sandals.

"Clara," Mom said, slicing through my reverie of sunshine and walks along the sandy shore.

"Yeah?"

"I know you're excited, but I—"

"Mom," I groaned, shaking my head. "You spend your life begging me to find someone. I really hope you're not about to talk me out of being happy right now."

"I'm not," she pressed. "I just hope you're thinking clearly about this one."

"Thinking clearly?" I frowned at my reflection.

"I am not one to discourage against dating a younger man," she went on. "After all, your father is younger than me."

"I know, Mom." She had only reminded me a thousand times throughout my life.

"But you were younger once, and I'm sure you can remember how men can be. They're not always looking for the same things you want," she said gently, and my shoulders sagged with the weight of my sigh.

"Weren't you the one trying to set me up with the diner guy?"

"Yes, but ... this is real, and I'm just making sure you don't set your expectations too high."

"I'm not expecting anything from this," I insisted, to convince both her and myself. "I've already decided that, if this isn't anything but a fling, I'm fine with that."

"I know," she said. "I know you say that. But ... maybe it's my intuition kicking in here, I don't know, but I think you might be hoping for something a little more this time around. And that's okay, I just want you to keep yourself a little guarded, that's all. Don't jump in before you're certain about how he feels."

Her concern, though well-meaning, made me laugh. My mother knew me better than just about anyone on the planet, and she, of all people, should know better than to warn me about falling in love too quickly. I could count on two fingers the number of times I'd been in love in my life, and in both instances, it had taken me over a year to allow the words to leave my lips.

"You have nothing to worry about, Mom," I told her, smiling once again at the hope in my eyes' reflection. "I'm just excited to see where this goes. That's all."

***

The rain had softened to a misty drizzle, as I headed from the parking lot toward the bookstore where I recently bought August's books. The conversation with my mother had plagued my brain on the ride over and coupled with my burst of self-conscious anxiety from before and Sylvie's warning to be careful, I was starting to wonder if I should just call him and cancel. There are only so many deterrents and red flags a woman can be faced with before she can't take anymore. But I pushed through it, reminding myself that great things in life don't always come easily, and a fling with August had the potential to be a *really* great thing. So, with my chin up and umbrella held high, I walked until I stood outside the door to the shop.

I couldn't remember if August had told me to meet him outside, but given the persistent drip of rain, sliding from the store's awning, I closed my umbrella and stepped inside. Soft, classical music filled my ears, and the scent of patchouli calmed my nerves. Despite it being close to summer, the air had cooled from the rain, and I welcomed the cozy warmth of the shop, as I meandered through in search of my date.

I had half-expected to find him, between the shelves and with a book in hand, and I would've welcomed the sight of him, glancing up at me from the pages, with his curls in his eyes. What I hadn't expected was to discover the source of the music: a baby grand piano, with August's fingers, dancing elegantly over the keys.

He wore a white shirt, speckled with drying rain drops, and suspenders, criss-crossed between his hunched shoulder blades. On his head was a fedora, and he wore it in a way that wasn't at all ironic or unnatural.

Every nerve in my body jolted at the sight of his slender frame, moving in time with the music, and with a shuttered sigh, I held a hand to my chest.

Brace yourself, I told my heart, as I stared, transfixed on the movements of his hands and shoulders. *This one has the potential to hurt.*

CHAPTER FOURTEEN

"How long have you been standing there?" he asked, when he finally looked over his shoulder, wearing a half-smile and a glimmer in his eye.

I blushed and waved a flippant hand, as I replied, "Oh, just long enough to hear you play 'Ode to Joy' and that last one." Then, I cocked my head and asked, "Which one was that?"

He chuckled as he answered, "'Helena' by My Chemical Romance."

Humming contemplatively, I replied, "I don't care for them much."

"Oh, no?" He lifted his chin with intrigue.

"My niece likes their music but," I pursed my lips with distaste, "they're not my thing."

He stood and grabbed his jacket from off the bench, hanging it over his arm. "Not mine either," he said coolly. "But everything sounds better when played on the piano, and that song is beautiful."

"It was," I said absentmindedly.

I had seen him before in the hospital, always wearing sweatpants and a t-shirt, and in his casual, work clothes at the coffee shop. He seemed to make every ensemble look good, but this version of August Gordon was undoubtedly my favorite. I'd seen younger men dress this way before, in slacks with a crisp button-down shirt, suspenders, and a hat. But they wore the attire as though they were playing a part in an old-fashioned movie, like it was nothing more than a costume. Not August, though. This was what he preferred to wear, what made him feel comfortable, and it showed in the natural way he readjusted the hat on his head and smiled out from beneath its brim.

"I hope you're hungry," he said. "Because I'm starving."

"I actually neglected to eat all day," I admitted with a flighty giggle. "I wanted to make sure I had an appetite."

He walked around the piano bench to stand beside me and said, "I neglected to eat, too, but that was only because I was nervous as hell."

"Nervous? About what?" I laughed anxiously, diverting my eyes in time to watch him cock his head, disbelief in his eyes.

"You're really playing up this clueless act, huh?"

I readjusted my purse, hanging from my shoulder. "What do you mean?"

"Nothin'," he laughed softly, and I glanced again at him, to see him smile and extend his elbow. Then, he asked, "Shall we?"

With a bob of my chin, I took his arm and allowed him to lead me back through the collection of shelves and displays, and out the door. We headed down the sidewalk, with my hand laying comfortably in the crook of his elbow, and found the Italian restaurant, Rossario's. August held the door and we stepped inside, where a hostess led us to a table by a latticed window, with an oil lamp flickering in its center.

"Your waiter will be right with you," she said with a bright smile.

"Thank you," August said, as he pulled my chair out for me.

The hostess left us to peruse the menus. I opened mine, while August sat down across the table, and as I flipped through the pages, he asked what I planned to drink.

"Oh, I'm not sure," I said, turning to the list of assorted wines and cocktails. "What about you?"

"I'll probably just get water," he said, then cleared his throat. "I'm actually bringing it up because I, uh, can't really drink. But I don't want to hold you back, in case you want to order a glass of wine or something. I know some people feel weird about that sort of thing, so I just wanted to make sure you know I'm fine with it."

I looked up from the alcohol menu and across the table, to see insecurity cloud the confidence in his eyes. But even though his admission was clearly one that left him embarrassed, he still looked directly at me, never diverting his gaze. He was studying me and watching for my reaction, as if this were a test and how I responded would determine if I passed or not.

"Not drinking isn't a dealbreaker for me," I replied honestly. "I really don't drink often either. I'll have a glass of wine after dinner now and then or a mimosa or two at Sunday breakfast, but that's about it. I can't even remember the last time I got drunk."

He folded his arms on the table and leaned forward, smiling with mischief in his eyes. "You do remember," he stated confidently.

"Oh?" I raised a brow at the accusation.

"Everybody always says they don't remember, but they do. They remember *something*."

I laughed, then pinned my bottom lip between my teeth, before saying, "Okay, okay. You got me. It was four years ago, with a guy I had been seeing. We got completely blasted on the beach one night and sang nineties power ballads at the top of our lungs until my neighbor threatened to call the cops."

The silver specks in his eyes sparkled in the flickering glow from the oil lamp. "So, you're a jolly drunk," he assessed accurately.

"Guilty," I said, playfully rolling my eyes.

He nodded, as his smile faded. "I wish I was."

"Are you the type who just falls asleep? That's my sister. She gets a few glasses of wine under her belt, and she passes out wherever she is."

"No," he said, shaking his head. "I'm the type you don't want to be around."

The light mood was darkened with his serious tone, but I didn't look away. This time, it was me who studied him. He was offering a slice of himself that he thought was important, and I made the conscious decision to take it all in. Every little, ugly piece.

"Is that why you don't drink?"

"Well, right now I can't drink because I'm being a good boy and taking my meds, as promised, and they don't play nicely with booze," he explained, and I nodded. "When I'm not on my meds though, I have a very small window where I'm pleasant to be around. But one little sip over the edge, and I am a complete piece of crap."

"You get angry?"

He nodded slowly. "Angry, belligerent, disrespectful …" He pulled in a deep breath and shook his head, disgusted.

"Are you violent?"

The question hardened his gaze and clenched his jaw, as if he hadn't expected it, and then, slowly, he began to nod.

"I see," I replied, matching the nod of his head with my own.

"But I'm the only one who needs to worry about that," he stated firmly. "Not you."

***

"So, tell me about this Sunday breakfast," he said, popping another piece of ravioli into his mouth.

110

Cutting into my eggplant rollatini, I laughed. "I mentioned that about half an hour ago, and *now*, you want to know about it?"

"I have a good memory," he said with a nonchalant shrug.

"Well, there really isn't much to tell. My sister and her husband host breakfast at their house on Sunday mornings. That's pretty much it," I replied before popping the bite of eggplant into my mouth.

"You say that like it isn't special," he commented, while pulling a breadstick from the basket in the center of the table.

I swallowed and shook my head, watching as he clenched the breadstick between his teeth and took a bite. "It's really not a big deal. It's just my parents, my sister, her family, and me, so it's not—"

"But you all get together, every single week, to spend time with each other," he interrupted, his voice soft and almost morose. "And you *enjoy* it."

"We do," I replied quietly, beneath the sound of a tinny accordion.

"And you don't think that's special."

His voice now edged dangerously close toward incredulous laughter, and I pursed my lips as I grabbed my glass of white wine. I knew the cliff notes of his history, how both of his parents had died and that his family had shrunk drastically in a little over five years. I didn't know how sensitive he was to the topic and I didn't want to say anything that would make me seem cruel and heartless.

"I, um—"

"I'm not trying to bite your head off," he said, smiling gently. "I'm just saying, it's a rare thing, I think, for multiple generations of a family to genuinely enjoy spending time together. And I guess it would be one thing if you kept it strictly to holidays, only a few times a year or something, but every single week ..." His mouth curved into a wistful, lopsided smile and his eyes stared out, to somewhere faraway. "It's just nice, that's all I'm saying."

I relaxed with a nod of my head. "It is," I agreed, and finished my dinner in the comfortable ambience, while a sympathetic hurt ailed my heart.

***

After dinner, when the rain had subsided and the ground was still wet, we walked from the restaurant to the park at the end of the street. Streetlamps guided our way, until we passed through the wrought iron gate and onto a dirt path lined with daisies, lilacs, and tulips. August knelt and plucked a single white daisy from the flower bed and handed it to me.

"What is your favorite season?" he asked, as I brought the little flower to my nose and breathed in the sweet scent of the earth's perfume.

"Oh, um," I held it in my hand, loosely hanging at my side, "I like them all for different reasons, really."

"Fair enough," he said, nodding. "But there's gotta be one that makes you feel more alive than any of the others."

He walked beside me, with his hands tucked deep into his trouser pockets and his fedora tipped back, so that it sat precariously on the crown of his head. Standing side by side like this, I noticed the difference in our height and enjoyed that the top of my head only reached his shoulder. I always preferred men to be tall, but hadn't yet been with anyone over six feet.

August was, though, and I liked that. I liked that very much.

"I really love the summer," I replied.

"Oh, God, why?" he asked, wrinkling his nose with disgust.

"Well, my house is right on the water, so one of the things I love is just to be outside, on the beach. Listening to the waves and feeling the sand between my toes. It grounds me, I think. Like, after a long year, I need the sun and warmth to recharge my batteries."

He groaned and I laughed at the look on his face, as he shook his head and turned away. "I don't know how we're going to make this work now," he said, sarcasm dripping heavily from his words. "All is lost. We should just call it quits."

"I'm gonna go out on a limb and guess that you don't like the summer?"

"Hate it."

"Hate is a very strong word."

"And a strong word is required to describe how I feel about the summer," he said, stopping along the path to address me with his full attention and studious eyes.

"Hm," I replied, nodding with pursed lips. August took a step forward and we stood toe to toe. I looked up

113

to his chin, my heart pounding in my chest, desperate for attention and affection, as I said in an unsure, quivering voice, "I guess we should just say goodnight—"

August's lips kissed mine, and my words died with a pathetic whimper in my throat, as his hand, careful and controlled, laid against my cheek and his thumb brushed the inky tips of my lashes. He held me there, suspended in that moment and surrounded by flowers and rain-touched dirt, as I breathed in the scent of his leathery cologne and sweet, musky skin, until he lifted his face from mine. I opened my eyes, to look up at him and the intensity burning deep in the dark, silver-specked ring of his irises. I swallowed, unable to think about anything other than kissing him again, and stood on my toes, to press a soft, gentle peck to the corner of his mouth.

"Thank you," he said, when I was flat on my feet again.

"Why are you thanking me?" I laughed and licked my lips, savoring the taste of him and finding I liked it as much as I liked him.

"For letting me kiss you."

I blushed beneath the prying eyes of the moon, before he took my hand, interlacing his fingers with mine, as if he'd done it a thousand times before. Then, we began to walk again, moving further along the path, with my heart beating loudly in my ears and my lips buzzing with the aftereffects of his kiss.

"What's your family like?" he asked after a few moments of quiet.

Laughing and still wishing to have his mouth on mine again, I replied, "Nosy. My sister is my best friend and likes to dig *way* too deep in my business. My niece, Christy, who was also with me at the coffee shop, is amazing but also a little too curious for her own good."

"And yet, you still want to spend time with them," he commented lightly.

"What can I say? I'm a glutton for punishment." I laughed with a gentle shrug.

"What about your parents?"

I sucked in a deep breath of crisp, damp air. "Well, my dad kinda stays out of everything. He thinks the less he knows, the better. But he's very supportive otherwise, and he's always there whenever I need him to be. He actually helped me a lot when I first bought my house …" Just the mention of my little cottage on the beach encouraged my lips to spread into a wide, aching smile. "I bought this little rundown shack on the shore a little over five years ago, and ever since, my dad and I have renovated pretty much the whole thing together. We got some help here and there, but for the most part, it's just been us.

"It's nice, though, because now every part of that house has pieces of him tied to it. It feels morbid to talk about it, but sometimes, I think about how, after he's gone, he'll always kinda be there with me, you know? I'll walk through the house and think, oh, Dad touched that doorknob, or there's the doorframe that sliced his finger, or there's the faucet he spent way too long installing because the whole damn sink fell apart."

August's lips were curled into a sweet, easy smile. I was never one to bogart a conversation on a date, but right now, I couldn't stop myself. He just made it so easy to open up and speak, and I never once stopped to consider how dangerous that could be.

"Now, my mom," I continued. "She's a horse of a different color. She makes up for what my dad lacks in conversation. All she does is talk. And sometimes, it really pisses me off, but she means well. And even when she makes me mad, she still has this way of making everything better. When everything seems wrong, she makes it right again."

"They sound great," he commented softly, and I nodded.

"They are," I agreed. "I mean, apart from the fact that Mom will never leave me alone about finding a man to spend my life with."

August chuckled under his breath and lifted our hands, bringing my knuckles up to his lips and gently brushing a kiss against my skin. My heart pulsed with heat, pumping my body full of hope, need, and the desperation to make this work despite every warning I'd been given leading up to this moment. August Gordon was a dangerous man, I knew it before and I knew it better now, yet somehow, I didn't mind, just as long as it could last.

"Well," he said, squeezing my hand tighter and holding it to his own thumping heart, "I hope I can help you out with that."

CHAPTER FIFTEEN

The morning greeted me with a gentle caress of sunshine against my cheeks, streaming in from between the lacy, cream-colored bedroom curtains. Before I could even open my eyes, a smile was already spreading across my face, with an abundance of gratitude for the night I had with August and the weekend ahead. My lips begged to call him and demand that he come over to spend the day with me, kissing on the porch, with the sun on our skin and the salt in our hair. But that type of desperation didn't seem appropriate for a woman my age. That was something only kids would do, I thought. People with less patience and experience than me. So, I climbed out of bed, remembering I was meeting my mother and sister at my parents' house, while hoping that August would call and distract me instead.

I might not have wanted to seem desperate, but if he'd asked me to go to him, I would ditch my family without hesitation.

He never did call though, and when at my mother's house, a Cape Cod style home not far from mine, the door was thrown open before I could even make it up the stone walkway. Marjie stood there, with an expectant look blazing in her teasing eyes and her hands on her hips. As I pushed past her, I released a groan that edged dangerously close to playful laughter.

"*So?*"

"So, what?" I asked, heading toward the scent of coffee brewing in the kitchen.

"Aren't you going to tell me about your date?"

In the kitchen, Mom handed me a full, steaming mug and I took a sip as I sat down at the table, in the same spot I'd always sat in, ever since I was a child. I made myself comfortable, hanging my purse from the back of the chair and crossing my legs beneath the table, all while Marjorie gaped at me incredulously from the kitchen doorway.

She looked to Mom and shook her head. "Can you believe her right now?"

Laughing, I cradled the mug in both hands, bringing it back to my lips, before asking, "God, can you give me a minute? I only just got here."

"Well, I don't want to say anything, but you *could* have called last night," my sister said, sitting beside me, as she always did. "Unless you were a little ... *occupied.*"

Mom filled her mug and sat across from us. She didn't say anything, but she didn't have to. Every

118

question she wanted to ask was right there, written in the hopeful glint in her eyes and the skeptical furrow of her brow, and I sighed, knowing I'd have to spill the beans sooner or later. So, I opted for sooner. "He didn't come back to my house," I informed them, shutting that presumption down right away. "We went out to eat and had a very nice dinner. Then, we went for a walk through a little park near the restaurant, and it was lovely."

"*Lovely?*" my sister parroted in a shrill tone.

"Mm-hmm," I replied, take a sip of coffee.

Marjorie rested her chin in her palm and stared at me with a dreamy gaze. "And? Did he hold your hand?"

My cheeks warmed in the cool kitchen, as I swallowed, then said, "He did."

"Ooh!" She squealed like a little girl, turning to my mother. "He held her hand!"

"He kissed me, too," I confessed, offering the information, needing to tell someone about the impromptu kiss among the flowers.

"He *did?*" Marjie gasped.

I nodded, lowering the mug to the table, and feeling the giddy beginnings of new passion bubbling to the surface. "Yeah," I said with a wistful sigh, unable to contain my smile. "It was ... *really* nice."

"What do you mean by *really* nice?" she asked, sitting at the edge of her seat.

"Would you say there were sparks?" Mom asked, finally breaking her silence.

Laughing, I rolled my eyes. "That type of crap doesn't happen in the real world," I said. "That happens in romance novels and fairytales, not—"

"Sure, it does," Marjie said, and Mom nodded in agreement. "I knew I would marry Mark on our first date."

"When I met your father, I didn't like him right away," Mom said, retelling a story I had heard so many times throughout my life. "In fact, I couldn't stand him for a long time. But one night, at a party for a mutual friend, he cornered me by the buffet table and planted one on me, right then and there. Initially, I was disgusted, because men shouldn't just walk up to an unsuspecting woman and kiss her. But then, all of a sudden, it hit me that, while I couldn't stand him, I had also grown to love him, and three months later, we were married."

Although I had heard it before, I always loved the story of how my parents got together. It was unconventional, and by today's standards, my father would have been chastised for even considering kissing my mother without her consent. But to me though, it was imperfectly romantic. The story of an underdog who finally got the girl of his dreams. It was meant to be immortalized between the pages of a book, and if I had the ability, I would have written it myself.

I wished something like that would happen to me, I always had. But my standards were high, and my expectations of relationships were even higher. So, while I'd always had my fun with men, I had never known the passion and certainty of lasting love. I wondered if maybe those annoying little facts about my personality were what kept the sparks from flying and the fireworks from going off.

"So, when are you seeing him again?" Marjie asked eagerly.

"I don't know. Who knows if I'll see him again at all," I said, injecting too much indifference into my voice to be believable.

"Maybe you can invite him to breakfast," Mom casually suggested, peering at me from over the brim of her coffee mug.

My eyes widened as I gaped at her. "What? I've gone out with him once. I can't just ... invite him to come have breakfast with me and my *entire family*."

I wanted to, though. I wanted to pick up the phone and tell him how much I loved seeing and spending time with him, how I desperately wanted him to meet my family, and for him to be a part of every single aspect of my life. But I resisted with a bite of my lip and turned to my sister.

"How's Christy?" I asked, quickly changing the subject.

"Why not?" Mom demanded, bringing her mug to the table. Her head was cocked, her eyes narrowed with demanding curiosity.

I sighed, putting aside the genuine interest in my niece for a moment, and looked back to my mother. "Because it feels too soon," I said.

"Who says?"

"I do."

"Well, no one else can tell you how you feel. But if *you* want to invite him, if *you* want him to meet us after

121

only one date, then nobody here is going to tell you that's the wrong decision to make, if you choose to make it. I would hope you'd know that there would be no judgment from any of us, and that we'd be happy to have him."

The conversation died naturally, as Marjorie then answered my question about Christy. She told us how my niece had jumped headfirst into the joys of singledom and had already lined up several dates with different men. But even as she talked and expressed her concern for her daughter, what my mother said was never far from my mind. Even after I left my parents' house and stopped at the Fisch Market to do some grocery shopping, I continued to think about it.

Society had never before influenced my decisions or dictated how I chose to live my life. I did what I wanted, at my own pace and in my own way, and nobody could tell me otherwise. I dated men, moved as slowly or quickly as I wanted, and ditched them the moment I knew things were heading south. But everything about August Gordon was different. His age, personality, interests, past, and yes, diagnosis. He was unlike every single man I'd ever known and dated, and that gave me pause. All because I was worried about what others would think. But that wasn't how I lived my life, and why should I be starting now?

So, in the produce section of the Fisch Market, I pulled my phone from my bag and dialed his number. It rang twice before he answered, and I smiled at the sound of his voice.

"Clarabell," he answered in that same sultry voice I'd grown to love.

"Hi, August."

"To what do I owe the pleasure?"

I turned away from the apples, not wanting them to see me blush, as I said, "Well, I'm in the grocery store and thought I'd give you a call."

He chuckled and I closed my eyes, resisting the urge to swoon into an overflowing display of watermelons. "Hey, if fruit inspired you to hear my voice, I'll take whatever I can get."

"It's just that, I was having coffee with my mom and sister, and they asked if I'd like to invite you to breakfast tomo—"

"I'd love to."

His eagerness opened my eyes and I stared ahead at the round, dark green fruit in desperate need of ripening. "I wasn't sure if you'd think it was too soon, or—"

"Clara," he interrupted with another chuckle. "I don't need to think about anything other than the very simple fact that, I like you. As far as I'm concerned, that's all that matters … unless you think otherwise."

"No," I said, absentmindedly lifting a hand to my chest, to feel my heart and its thunderous beat.

"Then, I'd love to. Text me your address, and I'll pick you up tomorrow morning."

"Okay," I replied breathlessly, while knowing my eyes would spend the night, watching the clock and eagerly awaiting the moment I could see him again.

CHAPTER SIXTEEN

The next morning, my stomach was alive with a festering ball of nerves and my fingernails were in desperate need of another manicure, after I'd picked the fresh polish off. August was on his way. He was going to see my house for the first time, and I couldn't remember the last time I'd had butterflies this big, drunk with possibility and infatuation.

Agnes waited by my side on the porch, as I anxiously watched the street for his arrival. With every car that drove by, my hope dwindled just a little more, as if I truly believed he'd stand me up. It was foolish, but I was eager, so when his black sedan finally turned onto the street and headed toward my house, I stood, hardly able to contain the delight of seeing him again.

He parked at the curb and got out of his car. When I saw he was dressed in a pair of jeans and a short-sleeved button-down, tucked in at the waist, I smiled at his put-together, vintage style. Then, when he grabbed a white, straw fedora from the front seat and placed it casually on his head, my smile broadened further into a ridiculous grin.

"I want you to know, Clarabell," he said, casually walking up the path to my porch, "I don't generally wake up before noon."

"I'm sorry to inconvenience you," I said, as Agnes tugged at the leash, anxious to greet an old friend.

"It was tough, I'll admit. I almost didn't come," he confessed sardonically, slowly taking the steps. "But I gotta say, seeing you in that dress, makes the sleep deprivation worth it."

He then stood before me, smelling like leather and smoke, and his arms snaked around my waist, tugging my body to press flush against his. I reached around his neck and held my breath, as he lowered his lips to mine and kissed me with a day's worth of passion. He tasted like toothpaste, minty and fresh, and my knees weakened, as I savored every caress and swipe of his tongue. I begged him with countless sighs to suggest that we cancel our plans, free up our schedules, and do nothing but kiss lazily on my front porch to the tune of windchimes and Agnes's impatient panting.

"God," he groaned, reluctantly pulling away. "I don't think I'll ever get tired of kissing you."

I exhaled with a gasp and opened my eyes, to find his gaze pinned intently on me and a soft smile curling the corners of his lips. There was pride in his expression, like it satisfied him to know he could render me stupid and speechless with a simple kiss. With a trembling

125

hand, I brushed a strand of flyaway hair from my cheek and cleared my throat, then smiled into his persistent stare.

"I'm just grateful you're so good at it," I said.

"Have you been with a lot of bad kissers?" I thought about it for a moment, as he knelt and finally greeted Agnes. "A few stand out above the others," I replied.

"Jesus, how many guys have you been with?" He laughed, glancing up at me, as Agnes tried desperately to shower him with her own brand of slobbery kisses.

"I lost count a long time ago."

His eyes widened, as he stood slowly. "I didn't take you to be that type of gal," he commented, a coy smile on his lips.

"And what type would that be?" I asked, as he offered his hand and I accepted.

He took Agnes's leash and ushered me down the steps and to the sidewalk, where I pointed to the right, and he steered.

"I guess what I'm saying is, I didn't expect you to have been with many people," August said.

I shrugged, my arm brushing against his. "I'm not saying there's been hundreds of men in my life, and it hasn't been a constant thing. The last time I was with anybody was about four years ago," I explained casually. "Most of my experience with men was in college. I experimented a lot and figured some stuff out."

He shot a look at me, brow raised with intrigue. "And what did you figure out?"

Laughing, I said, "That I don't like a lot of men."

126

"Damn," he chuckled. "I guess I have my work cut out for me, then."

I glanced at him, standing a head above me and haloed by the early summer sun. The brim of his hat shaded his eyes, darkening their color and adding a bit of mystery to his already wonderous persona. His jaw was sharp and prominent, his lips seemed to be permanently curled in a satisfactory smile, like life was forever good and never bad. He walked with enviable confidence, head held high and back ramrod straight, radiating pride and just enough arrogance to be attractive.

Holding his hand tighter and enjoying the warmth of his palm against mine, I pressed my shoulder to his arm and said, "I don't think you have anything to worry about."

"Ah, there's always something to worry about, Clarabell," he replied. "Life just gives us moments like these sometimes, to lull us into a false sense of security. But that's okay. I like moments like these, they give me something to hold onto when shit hits the fan. I just know better than to put all of my trust into them."

***

We walked up to Marjorie's house, hand in hand, with Agnes happily leading the way. The door was already open to us, and the moment we stepped inside, August's confidence seemed to diminish a little. He hung back, letting me walk ahead through the house and to the empty dining room, and when we entered, he stood in the doorway, frozen, as I unclipped Agnes from the leash.

"Hey, guys!" Marjie said, hurrying into the room from the kitchen, arms loaded with bowls of food. "We're sitting on the deck."

Over my shoulder, I glanced at August and shrugged nonchalantly, before proceeding through the open doors and out onto the deck, where my family was already seated. They chattered about passing the orange juice and are those eggs and where is the syrup. Nothing but a cluster of voices that hardly made any sense at all, until they spotted us, carefully moving around the table to the two empty chairs, and just like that, they stopped. All was then silent, aside from a nearby bird, who hadn't gotten the memo. As August pulled out my chair, I realized with a stifled groan that it was now on me to make the moment less awkward.

"Hey, guys," I said, filling my voice with enough sunshine to brighten the darkest corners of Hell. "So, I wanted you all to meet August."

My father was the first to stand and greet him, with a welcoming reach of his hand across the table. My sister's husband followed suit, and despite August's earlier apprehension, he accepted graciously without hesitation.

"Nice to meet you, man," Mark said. "Sit, make yourself at home. Can I get you anything?"

August took the chair beside me and shook his head. "No, thanks. Everything here looks great."

My eyes shot across the table, to the three women I trusted more than anybody else. They watched him with inconspicuous glances over their champagne glasses and I knew, knowing them, that they were studying every move he made, picking every word he said apart, and reading too deeply into them all. It was all out of love and care, and I knew they meant well, but it made me nervous. I just wanted them to like him.

"So, August," Mom finally said, after our plates were all loaded and the eating had begun, "Clara says you're an author."

He snorted, then nodded. "Yeah, I guess you could say that."

Christy laughed from beside her grandmother. "You don't seem too happy about it."

The conversation I'd had with August at the hospital came rushing back to me then. His disdain toward the medications he was on. His stifled creativity. His hatred toward the book he recently released. I worried that the mention would trigger a burst of anger, and I readied myself to change the subject if things got too heated.

"Oh, it's not that," he replied, smiling reassuringly at my niece. "It's just not all it's cracked up to be, I guess."

"What do you mean by that?" Mom asked.

August took a slow sip of juice and cleared his throat, then said, "Well, I grew up knowing I wanted to write. It's all I ever wanted, and when I was nineteen, I was lucky enough to get a contract with a very sought-after publishing house. They wanted five books from me in a ten-year span, and I thought I had it made. They had offered me a small advance, so I figured I'd make that back in no time and start raking in the royalties, no problem."

"I take it that's not exactly what happened," Mark said, listening intently.

129

August shook his head. "My work isn't very …
marketable, let's say. So, they've barely made back what
they originally spent on me, and the royalties that I
thought would be pouring in are more of a, uh … slow
trickle. So, to really fit the starving artist stereotype, I
work at a coffee shop to make ends meet, while I
struggle to write my fifth book and hope that's the one
that'll put me on the map."

Marjorie's lips spread into a smile, as her eyes
volleyed from mine, then to his. "Well, if you're as good
as Clara says you are, then I'm sure you'll make it big
someday."

My mouth stopped chewing as soon as the words
had been said. August had no idea I'd read his book. It
felt so personal and I hadn't found the right way to tell
him. Now, he knew. I didn't know what to expect from
his reaction, knowing how he felt for his recent book,
and I waited with a spine so straight it ached.

I could feel his eyes on me, burning a hole straight
through to my quivering heart, as he said, "I can only
hope."

***

"I like him a lot," Marjorie declared, as I helped her clean
the table.

The guys—our father, Mark, and August—had
decided to busy themselves by playing a rousing game of
horseshoes with the girls, while Mom, Marjie, Christy,
and I cleaned up and gossiped. We stood in the kitchen,
staring out through the large, bay window and watching

the men. My stomach was full of butterflies and food, both competing for space, and I smiled at the words my sister spoke.

"Really?"

She nodded assuredly. "Oh, God, yeah. He's ridiculously good looking, in this ... understated way—"

"Right? He's freakin' beautiful," I gushed, then clapped my hands over my blushing cheeks and laughed beside myself.

Christy wrapped her arms around my shoulders and squealed. "Oh, my God, I *love* this side of you," she said, squeezing me tightly.

I looked over her head at my mother, standing on the other side of the window, a cup of coffee in her hands. She kept a watchful eye over me with a gentle smile on her lips. I waited for her assessment to come, but she kept silent. That is, until Marjie and Christy went outside moments later, leaving us alone.

"What do you have to say, Mom?" I asked, crossing my arms and smirking.

"What?" She was pretending to be clueless, widening her twinkling eyes and pressing a hand to her chest.

"You have something on your mind. I can tell. So, just say it."

She pursed her lips and tipped her head, further studying me, before finally saying, "Clara, I have seen you with quite a few men over the years."

I nodded, swiping my tongue over my teeth, then said, "Yeah. I guess you have."

Her lips spread with a gentle smile, and replied, "And not once have I seen you act the way you are with him."

The nerves I'd been battling all day wound tighter together, knotting and aching in my gut. I turned from my mother and glanced out the window, to watch August toss a Frisbee to Mark and laugh as Agnes made a solid attempt at snatching it out of the air. He had lost his fedora at some point and now it was perched on the head of Lydia, sitting on the grass with her twin sister and watching the game. Christy and Marjorie bathed in the sun on a couple of lounge chairs, chatting with my father, and it hit me hard and fast how natural this picture looked. It was the perfect image of a happy family, enjoying a warm, beautiful day in early June. It was welcoming and beckoning me to join with the promise of hugs and laughter. And August easily fit into it, like the piece that had always been missing.

This was exactly what I wanted. I wanted him, I wanted it all. Still, I remembered that he fell hard and fast, he warned me of it himself, and I knew I was plummeting right along with him. But that's not what scared me and kept me from embracing the rush of a quick transition into love.

It was what he had said earlier, about there always being something to worry about, and I was terrified about what was waiting for me around the bend.

CHAPTER SEVENTEEN

Sylvie waited for me at the elevator, her eyes pinned to the watch on her wrist. It was rare for me to run late on workdays but today was one of those. The morning had been full of unfortunate events. A broken coffee machine, a disgusting incident involving cat vomit and bare feet, a curling iron on the fritz, and bumper to bumper traffic on the highway. Yet all the while, I couldn't contain the permanent smile affixed to my face.

"I am *so* sorry," I emphasized, rushing off the elevator and toward my friend. "It's been a morning."

She waved a hand, shooing my apology away. "Don't worry about it. We just had some issues over here, too."

"Oh, no," I sympathized, as Agnes took a seat on my foot. "Everything okay?"

She nodded reassuringly. "Yeah. Or at least, it will be ... I hope. We have a new patient. She just admitted herself this morning, and she has been ... well, let's just say, she's a little difficult. But everything's quiet for now, thank God."

Then, she asked, "How was your weekend?"

She wasn't just simply asking a friendly question. The expectant look in her eyes told me she wanted to know if I'd seen August, how our date went, and if I was planning on seeing him again. I turned away, knowing my face was red with the thrill of a new, promising relationship, and I grinned.

"Well, I had a date on Friday."

"With ..." She gestured enthusiastically for me to go on, and I rolled my eyes.

"Yes, with August," I offered, laughing and turning back to her. "And before you ask, *yes*, it was lovely. And *yes*, I plan on seeing him again. In fact, we just had breakfast with my family yesterday."

Sylvie was clearly happy for me, as relief washed over her features with her breathy sigh and smile. I searched for any sign of unease, concern, or disapproval, and when I found none, I relaxed with a returned grin. She wished me well and offered hopes that this could be the start of something wonderful for both of us, and with that, we went about our days.

Agnes and I visited a couple of new patients who had been admitted over the weekend, but all the while, I missed the friend I had in Phoebe. I wondered how she was doing and made a mental note to send her a message soon, and hoped I could soon make that type of connection with someone else.

The workday was short, and when it was over, I joined Sylvie for lunch. While she ate a salad, she groused about her husband and his continued inability to be left alone with their son, and I filled her in on the familial drama surrounding Christy and her newfound love for dating random men. After the tea had been spilled, I left the hospital with the confidence that the rest of the day would make up for my unfortunate morning.

Agnes and I returned home, and while she napped with the cats, I put on some music, did the laundry, and mopped the kitchen floor. I vacuumed, scrubbed the bathrooms, and wiped the windows down until the sun shone through without a single smudge in sight. I cleaned until the moon greeted the sky and the air grew cold, and then, I closed the windows to a whipping wind and cooked myself some dinner to the tune of cackling gulls in the distance.

After dinner was eaten and the dishes were cleaned, I curled up on the couch with *The Old Man and the Sea*. I breathed in the comfort of a well-loved book and devoured the words, until my phone buzzed from beside me. I couldn't stand being interrupted from my reading, and normally, I wouldn't have answered at all. But when I saw August's name light up the screen, I accepted the call immediately, surprised that I was, for once, more excited to hear someone else's voice than read words I'd read a hundred times before.

"Hi," I answered with a smile, tucking the bookmark into place, and closing the book.

"Hello, Clarabell."

His liking for my name squeezed around my heart, as I replied, "How are you?"

"Well, I just got home from work a little while ago, to find that Nana had made chicken cordon bleu, which is one of my favorites. Then, after dinner, I took the most refreshing shower of my life, and just now, I got to thinking, what could make this night even better? And you know what I said?"

I smiled wider at the uplifting sound of his tone. "What?"

"Hearing your voice."

"Well, you're lucky I answered at all," I teased. "You caught me in the middle of a chapter."

August groaned with disgust, long and loud. "Oh, God, that's the freakin' worst. I'm sorry. You want me to leave you to it?"

I shook my head profusely. "No, it's okay. I've read this book a few times, I know what happens."

"You know, I would've texted instead, but I hate texting."

"Do you, really?" I asked, crumpling my forehead with curiosity.

"Despise it. And I'll tell you why, if you want, but you have to tell me that you're prepared for a tangent. I'm really passionate, and this could get lengthy." His words faded into a chuckle, and I grinned.

"Should I get a drink? A snack, maybe?"

"Definitely. Two snacks, if you have them. Tell me when you're ready."

I laughed, pulling my knees up and hugging them to my chest. "Lay it on me."

With a dramatic pause and audible inhale, he began, "So, this is going to sound painfully ironic coming from someone who would love to make a living as a writer, but I personally believe that we, as a society, have invested *far* too much into the disconnect of the written word and technology. Think about it. Social media, text messages—Hell, even email. We have allowed for all of this digital crap to take over and replace the necessity of human contact. People *need* contact, whether they want to realize it or not. People need to feel as though they are talking to another person and not a, a, a *machine*. They need face-to-face, voice-to-voice contact. God, even just a handwritten letter is better than receiving an email."

I let him take a breath, and when it seemed he wasn't going to add anything more to his spiel, I said, "Well, for argument's sake, an email or a text is better than nothing at all, isn't it?"

"Oh, absolutely. Don't get me wrong. There's a time and place for all of it. Computers. The internet. Cellphones. All of it serves a purpose, without a doubt. But it's horribly abused, and it's being used to replace all of these basic human needs that have been around since we were living in caves and inventing the fucking wheel," he said, his tone elevated with passion. "I'm not saying nobody should ever text each other, or email, or connect with their cousin across the world on social media. Not at all. Sometimes it's all we have, there are no other options, and that has to be good enough. But it just seems to me that too many people take these things and think they're good enough. Like because they got a text from Grandpa, they never have to hear his voice again. Or because they had a video chat with Uncle Jim Bob, they never have to hug him again. But if we allow ourselves to *truly* feel that way, if we allow this shit to *really* take over, then we will live in a cold fucking world, colder than it already is. Our compassion toward each other will end with a meaningless, generic post on Tweeter or, or … whatever the hell it's called, and nobody will have any clue how to sign their own goddamn name. And I don't know about you, Clara, but I don't want to live in a world like that. I think that's exactly where it's headed though, and that scares the hell out of me."

August's passion bubbled through the phone in bursts of agitated breath, while I sat, hugging my knees tightly to my chest. Staring ahead, unblinking, toward the Persian Tabriz rug I'd bought at a flea market so many years ago, I could no longer remember how old I had been. It was an antique, around eighty years old at the time of purchase. I had seen it from two booths over, big and bold and cherry red, and I'd wandered over, not caring at all about the number on the pricetag and knowing that, no matter what it said, it was coming home with me. It was stunning, with its pops of burgundy, green, blue, peach, and pink. Little bursts of color that matched nothing in my sandy house on the shore yet managed to complement it perfectly, the way Lucille Ball complemented Desi Arnez, and I loved it. Not only for its beauty but its history as well. Someone, maybe even multiple someone's, before me had owned and loved this rug enough to keep it in such beautiful condition. And the same could be said for so many of my belongings. Things I'd picked up in various antique stores, garage sales, and flea markets. Trinkets, dishes, books, furniture. They were symbolic of where we've been, lovely little pieces of the past, and as I stared into the intricate, Oriental design in my rug, I thought about how right August was. I already knew it—hell, I'd been harping on about it for years. But I had never stopped to realize I was playing right into it myself, simply by exchanging my beloved handwritten letters for emails and phone calls for text messages, and that made me so sad.

"Wow," I said, my voice a breathy whisper. "I never thought about it like that before."

August laughed, lightening the mood with the sound. "I'm sorry. Like I said, I'm really passionate."

"You are, but you're not wrong either."

His sigh was again audible, and just the tiniest bit sad. "I just think we, as a society, need to learn to appreciate each other a little more. Everyone. Not just acquaintances or people we meet on the internet, but friends and family, too. We take everybody for granted. We just … shove them behind a screen and treat them the way we would treat the stupid, robotic voice at the self-checkout. And let me tell you, you rarely know when you're going to hear that person's voice for the last time, and when that time comes and you waste it on a fucking text, you're going to wish you had called. You're going to wish you had a second chance to hear their voice. But we don't get second chances in life, not really, not for stuff like that. So, that's why I called you, Clara. Because

I didn't want to waste this moment, if it happens to be the last, on a fucking text."

He barely took a breath when he rambled, elevating his words erratically to emphasize the passion and truth behind them. I wondered beyond any current business of mine where it had all stemmed from and how he had adopted an appreciation for the old ways, the same way I had. Whatever it was, I enjoyed the time I spent talking to him all the same, and when I knew that he had taken a moment to breathe, I spoke.

"I appreciate the way your mind works," I said. "You're a dying breed."

"So are you, Clarabell," he replied. "And I think that's why I like you so damn much."

We talked for another hour, comparing our Hemingway libraries, and discussing our favorite songs from before either of us were a thought let alone born. At some point during our conversation, I had laid back on the couch with a hand on my stomach and one foot kicking in the air, just listening to the sound of his voice. I thought I liked him so damn much, too, and decided that, when I was out of work the next day, I would call Phoebe instead of text.

CHAPTER EIGHTEEN

"Hey, Phoebs!"

"Oh, my God, Clara!" She squealed, and I smiled, happy to hear the sound of her jubilant voice as I drove home from the children's hospital. "How are you?!"

"I'm good! Just got out of work, so I thought I'd give you a call."

"You have no idea how happy this makes me. How's Agnes? Oh, God, I miss her so much ..."

With my eyes on the road, I reached into the backseat and gave Ag a loving pat on the snout and said, "Aw, she misses you, too. Maybe we should come see—"

"Oh, my God, yes! You *have* to come see me one day, whenever you can, whenever you're not busy. My stepmom—I told you about her, right?"

"You did," I said, driving past River Canyon's bustling main street and onto Oak, while remembering the brief mentions of her father's wife.

"Well, she went out and bought me a freakin' *Macbook*. Isn't that *amazing*?!"

I narrowed my eyes and pursed my lips, recalling something Phoebe had told me months ago, about an ugly experience she'd had. A couple of mean girls from her high school had created a horrifically nasty post about her on an online forum, and the relentless and unwarranted teasing regarding her physical appearance had driven Phoebe to self-harm. Her father had taken her phone away and put parental controls on the family desktop computer. He blocked his daughter from social media as a way to protect her from the persistent nagging of her brain, wondering what the bullies had to say about her hair, body, or boyfriend. I questioned why her stepmother would think it was a good idea to get Phoebe a computer of her own, when the girl I had seen a week ago didn't seem like she was ready, and I wondered what Dr. Sherman would think about that. I didn't say anything though, and just enjoyed the sound of her happiness for the time being.

"That's awesome, Phoebs. I have a Macbook, too. It's the best computer I've ever had."

"That's saying a lot, when you've been around since people rode dinosaurs to work," Phoebe teased, a grin in her voice.

I glowered at the phone, sitting in the cupholder. "Hey, respect your elders, young lady," I jabbed, before laughing. "Maybe I can come by soon. I have to see what's going on with work and my family, but—"

"I would love it so much, you have no idea," she gushed. "I mean, we would have to meet somewhere else, 'cause I wanna see Agnes and my dad would like, die if she came into the house, but—"

"Your dad's allergic to dogs?"

"Seriously allergic. I didn't tell you that?"

Phoebe never talked much about her dad. Never had. "No, you never mentioned that."

"Yeah, like, this one time, we went to my stepmom's brother's house for a barbecue and Dad didn't know he had gotten a puppy. Like, my stepuncle wanted it to be this big surprise that he had gotten this dumb little hairball. Dad walked into the house and it was like, two seconds later, he started coughing and saying he couldn't breathe. It was *crazy*. We had to call an ambulance and everything."

"Holy crap, Phoebe," I said, shaking my head with disbelief, as I pulled into the driveway.

"Yeah, well ..." Phoebe sniffed a little indifferent laugh, automatically changing her tone. "He's fine, so it's okay."

I wanted to ask more about her father. It ate away at me, not knowing the hidden depths to their relationship and her feelings toward him. In the hospital, it seemed wrong to pry. It wasn't my place. She always handed me the topics she wanted to talk about, and I went with them, ignoring my inner nag and her endless questions. Now, in the car, over the phone, I wished it seemed different and more casual, but it didn't. Not the way it did with August.

143

My connection with Phoebe hadn't crossed that line between friendliness and professional yet, and so, I left it alone.

"Hey, so I gotta get going," I said, grabbing my bag from the front seat and climbing out of the car. "I have groceries to put away and a dog in desperate need of a bath."

"Yeah, I gotta go, too. I'm gonna work on some stuff for TikTok."

"TikTok?"

She laughed like I was adorable. "You're not on TikTok?"

"No?" I opened the back door and let Agnes run herself up the walk and onto the porch. "Should I be?"

"Oh my God, Clara! You *have* to get on there. I've been talking to this ridiculously hot guy from Australia. Maybe you could find a boyfriend on there, too."

With the phone pinned between my ear and shoulder, I opened the trunk and hoisted out the two bags of groceries, and thought of August. My cheeks immediately warmed and I bit my lip, hesitating in my response and not knowing if I should divulge anything about my infantile relationship, if that's even what it was at this point. But I wanted to. I wanted to tell someone else. Hell, I wanted to tell everyone.

"Actually, I've been seeing someone."

Phoebe wasted no time in releasing an ear-piercing squeal, nearly rupturing my ear drum. "Clara! That's freakin' amazing! You gotta tell me everything!"

I laughed, as I took the stairs to the porch. "Next time, next time. Right now, I have ice cream melting in my arms. I'll call you soon, okay?"

"O-kay," she groaned playfully. "I love you and I miss you."

"Same here, Phoebs," I said, as I hung up, and smiled.

I was glad that I had called.

***

"Clarabell."

I smiled at my name coming through the speaker and put the phone down, to return both hands to my dinner, frying on the stove.

"Hi, August."

"What are you doing?"

"Well," I said, using the spatula to flip the leftover chicken breasts in the pool of spitting oil, "right now, I'm frying up a few chicken cutlets and roasting some potatoes for dinner. What are you doing?"

"I want to see you."

The spatula stilled against the cast iron, and I watched the tiny bubbles rise and then burst. "Like, this weekend, or—"

"No. Like, right now." His tone was so earnest, urgent, and raw, it highlighted every word with the type of desperation only lust can bring on, and I quickly licked my drying lips before replying.

"O-oh, um, I—"

"If now isn't a good time, that's fine, don't feel bad about turning me down," he said, laughing easily. "But I miss you, and I'm learning quickly that I dislike that very much."

I flipped the chicken, and it greeted the pan with a fresh chorus of sizzles, while I thought about his proposal for a moment. I wasn't shy, and I wasn't opposed to an impromptu visit from a romantic conquest that often ended with one or both of us naked. And considering the fact that it'd been a long time since I'd had a night like that, I couldn't lie and say it wasn't appealing. But trysts were for the weekend, when there was no work the next morning and the alarm clock wasn't an issue. If I was going to enjoy August's company, I wasn't sure I wanted to do it with bedtime looming over me, like a strict and scowling parent.

"I don't like missing you either," I found myself saying, anyway. Because even though the clock was loud, my heart couldn't help but be just a little louder.

***

"Hey," I said, opening my door as August headed up the porch steps.

"Hi," he replied, before grasping my face in both hands and kissing me with luxuriously slow patience, savoring every taste, touch, and moan. He hummed against my lips, a delicious sound of approval, and I responded with a swoony sigh. Then, with his forehead pressed to mine, he said, "It smells good in here."

"There's dinner in the kitchen, if you're hungry." I licked my lips, tasting our personal blend of mint and cherry Chapstick.

"Starving," he growled, pressing his mouth to mine again and groaning from somewhere deep inside. "Fuck. Okay. Give me the grand tour or else we're never leaving the doorway."

With knees like jelly, and fires building both low in my belly and between my legs, I wouldn't have minded. Eating my mother's leftover chicken took second place to enjoying August's kisses inside the entryway. But instead of saying so, I laughed and took his hand to lead him across the red Persian rug and through the living room. I gestured toward the couch and the wall of shelves encasing the stone fireplace, and he made comments about how nice it all was and how he needed to peruse those shelves and look through those movies. Then, we entered the kitchen, where the windows were open to the waves and the screen doors welcomed the salty breeze inside, and I looked over my shoulder at August to find a grin spreading wide across his face.

"You have a very beautiful house, Clarabell," he commented softly.

I laughed, taking him to the table, where I already had dinner laid out for two. "You've only seen the living room and kitchen so far."

Pulling out my chair, he said, "That's all I need to see, to know that you have a fucking beautiful house." Then, he narrowed his eyes, as he sat down, and looked around at the floor. "But ... where are all your animals? Where's Agnes?"

"Oh, well, the cats are shy. They'll come out eventually. The bird and fish you already saw in the living room, and Agnes is ... huh, where *is* she?" I pursed my lips and peered around the corner and down the hall, then smiled. "There she is! Hey, Ag. Look who came to visit us."

Agnes stopped just inside the kitchen, stretched her front legs out and yawned. August laughed, a genuine sound that played nicely with the sloshing of salty water against the shoreline, then slapped his thigh.

"Don't look so happy to see me!" he exclaimed jubilantly, shaking his head. "Get over here, girl. Let me mush your adorable face."

Now awake and eager to please, Agnes bounded over, laying her head in his lap, and he stroked her ears as we ate.

While he was on the way over, I had scurried around the house like a busy squirrel readying for Winter. I set the table, fluffed the couch cushions, and made sure every little thing was in place and ready to be met by his eyes for the first time. I had anticipated an awkward interlude between his arrival and the onset of comfort, but now, sitting at the table and eating my mother's food in his company, I found nothing uncomfortable about him being in my house. It was as if he'd always been a part of it, like he belonged there, just as much as the crown molding and red Persian rug, and I kept glancing at him and wondering how that could possibly be.

"So," he said in conclusion, wiping his mouth with a napkin and discarding it onto his cleared plate, "can I see this beach of yours?"

The question wasn't meant to be an insinuation, I don't think, but the room grew instantly hot, despite the windows and doors being wide open to a pleasant breeze. I swallowed, as I stood and collected our dirty dishes and put them in the sink.

"Of course," I said, holding onto the calm in my tone. I glanced at his short sleeves, remembering he hadn't brought a jacket and asked, "Do you want a sweatshirt? Or a blanket, maybe?"

He shook his head, standing from the table. "No, I'm good."

Unlike him, I was sensitive to the faintest chill, so I grabbed a blanket from the couch. It was an old quilt my grandmother had gifted to me as a young girl, and I wrapped it around my shoulders. Then, together, August and I left through the sliding back door, with Agnes pouting on the other side of the screen. We left the deck, descending the long staircase down to the rocky shore and leaving the house behind to stand in the dusky glow of the moon.

"Wow," August muttered quietly, with his hands tucked into his pockets.

"I know," I replied, standing beside him, clutching the ends of the blanket against my chest.

The wind whipped our hair this way and that and the waves crashed noisily against the rocks. My bitten cheeks told me it was almost too much to be standing on the shore like this, and that we should get back inside where we had the shelter of the walls, but with narrowed eyes, we continued to stare out across the blackened watery landscape.

"I love the ocean," he finally said minutes later. "It's so powerful, nothing can touch it."

"Well, people do," I offered. "With all our garbage and whatever the hell else."

"Oh, sure, right," he said, nodding. "But that accounts for so little what's out there. There are leagues upon leagues of untouched water on this planet, so much we haven't seen, so much we could never even begin to discover it all."

I slowly nodded, my gaze aimed out toward the rippling water and folding waves. My lungs opened, taking in the scent of salt and brine, and I closed my eyes to the stillness of the night. Pressure spread across my lower back, and fingers splayed and curled inward, as August's hand moved up my spine to the nape of my neck. With eyes still closed, I opened my other senses to the capabilities of touch, scent, and taste. His mouth found mine in the night and my lips parted to accept his tongue. He kissed me slowly, lazily, as if the beach was suspended in time and we had every moment gathered to use as we wanted. I sighed, melting into his touch, and giving in to the power his kiss had over my breath, heart, and legs. He held me up, keeping one hand at the back of my neck and the other around my waist, because what control August lacked in taming the ocean, he made up for in his ability to control my gravity.

His kisses shifted, moving from the corner of my mouth to my cheek to trail over my neck and to my shoulder. I kept my eyes shut, curling and uncurling my toes to the thrum of my heart. A desperate lust unraveled, as my hands released the blanket, letting it fall to the sand, and found the lengths of his windswept hair, holding his mouth to my neck and hoping he wouldn't stop there.

"Clarabell," he muttered, pressing my name to my throat. I answered in an incoherent mutter of sighs and moans. "I want you so bad. Can I, please?"

My lips parted to his open mouth against my chest, dipping, licking, and sucking, and I savored the words he had spoken. Forty-two years on the earth had led me to many partners, more than I could realistically remember, and never once had I been asked permission. Never once had I been taken against my will, and for that, I knew I was lucky. But every encounter had still been assumed, neither of us saying no or asking permission, until now, and my legs shook and begged to accept with a resounding yes.

I pulled at his hair, leading his lips back to my waiting mouth, and kissed him again, slow and long and deep, before replying, "God, yes."

With a low, primal groan, he kissed me again, pulling me from the shore. I giggled into his mouth and felt like a girl, swept away and smitten, as he led me up the stairs and to the deck, where he laid me down. Then, to the melody of the waves caressing the shore and the wind singing the song of the sea, he took me and made me his.

CHAPTER NINETEEN

I woke up to him in my bed. Gloriously naked and with one arm stretched out across my bare chest. There was something nice and natural about having him there and seeing that he hadn't skipped out in the middle of the night after I'd fallen asleep. With the warmth of his body seeping through to my heart, I smiled into the streaks of brilliant sunlight, slicing through the curtains and across the bed.

He moved beside me, wrapping his arm tighter around my chest and nuzzling his nose behind my ear. "Good morning," he murmured, his voice heavy and rasped with sleep.

"Good morning," I repeated, sighing and closing my eyes again to shut out the morning and sun.

"You're even more beautiful in the morning," he softly muttered, pressing a kiss beneath my ear. My chest clenched with an unexpected burst of emotion at the compliment, remembering not too long ago, when I was worried what he'd think of me when the makeup had been wiped away and the wrinkled truth behind my age was revealed.

"Thank you," I whispered, not knowing how else to reply.

"You're welcome," he said, before sighing against my skin. "I wish we could stay right here all day. I don't want to miss you, and I know the second I leave, that's exactly what I'm going to do."

I nodded, pouting. "I know. I'm going to miss you, too." Then, rolling beneath the weight of his arm to face him, I opened my eyes to his drowsy smile and asked, "Can you come over later?"

He reluctantly frowned and shook his head. "I would if I could, but I have work tonight at the coffee shop, and then I really do have to try and make some headway in this manuscript. My editor has been on my ass about it, and I really haven't gotten much done."

"Oh," I said, sticking my bottom lip out further and pressing my hand over his heart, to run my fingers through his dark and course chest hair.

"But," he said, leaning forward to press a kiss to my downturned lips, "can I see you this weekend?"

I nodded eagerly. "Friday?"

Another kiss and another smile. "I'm already looking forward to it."

***

153

"Patty?" Sylvie said, leading Agnes and me into the room. We waited at the door while my friend approached the elderly woman, sitting by the window with a bouquet of white roses. Sylvie crouched beside the chair and placed a hand on her knee.

"Patty, remember I told you about Agnes and Clara?" The woman barely nodded. "Well, they're here. Do you want to visit with them for a little while?"

The woman turned then, her eyes hooded by exhaustion and an overwhelming amount of sadness, and she took in the sight of the patient Yellow Lab and me. She studied us for a moment, before offering another barely-there nod, and Sylvie patted her knee with care and reassurance.

"You don't have to say anything," she told Patty. "They're only here to visit. No pressure on you or anyone. Okay?"

Patty didn't bother to nod again. She simply directed her gaze back out the window, and Sylvie stood, waving us in. I took the unoccupied chair and dragged it over, situating it closer to Patty but not close enough to be intimidating, and loosened Agnes's leash. The dog immediately felt the slack and walked carefully toward the old woman. Patty didn't hesitate, she held her knobby-jointed hand out to her new four-legged friend, and Agnes accepted the invitation with a wag of her tail.

"Good girl," the woman said softly, petting Agnes and never looking at me.

"It's nice to meet you, Patty," I said, taking a seat. "I'll just be right here, if and when you need something."

Sylvie gripped my shoulder and mouthed, "Good luck," before heading out of the room, leaving me to hopefully make a little progress with the woman who refused to say much. Sylvie had given me the rundown when I'd first arrived. Patty had arrived over the weekend, following a breakdown after the sudden death of her daughter. Her husband had called paramedics, afraid she would hurt herself, and she'd been promptly admitted to the psych ward. Ever since, Sylvie had struggled to get the woman to talk, and now, it was Agnes's turn to try.

"How old are you?" Patty asked after only a few minutes of stroking her hand over Agnes's head.

"Me?"

She looked up at me over her large nose. "Is there someone else in here I'm unaware of?"

I smiled at the sharp edge in her voice. "I'm forty-two."

Nodding, she slid one of Agnes's ears through her fingers. "That's what I figured. You married?"

"I'm not, no."

"Boyfriend?"

I closed my eyes and was back in my bed, wrapped in August's arms, with his kisses warming my neck. "Yes."

"What's his name?"

"August."

"Hm," she answered shortly, nodding. "My husband's name is Augustus. Augie."

"Small world."

"Hm." She nodded again. "Your name is Clara?"

155

"It is."

"Clara and August, August and Clara," she muttered thoughtfully. "How long have you been together?"

"Not long, just a couple of weeks," I said, watching her as she watched Agnes. I hoped that by talking about myself, she would eventually offer something about her. A piece of her life, a sliver of what had brought her here.

"I guess when you reach a certain age, the length of time together matters less. You stop keeping track," she said.

I smiled, remembering boyfriends of my youth and counting our time together down to the minute. "That's so true."

"When we're older, the time apart is so much more significant, isn't it?"

A cloud darkened her eyes the moment the words were spoken, and I reluctantly nodded, afraid she wouldn't say anything more.

She didn't.

***

Later that night, after dinner and drinks at my sister's dining room table, Marjorie took a long pull from a bottle of beer, draining half of it in two, hearty gulps. My sister wasn't one to guzzle her booze, generally only welcoming intoxication when life was really taking its toll. So, when she lowered the bottle to the table, I took it from her and demanded to know what was going on.

"Christy has been on three different dates since Saturday," she told me.

"All with different guys?" I asked, narrowing my eyes with surprise and suspicion.

She nodded. "And she's coming home late. I haven't asked, but I'm pretty sure she's sleeping with them, and it's none of my business but ... I don't know ..." She wiped a hand over her mouth, rubbing away the last of her gloss. "She's only ever been with Josh, and now, the second she's broken up from him, she's trying to sleep with every single guy in Connecticut or something."

She was right. It was none of her business. If Christy wanted to try a few different men on for size every night of the week, that was her choice to make. But I understood my sister's motherly concern, especially when I considered that Christy was so ready to jump into lifelong commitment with her ex-boyfriend just a few weeks ago. It seemed a little too fast, too soon, even to me, and I furrowed my brow.

"Do you want me to try and talk to her?"

Marjie thought about it for a moment, then shook her head. "Not yet. If she comes to you, then yeah, I would appreciate it. But wait for her to say something. I don't want her thinking I'm sitting here, gossiping about her."

"Well, I mean," I pursed my lips and tilted my head, "you kind of are."

She sniffed a defeated laugh. "I'm just worried about her. She's hurting, and I'm afraid she's expressing it in a potentially destructive way. She doesn't even *know* these men." She shook her head and downed the other half of her bottle, before saying, "I feel sick thinking about it. Let's talk about something else. What's going on with you? How's your new career in cradle robbing going?"

I laughed as images of August filled my head, naked and nestled comfortably between my legs. "Fabulously."

"Oh, yeah?"

I bit my lip, then said, "He came over last night."

"And?"

"*And*," I drawled, "he left this morning."

Marjie's jaw dropped, and her eyes lit with excitement and envy. "Oh, my God, you lucky bitch. And it was, you know ... good?"

I laughed and nodded. "Yeah. It was good." Very good in fact. The best I'd had in memorable history. August had a way of making every part of my body feel cherished, while coaxing climax after climax out of me with the skill of someone experienced, but I decided to keep that to myself.

"So, what do you think? Could this be it for you?" Marjie asked, raising a brow and nudging my ankle with her toe.

I shrugged. "I don't know what's going to happen six months from now, Marjie," I said, wrapping my hand around my bottle of beer. "But I will say that, this is it for the moment."

She nodded but her smile soon dropped away until all that remained was her worry. "I hope Christy settles down soon. I hate thinking about what kind of trouble she could get into doing what she's doing. I want ..." She blew out a breath and wiped a hand over her eyes. "I want *her* to find someone to make her happy for the moment. If she needs to find someone at all."

"She will, Marj," I assured her, resting a hand on her knee.

My sister offered a short nod, before reaching over for my unfinished bottle of beer, and said, "Yeah, well, I just hope it happens before she gets herself in trouble."

CHAPTER TWENTY

His lips were gentle, as they mapped their way around my body, sensuously soft and careful in every movement. With eyes closed, my mouth opened in a whispered gasp, hovering somewhere between awake and asleep. He laid beside me, landing in a nest of sweaty sheets and rumpled blankets, and wrapped an arm around my waist. I tipped my head, pressing my ear to his chest to find his heart and its melodic, steady thump-thump-thump, and sighed into the dark.

"My God," I whispered in response to his shower of kisses on my forehead and hair.

"Mm-hmm," he murmured with sultry agreement, holding me tightly to his warm, naked body.

The room fell barren of all noise but for our hammering hearts and calming breath. I listened for the waves through the open bedroom window but found our bodies too loud, still buzzing from the sex and thrill of the weekend, and I smiled, unable to remember the last time I had felt quite like this. I remembered what he had said, about falling hard and fast, and I swallowed against the reality that the ailment must have been catching.

Abruptly, he sat in bed, and I opened my eyes to find him leaning over the side of the bed, rifling on the floor for something.

"What are you looking for?"

"My pants," he said hurriedly, snatching them off the floor and pulling something from the pocket. He dropped them back down and propped something onto his knee. In the dim glow streaming from the open doorway, I watched a pen quickly jittering away against paper, and I realized he was writing.

"Struck with inspiration?" I asked, poking him in the side with my toe.

"Mm," he muttered, nodding. "You seem to do that to me."

"Oh, I do?"

He closed the little notebook and laid it down on the bed, before turning to face me. "Before I met you, I had hit a wall with my current work in progress. Every time I would sit down to write, it was like trying to run on sand to get anything done, and it's been like that for weeks. But then, the other day, when I had *this* for the first time," his fingers skated in languorous circles over my sensitive side, bringing me to twitch and giggle, "the wall crumbled, and the story has direction again."

"You're welcome," I laughed, grabbing his hand, and bringing his fingertips to my lips. They smelled like me, and I loved how much I liked it. "What is it about?"

He hummed with approval as I pulled one finger into my mouth, sucking my taste from his skin. "It's about a man who falls under the spell of this very sexy older woman."

"I see," I said, nodding and moving onto the next finger. "So, it's autobiographical."

"Something like that," he muttered, voice gruff and laced with lust.

Pulling his fingers from my mouth, I moved his hand lower and lower until it rested over the heat between my legs, silently asking for more. I had never wanted more from my last boyfriend, with the blond highlights and zero conversation. We had sex, we'd roll over, we would go to sleep. But not with August. Now, my libido was alive and rejuvenated, like it was twenty again, with an insatiable hunger for his mouth, fingers, and the rising appendage between his legs. Lucky for me, he obliged with his own greedy hunger, dipping his head to kiss me with lips and tongue and startling nips of teeth. I threaded my fingers through his unruly mess of curls, holding his head against me until the thickness of his tongue wasn't enough.

"Come here," I commanded, digging my fingers into his shoulders.

August was always willing to do as I said, and he lifted his head, crawling upward to cover me with the heat of his skin, and kissed my lips in perfect unison to his body sliding effortlessly into mine. I groaned with him and initiated another fervent, feverish round of sex, all but losing my mind to the clatter of my headboard against the wall and our heavy, labored breath.

"Fucking hell," he said with a taxing sigh, resting his head against my shoulder. "I'm telling you now, I think I need a nap before round four."

I laughed, brushing his hair from his forehead. "Well, I think *I* need to eat something before I can think of sleep."

The mention of food lifted his head and lit approval in his eyes, and naked, we headed down the hall and into the kitchen. I opened the fridge while he took a seat at the island, and when I held out a bowl of cut fruit, he waved his hand with the demand to bring it over.

As I grabbed two forks, I said, "So, I'm the perfect muse, huh."

"You are," he replied, as I sat beside him, and we dug into the bowl of grapes, cantaloupe, honeydew, and pineapple.

"I bet you say that to all the girls," I teased, spearing a pineapple, and popping it into my mouth.

August shook his head. "No. Not all of them."

His sincerity had sparked curiosity, so I asked, "Who was your last?"

"My first wife," he answered, so matter of fact. "She inspired a series of short erotic stories I had published in my college newsletter. Which is probably the *last* thing you want to hear about."

Without an ounce of envy, I shook my head. "You have your past, and I have mine. It can't be erased. So, as

163

long as neither of us are living there, I don't see any harm in talking about it."

"Hm," he muttered, cocking his head, and taking me in through hungry, hooded eyes. "You're something else, you know that?"

Snorting, I shrugged and bit into a slice of cantaloupe. "I'm just experienced in this department. Jealousy over the past will get us nowhere. It's a waste of time."

His lips spread slowly into a fond smile. "Agreed."

"So, when can I read these erotic stories?" I laughed, jabbing his side with my elbow, and he laughed heartily.

"Oh, that's *definitely* never happening," he said, continuing to laugh. "Honestly, I never should've published them in the first place. It would have been less vivid to throw pornographic pictures of us around campus. But I was young and stupid, and I was proud of what I had written, so," he thrust a hand into the air, "out they went into the world."

I nodded. "So, then what is it that you're writing now?"

"I told you," he said. "It's the story of a younger man who falls desperately in love with an older woman."

My eyes met his and I told myself that he wasn't right now confessing his feelings for me. That he hadn't just told me he loves me. But that was difficult to believe, when what I saw there, in all of his silvery stars, was the affection of a man, so taken and smitten by the woman he was with.

"But it's not erotic?"

It was his turn to snort. "Well, if we keep going the way we're going, it might be. But right now, no. It's just ..." He pulled in a deep breath and pursed his lips. "It's lovely, that's what it is."

I wondered what he was writing about, as I speared another piece of fruit. If he had been so comfortable being candid about his sexual relationship with his ex-wife, what was to stop him from documenting every line on my face, every lump of cellulite in my thighs, every centimeter my breasts had sagged? And what was to stop him from presenting it to the world, printed neatly between the pages of his next potential bestseller?

But then, I caught the look in his eye, the way he glanced at me when he thought I wasn't looking. The fire that burned there and the forever building amounts of lust. No man wearing a look like that would jeopardize his relationship in that way, and I had to believe that, as I speared another piece of pineapple.

"So, what would you think about meeting my grandmother?" he asked abruptly, tearing me away from my thoughts and fruit, and all I could say was, "Okay."

No man without the desire for commitment and respect would want his girlfriend to meet his grandmother, I thought, and I couldn't stop myself from grinning.

***

The gentlest of breezes rustled the leaves of the cherry blossom tree that hung over the flagstone walkway. It brushed against my cheek, like the caressing fingers of a lover, as I followed mine up to the door painted a bright, lemony yellow. A butterfly fluttered past my hand, reminding me all too much of the ones forever wreaking havoc in my gut.

"You've been quiet," August said, glancing over his shoulder with a raise of his brow.

"I'm nervous," I admitted, smoothing my lavender sundress over my chest as I wondered if maybe I should have opted out of the push-up bra. Or maybe I should've chosen a different dress. Or maybe we shouldn't have come at all.

"Don't be," he said with a warm chuckle, wrapping his arm around my waist and pulling me forward, to stand beside him at the door. "You know those old grandmas who just bake cookies and dote over their grandchildren all day?"

"Yeah," I replied hesitantly.

"That's Nana. Trust me, she's going to love you."

"You don't know that," I muttered with a groan, and he laughed goodnaturedly.

"Yes, I do. She's incapable of disliking anybody." Then, he kissed my cheek, and asked, "You ready?"

A persuasive glint in his eye encouraged me to nod with complete disregard toward the nerves that continued to nauseate me. He opened the door and revealed a living room I would've been proud to call my own. Bright, sunny furniture, a plush sandy carpet, sky blue paint, and an intricate model ship above the crisp, white mantle welcomed me in with open arms. August chuckled again, as I clutched my hands to my chest at the sight of an antique ship wheel, hanging above the sofa.

"This is so beautiful," I marveled, brushing my fingertips over the carved wood.

"And would you believe I only paid a dollar for it?"

I turned at the sound of the warbled voice to see a hunchbacked, old woman enter the room, carrying a tray of cookies. Her hands shook, rattling the silver platter, and August rushed to take it from her.

"Thank you, honey," she said, patting his arm before taking a seat on the couch. Then, she turned and offered a little smile to her grandson with a patient, expectant look in her eyes.

"Nana, I told you about Clara," August said, placing the tray onto the glass coffee table, beside a white lantern.

"That's right, you did," she replied, clapping her hands before laying them neatly in her lap. "Clara, it's lovely to meet you, dear. Sit, sit." She gestured toward the spot beside her, and I accepted graciously.

"It's nice to meet you, too ..." I raised my eyebrows in question, and she replied, "Oh, just call me Nana. Everybody does."

I quickly learned that Nana laughed a lot and smelled of roses, and I liked her immediately and immensely. On that Saturday afternoon, we sat together in the sun-drenched living room, eating cookies and visiting like we'd known each other forever. We talked about the beach and Connecticut in the summer, my job as a therapy dog handler, and her passion for painting lighthouses and seashells. She spoke of August's gift for writing, how she had always known he would be an author, and all the while, August blushed and kept his gaze diverted.

After two hours of chatting, Nana announced that she would be late for her Bingo game if we kept distracting her. August asked if I'd like to have dinner with him, and of course, I said yes.

"Just give me a second," he said with a smile, before disappearing up the stairs.

Nana laid a hand on my knee, drawing my attention back to her. "Clara," she said, using my name with urgency, like she was about to spill a secret, and I turned to her.

"Yes?"

She frowned, deepening the lines etched around her mouth as she looked to the stairs. Then, she sighed, and said, "He has a way of seeming confident, but he's not as strong as he appears. I know I don't have to tell you this. Of course, I don't. I know how you met, but ... he's very sensitive, Clara. He can be very ... fragile."

I nodded, barely bobbing my head. "I understand," I replied quietly.

"He's so taken by you," she said, meeting my eyes with concern. "He's smitten, and ... I just need you to be careful with his heart. Please, do that for me. Even if you have to hurt him one day, please do it gently."

I swallowed at the serious sound of her voice. "Of course, but, but I won't—"

She held up a hand, stopping the words from spilling from my lips. "Don't say anything that you can't promise. Just tell me you'll be gentle, that's all."

168

Opening my lips again to protest, she pressed her hand firmly against my knee, and said, "*Please*," urgency laced between every letter of the word. She was so persistent, so fraught with worry and concern, all I could do was swallow against the tumultuous feeling, rising in my throat.

"Okay," I said, nodding. And then, before she could say anything more, August came down the stairs, smiling at the sight of us sitting closely together. Completely clueless of the fear that now threatened to drown the happiness in my heart.

CHAPTER TWENTY-ONE

"Hi, Patty. How are you today?"

The woman sitting by the window quickly flitted her gaze in my direction before staring back out toward a lone tree in the distance. She barely shrugged her shoulders as her hand absentmindedly went to Agnes's head.

"Oh, you know. Fine, I guess."

"Oh, yeah? That's good," I said, taking a seat. "What are you doing this weekend?"

"Oh," she replied in a flighty tone. "Same as usual."

Patty's usual, I had heard, was to spend the weekends staring out the window, while her husband and son tried desperately to get through to her. Which wasn't much different than what Sylvie and I had been trying to do all the days in between. In the three weeks since she'd arrived at St. Mary's, she had kept her conversational skills to a minimum, and I was beginning to wonder if it was that she just didn't have much to say.

"I'm spending the weekend with August," I said, filling the air with small talk. "We're going to check out this antique bookstore by his grandmother's house tomorrow, and then, I think we're going to camp out on the beach."

"That's nice," she said, keeping her eyes on the tree.

"It should be," I agreed. "The weather is supposed to be beautiful. Good for a night outside."

"My daughter loved camping."

My ears perked at the mention of her late daughter. In the weeks since I'd met Patty, she had never mentioned her or the trauma and tragedy surrounding her death, and although I knew that was the very reason she was here, I hadn't pushed for information. But now, with an invitation presented to me, I gently grabbed for it with the intention to run.

"Oh, really? Did she camp a lot?"

Patty swallowed, before quickly nodding. "Sh-she did. She and her husband … they would go every year. Every summer, they would take their trailer and park all, all over Connecticut."

"That sounds so nice. Did you ever go with them?"

She closed her eyes to the tree and swallowed again. "Every year."

A tear clung to her lashes for a moment before sliding along her cheek and dripping from her jaw. It landed onto her lap, in a spot soaked in early summer sunlight. I pretended to know what was in her heart or plaguing her mind, and imagined how difficult it must be to know that summer was here, and her daughter was not. There would be no camping trips this year, or any year after. Another tear escaped her eye, meeting the other in her lap, and I reached out to lay my hand over her knee. Patty didn't react to my touch, other than to hasten her hand's movements against Agnes's head.

"Would you like to tell me about her?" I asked, taking a risk. The worst that could happen was, she'd clamp her lips shut and our session would be over. I'd be back on another day, and we could try again. But I just had to keep trying.

To my surprise, Patty opened her eyes and turned to me, her lips twitching. Tempted to smile. "You remind me of her. Pretty. Smart."

"Oh, yeah?"

"She was always smiling." Her lips were unleashed then, spreading into a grin. "She had the most beautiful smile. And her laugh ... no matter how sad I was, she could always make me happy again with that laugh."

"She sounds wonderful," I commented softly, knowing the eventual break in her joy was coming.

"She w-was," Patty said, nodding quickly. "I spent so much time with her. She, she was my best friend, you know. And how I didn't know ... how I didn't ever *see* ... I-I don't know how I'll ever understand."

"I'm not sure you can ever understand," I said, keeping my hand still on her knee.

"They tell you to look for the warning signs, don't they? They tell you to watch out for all, all, all these *things*. But there was nothing there to see. Her husband would have noticed. *I* would have noticed."

"Some people wear their depression on the outside," I told her. "But others, they keep it buried down deep, so there's nothing for others to notice. That doesn't make it their fault, or yours."

"But *why*?" she nearly shouted, her forehead crumpling and her tears falling quicker now. "Why wouldn't she let me help her?"

"I don't know, Patty," I replied, not knowing what other answer to give. "But what I do know is, it wasn't your fault for not knowing. It wasn't anybody's fault, not even hers."

She closed her eyes again and turned away, before nodding. "I-I know. I do know that. I just wish I'd known, that's all I'm saying. I would have done everything differently, I would have gotten her help, and …" She took a deep breath, her lungs quivering. "I just wish I had known."

***

The plush fabric of the blanket was soft and luxurious against my back, while August's hips rocked against mine, in time with every gentle caress of the waves to the shore. Our kisses were sloppy and slow, lazy, an accurate albeit euphoric representation of the way summer makes one feel. I turned my head, aware of the soft yet gritty sand beneath the blanket, and smiled toward our fire, flickering wildly and reaching toward the sky, as August's lips traveled along my jaw and to my ear. Frank Sinatra crooned away from my portable speaker, sitting in the mouth of our cozy tent, and the stars looked down from up above, playing voyeur to his hands, roaming freely along my naked curves and into my unkempt hair.

This was a perfect night, with the most perfect campout mere feet from my house. It could only have been made possible with the perfect man, and with that thought, I realized he was exactly that. The perfect man. Everything I had ever wanted, rolled into this package of sinew and bone, skin and muscle, curls and silver flecks.

"Clarabell," he murmured into my ear, nipping the lobe with his teeth. "How the hell do you always feel so good?"

"I'll tell you my secret when you tell me yours," I retorted coyly, wrapping the tendrils of his hair around my fingers. He lifted his head as I turned to face him again, meeting his eyes and the galaxy that lived within, and in that moment, I experienced a miracle.

It came without invitation, as every cell in my body seemed to bloom with acute awareness. Every inch of me now knew every inch of him, every beat of my heart spoke to every beat of his, and when his lips touched mine, every star watching from above burst in sparks of color and glory. It could be nothing but the fabled fireworks my mother and sister had spoken about. The ones I'd heard about for years and never knew, until now, weeks into our relationship.

There they are, I thought, as a sob broke away from my lips, surprising us both.

Abruptly, he pulled away and searched my eyes with concern. "What's wrong?"

I swallowed, afraid tears weren't far away and determined not to be that woman who cries during sex.

"Nothing," I said, shaking my head and moving my hands from his hair to the sides of his face. "I'm just really happy. That's all."

"I am, too," he replied, kissing the tip of my nose. "More than I've been in … *God*, forever, probably."

"I …" I pulled in a deep breath and bit my lip, fighting the wave of emotion that continued to threaten with pulls at my throat and burning pricks against my nose. "I think I'm in love with you."

The battle was lost, and my voice quavered. I laughed at my own expense and lifted my head, burying my face in his shoulder to hide my reddening cheeks, as his hips stilled against mine, suspending our bodies at the cliff's edge.

Damn my emotions and words and their insistent need to be said at a time like this. Damn them to Hell.

"Hey, hey, hey," he said, pulling away and kneeling between my knees. Without his shoulder there to hide against, I covered my tear-streaked face with my hands, but August wrapped his fingers around my wrists and gently pulled them away. "Clara, hey. Don't cry."

"I-I can't help it," I whispered, keeping my eyes shut and turning away. "I shouldn't have said anything. I'm sorry. I just—"

"No, come here." He didn't wait for me to come to him, as he reached out with his arms and scooped me up. Sighing, I knelt before him, our bare knees touching on the soft blanket, and kept eyes on the flames, reaching for the sky. "Look at me," he commanded, pressing his palms to my cheeks and carefully turning my head to face him. Then, when I finally mustered the bravery to meet his gaze, he smiled and calmed my hammering heart.

"Nobody else has ever said it first," he said. "I told you, I fall hard and I fall fast, and I'm always the one to take that initial leap."

The realization that he might not feel the same way, crashed against my lungs and burned my chest with the impact. "Oh, right," I whispered and gnawed at my lip.

"I was determined to hold back with you, though. I didn't want to be the first because I knew how you initially felt about being with me. I didn't want to screw this up by moving quicker than you wanted to go, especially if you didn't want it to be more than just, I don't know, a fling. And I didn't want to get hurt again."

"I understand," I replied, wishing desperately that I could turn back the hands of time and take back every stupid word I said, as a big, fat, telling tear fell from my eye.

"Please, don't cry, Clara," he said, kissing the tear from my cheek.

"I can't help it," I whispered, closing my eyes to the feeling of his lips on my skin and hoping this night wouldn't be our last.

"Would it help if I said that I'm also in love with you?"

I groaned, opening my eyes to stare at him, incredulous. "I don't want you to say anything if you don't—"

August laughed, shaking his head and grinning. "I'm not," he said, pushing his hands into my hair. "I am so in love with you, Clara, and it has been one of the greatest challenges of my life to keep my fucking mouth shut about it. But now, the cat's out of the bag, and I don't intend to stop reminding you of just how much I love you for a long, long time."

Every beat of my heart sang in unison with every beat of his, as I reached for him with aching fingers. We kissed with a passionate urgency, in the way only new love can, as his back met the blanket and my thighs clung tightly to his hips. We finished what we had started beneath the voyeuristic sky, and with every moan and thrust, I begged the stars with a silent passion for what he said to not just be the fleeting words of a man who loved falling in love. I wanted them to be a promise, one he wouldn't take back, and I wished for it to be true.

***

Wrapped in the comfort of his arms and the summer's warm embrace, I opened my eyes to the cover of the tent. It was still nighttime, and I wanted to be sleeping, but I was aware I had woken for a reason—why? What had woken me up from a wonderfully deep sleep?

"Your phone," August grumbled, his chin moving against the top of my head.

"What?"

"It's ringing."

"Shit."

Suddenly aware of the irritating chime, I reached for the offending device and forced my eyes to focus on the name lighting up the screen. "Phoebe?" I croaked through a throat scratchy with sleep. "What the ... why would she ..." I muttered incoherent, incomplete phrases, as I answered the call and pressed the phone to my ear. "Hello? Phoebs?"

"C-Clara?"

The warbled sound of Phoebe's voice crackled through the speaker, accompanied by the rush of running water, and just like that, I was wide awake.

"Hey, Phoebs," I said, sitting up, with August's arm falling into my lap. "What's up?"

"Clara, I ... I-I don't know w-what to do. I-I-I can't keep doing this. I just, I just c-can't."

The force of my heart, slamming violently against my ribs, echoed through my bones and into my ears, as I replied, "What can't you do, honey? Talk to me. What's going on?"

August was awake now, too, and he sat up beside me, his concern plainly written in his eyes. He brought his ear closer to the phone, listening in, and I didn't stop him from eaves dropping.

"I w-want to die," she said, and I realized she was crying. "There's nothing for me here. No-nobody cares if I'm h-here or not."

"Oh, Phoebe, honey," I said, coaxing my voice to remain calm. "I care. You know I do. That's why you called me, right? Because you know I care?"

"I ..." She hesitated, breathing loudly into the voice, sobbing. "I-I don't know why I c-called. Clara ..." She hiccupped and made the guttural sound of a person in deep, devastating pain. "God, Clara, I'm s-so, so fucking sick of feeling like this. I just want it to stop. I need it to fucking stop."

178

Tears bit angrily at the backs of my eyes and the breath in my lungs stuttered on its way out. I shuddered, cold despite the heat of the night, and August wrapped an arm around my shoulders. I needed to talk her down from this cliff before she jumped, I could never live with myself if she jumped, and I held onto the simple fact that she had called me, as I said, "Honey, will you let me come get you?"

"R-Right now?"

"Yes. Right now."

She sniffled. "Will, will you b-bring Agnes?"

I was already crawling out of the tent and running back to the house, as I said, "We're on our way."

CHAPTER TWENTY-TWO

Phoebe's father's house was dark when I pulled up to the curb, except for a small, iron lantern beside the front door. I gritted my teeth at the thought of knocking on the door, hoping Phoebe would come outside without me having to disturb the whole household. But after several minutes of waiting with Agnes whimpering in the backseat, I realized she wasn't coming. Afraid that she had done something to hurt herself, or worse, I hurried to unbuckle my seatbelt.

"I'll be right back, girl," I said to Agnes, before leaving the car and running up the path to the stoop.

I wasted no time in beating my fist incessantly against the door, praying someone would come, and when the adjacent window suddenly illuminated with a soft light, I sighed with temporary relief. The door was thrown open and there I saw the scowling face of a man I had never seen before.

"Who the hell—"

"Mr. Walters?"

He narrowed his sleepy eyes with suspicion. "Yeah …"

"My name is Clara McKinley. I'm a therapy dog handler from St. Mary's." He nodded with recollection. "I just got a call from—"

"She's taking me to the hospital." Phoebe's voice came from behind her father and Mr. Walters turned around, startled, revealing the shriveled form of his daughter. Her complexion was sallow, and her shoulders were slumped, with a backpack hanging from her hand. The man's arms drooped at his sides as his defeated sigh filled the room with an audible exhale.

"What happened?" he asked, as Phoebe pushed past him and the heartbreak in his eyes.

"Don't worry about it."

"Phoebe," he said, speaking firmly. "Tell me. What happened?"

"Same shit, different day, Dad," she muttered, walking by me and toward my car.

Her father turned and stared at the back of her head. "But I thought you were doing better," he called after her. "You said—"

"I say a lot of things, Dad. You just don't care enough to pay attention to what I'm *not* saying," she called back, and with that, she opened the passenger door, then slammed it behind her.

The moment hung in the air, thick and heavy. Mr. Walters stared at his daughter, clenching his fists and releasing them. He seemed torn, not knowing what to do or how to react. I knew I should say something, I knew I had to, but exactly what wasn't coming easily. Still, I comforted people for a living, and I felt the need to comfort him now.

"I'm sor—"

"I *do* care," he interjected. To me or himself, I didn't know. "I just don't know *how* the hell to care anymore."

I didn't know what to say to that, and I responded by simply biting my lip and nodding.

"I know she needs help," he went on, now addressing me with the pain worn in the lines on his face. "And I think I'm getting it for her every single time I take her to that hospital whenever she asks, but then, she's released, and a few weeks later, we're back here again. I don't know what the hell I'm doing wrong, but what I do know is, I'm failing that girl."

I pulled in a deep breath and wetted my lips, as I glanced over my shoulder, to catch Phoebe climbing into the backseat and wrapping her arms around Agnes's neck.

"Does she ever say anything to you?" he asked quietly. "About what I could be doing differently?"

Confronting the father of a patient at three in the morning wasn't on my list of things to do that weekend. I longed to be back on the beach, sleeping in the arms of my boyfriend. I desperately wanted to be transported there instead of this doorstep, as I sighed and brushed a few strands of hair away from my forehead.

"I'm going to be blunt with you," I said plainly. "Phoebe never says anything about you, and I've always wondered why. She only ever talks about her mom."

"Her mom?" He scoffed, and I turned to watch him shake his head, incredulous. "God, I can't even imagine why. Her mother hasn't been in the picture in ... Jesus, her whole life, just about."

***

"What were you talking to my dad about?"

I glanced to the girl with black rings of makeup smudged around her eyes and streaked in messy lines down her cheeks.

"He asked if you ever say anything about him," I answered honestly.

"What did you say?" she asked, while moving back into the front passenger seat.

"I told him you've never said anything about him."

She nodded with satisfaction. "Good."

"Why is that, Phoebs? Why don't you ever say anything about him?" I finally asked, after months of wondering.

"Because there's nothing to say," she replied bluntly.

People have a way of hiding their true selves behind dishonest facades. They become skilled at playing the role expected of them and only let the realest side of themselves out to play when they feel most at ease. I knew I had only just met Phoebe's father, and who was I to decide if that man at the door was an accurate portrayal of his true self? But I had caught him off-guard.

He was vulnerable, half-asleep, and most people in that state don't have the time or energy to muster a false persona. His concern felt genuine, and the love he had for his daughter appeared too real to be imagined.

"He seems very worried about you," I told her gently.

She snorted. "Yeah, okay."

"What happened tonight, Phoebs?"

I glanced to see her purse her lips and shake her head. "Nothing. It's stupid."

"Well, it was enough to make you upset, wasn't it?"

"Yeah, well." She sniffed and rubbed her nose with the back of her hand. "It's just that nobody wants me around. That's all it was."

"Who doesn't want you around? Your dad seems to—"

"God, fuck my dad, okay? Stop talking about my fucking dad."

"Okay. I'm sorry."

She crossed her arms and slumped against the seat. Then, she said, "I called my mom earlier, okay? She told my sister she could come to Florida for the summer, and I called and asked if I could go, too."

Keeping in mind what her father had said about her mother's absence from her life, I treaded lightly as I asked, "What did she say?"

Phoebe pulled in a deep, quavering breath, before exploding in a burst of anger and kicking the dashboard. "She fucking said no, that's what she said! She said no." Tears spilled from her eyes, further smearing the makeup on her face. "She says I'm a handful. Sh-she says I'm

184

better off staying here because my dad knows what to do with me," she cried, using air quotes. "I k-keep telling her I-I'm going to get better. I would be better, if she'd let me fucking stay with her, but she, she d-doesn't believe me. She just says if I was more like Taylor, she'd f-feel different. She only wants her and not me."

My heart shattered at Phoebe's desperation to please her mother, to be with her and prove to her that she could be exactly what she needed her to be. I ached for her and the competition with her sister, unable to believe that a mother could so willingly pit her daughters against each other in such a cruel, heartless way. Had it always been like this, ever since the girls were small children? Was this how Phoebe had grown up, craving the attention of her mother and resenting her father for being the only parent in her life who genuinely cared?

I held her hand as we made our way to the hospital and Agnes kept her head on her shuddering shoulder. With a tight hug, I dropped her off and promised I'd see her on Monday, and before I drove back home, I sent a message to Sylvie.

Hey, sorry to text you so late. I just dropped Phoebe off at the hospital. I'll explain more later, but I really think we should get her and her dad into therapy together. I have a strong feeling that might help a lot. Or at least I hope so.

***

185

By the time I got back home, the sky had painted itself in shades of orange, red, and pink, as the sun peeked over the horizon. I headed through the gate of my picket fence to walk down to the beach, only to find that the camp had been cleaned up and the fire had been put out. Sighing with disappointment, I trudged my way back up the stairs and through the back door. The house was quiet and still upon entering, but as I walked through the kitchen, Bumby, the black and white lummox, wandered slowly down the hall from the bedroom.

"Hey, Bumb," I greeted him, only to be ignored.

August was fast asleep on my bed, surrounded by the other three cats. Agnes wandered in after me and dropped exhaustedly onto her bed, falling asleep immediately with a heavy sigh.

I knew exactly how she felt.

The room was enveloped in such an excruciating quiet, I tiptoed around in fear of disturbing them all, as I carefully peeled off my clothes. I gritted my teeth, pulling back the sheet and hoping I could just climb in without waking anyone up. I cursed beneath my breath when one of the cats, startled by my intrusion, jumped from the bed in a hurry, waking everyone else, including August.

He lifted his head, eyes squinted and half-hidden behind his tousled curls. "Hey," he mumbled, yawning and pushing his hair back from his eyes. "How's Phoebe?"

I made myself comfortable under the weight of the quilt and pressed my naked skin to his. "She's okay," I said, laying my head on his shoulder. "I think so, anyway. She was better when I dropped her off at the hospital than she was when I spoke to her on the phone, so I guess that's something."

"It is," he replied, nodding.

A weight heavier than the blanket settled against my heart as I closed my eyes and sighed, breathing in August's salty scent, the beach still clinging to his body. I wrapped an arm around his waist and hugged him tightly, selfishly saddened by the abrupt interruption to what should have been a perfect night. He combed through my hair with his long, nimble fingers and asked what was wrong. I hesitated in telling him, not wanting to get into it when I could be finding sleep again, but he was insistent.

"I'm just sorry I left," I said by way of admission, and immediately felt guilty for saying it at all.

"What?"

"No, that was awful. I shouldn't have—"

"Don't ever be sorry for telling me the truth," he replied. "And don't ever be sorry for helping someone, either."

"But our night was ruined and—"

"Clarabell, do you know how my father died?"

I opened my eyes to the darkened room and stared ahead at nothing in particular, as I said, "I read that he … took his own life."

"Right. You read that online. On my website, yes?"

"Yes," I said, nodding.

"Well, what my website doesn't say, is that he didn't call anybody before he grabbed his gun and shot himself in the head. It also doesn't say that I have spent nearly

187

twenty years wondering what would have happened if he had."

Despite laying down, my heart plummeted toward the murky, gurgling depths of my stomach, and together, they flipped with nausea and gut-wrenching guilt. I shouldn't have said anything. I shouldn't have opened my damn mouth at all. I worked with patients in a psychiatric hospital. I made a living by helping people, and I could hardly believe I had allowed even a fraction of a second to be wasted on regret over doing just that.

"God, August," I groaned, laying a hand over my face. "I'm such an asshole."

"No, you're not. And I'm not trying to make you feel like one. You're human. All I'm saying is, there are calls to ignore and things to put off, but that one? You answer it, you go help if you can, and you don't ever apologize for it."

"Okay," I whispered, knowing he was right. Of course, he was.

The room fell silent. Somewhere in our conversation, the cats and Agnes had found they'd had enough of our racket and left the room, leaving us alone. After a few minutes, I thought August had fallen asleep. I allowed my body to grow heavy, while my mind continued to race with the events of the night and the regret of having said anything. I had known about August's father. Hell, I knew about *him* and why he had been in the hospital, so how I could think for a second that I should've said something so insensitive in the presence of someone familiar with the pain from simply living was inexcusable. That wasn't me, and for a second, I wondered if being happy and smitten had really pulled me *that* far away from who I was, when August spoke.

"I love you, Clarabell. I love so much about you, but I think the thing I love the most is your selflessness. Your dedication to helping other people and the attachment you have to your family and patients—myself not included." He chuckled, before continuing. "You told me that what you want to do with your life is save others, and I really hate the thought that I could ever be the reason for you to hesitate. Even for a second. Because I know that's not you, and I never want to be the reason for you to change."

Swallowing against a rapid rise of emotion and nodding, I cleared my throat and said, "I love you, too, August, and I promise, I won't change."

CHAPTER TWENTY-THREE

Saturday was spent sleeping in and making lazy love in the kitchen while dinner simmered in the slow cooker I'd recently found the inspiration to buy. We ate on the back deck, listening to the sea gulls and the sloshing sea. We laughed at Agnes, as she chased the birds and they taunted her with cackles and flapping wings. It was lovely, and whenever a comfortable lull touched our endless stream of conversation, I caught my mind saying, *this is nice.*

"What are you thinking about?" August asked, before bringing his glass of lemonade to his lips.

"Oh," I said, smiling. "Just that … I'm really happy."

He lowered the glass and returned my smile. "I'm glad. So am I. This is really good, I think ... what we have."

"It is," I said, placing my elbows on the table and folding my hands, touching them to my chin.

"It makes me wonder if I've ever truly been in love before," he went on, a thoughtful expression creasing the lines between his brows. "All of those times with other women, they almost feel like a waste to me now. Like I wish I had just met you before I spent a second with any of them. But then," he pursed his lips contemplatively, before continuing, "I have to wonder, maybe I needed those experiences, to know that this is real. You know what I mean?"

I did, and I nodded. "Do you know that I was proposed to a couple times?"

He shook his head. "You didn't tell me that, no."

"I had two boyfriends, one in my twenties and another in my thirties, who actually asked me to marry them."

"What did you say?"

I laughed softly. "I said no. Both times. I didn't even hesitate."

"You weren't happy with them?"

Shrugging, I looked out toward the ocean, to watch Agnes splashing along the shore. "It wasn't that I was unhappy. I liked them, loved them even, but I would always catch myself wondering if there was someone better out there and if I should keep looking. That's always been my biggest problem in relationships; I'm always questioning what I'm missing out on. So, when they proposed, I said no. Because I figured that, if I ever had to think something like that, even for a second, then they weren't the person I was meant to be with."

"But that's natural," August countered, and I turned back to him, surprised by his challenging tone. "Commitment isn't something to be taken lightly, and it's a very human thing to question if you're making the right decision."

"Yes, I believe they call that *cold feet*," I said, laughing as I picked up my glass of lemonade. August smiled, as I continued, "There's a big difference between allowing your nerves to take over for a moment and constantly asking yourself if you're only settling because you feel you have to."

"Ah," he replied with an understanding nod.

"That's how it's always been for me," I went on. "In any relationship, really. Like, this guy I was seeing a few years ago, we had so much fun for a few months. But when I sat down to think about where the relationship was going, I realized I didn't see it going anywhere at all. Then, I'd look at, oh, I don't know, Paul Newman or Marlon Brando, and I'd think about how I'd trade every man in existence today to have a man like that. And that's the moment when I'd know, yep," I nodded, "it's time to be single again."

Any man without an ounce of confidence would've heard his woman say something like that and feel threatened. He would have wondered if his days with her were numbered and if he should just cut the cord now to save himself the wasted time. But August's lips curved into a warm, adoring smile and he simply chuckled, shaking his head.

"You're a rare one, Clarabell," he said, rasped affection laced through his tone.

I laughed and shook my head. "I'm picky."

"It's not a bad thing to know what you want," he replied. "And if what you want is Gregory Peck, then you've got him, as long as you'll be my Audrey Hepburn."

I laughed again at the reference to *Roman Holiday*, a favorite of mine. "They never end up together," I pointed out, smirking from across the table.

"No," he agreed, nodding. "But I never liked the way it ended anyway, and who's stopping me from rewriting it?"

***

I thought it was thunder that woke me up that night, surprising me with a loud crack and stealing the breath from my lungs. But as I sat in bed, steadying my frantic heart, I looked out the window and realized it wasn't raining. Yet another resounding bang broke the silence from somewhere in the house, and frightened, I looked around the room for August, only to find he wasn't there.

"August?" I whispered, laying my hand against his side of the bed, as if I believed he might actually be there but just invisible to my eyes. "August?"

There was no answer to my questioning call, but then I heard him, talking beyond the bedroom door. Realizing he must have been on the phone, I settled with a sigh, laid back down, and peered at the clock, seeing that it was after midnight.

"Another night of no sleep," I muttered begrudgingly to the universe.

"Dammit!" I heard August shout, and then came the sound of a chair violently scraping against the kitchen floor. "No, no, no. Fuck, I gotta get this right. I gotta get this right now. Now, fucking *do it!*"

It didn't take long to now realize that he wasn't, in fact, on the phone, and I wondered if someone else was in my house. But no other voice responded to the anger in his, and it occurred to me that he was talking to himself.

Climbing out of bed and tying my robe loosely around my waist, I made my way down the hall toward the kitchen. There, August stood, naked, at the table, with one of the chairs shoved far behind him. His arms were ramrod straight and his hands were planted firmly to the table's surface, framing the open laptop. With his back to the hallway entrance, he didn't notice me at first, as I shuffled in and rubbed my eyes, trying to adjust to the blinding light cast from the computer's screen.

"Hey," I said, and he turned quickly on his heel to stare at me, his eyes wide and his brows lowered in anger. The look on his face startled me and I smiled. "Sorry, I didn't mean to scare you."

Without a word, he looked back to his computer and aggressively tapped one of the keys. As I moved closer, I saw a word processor open on the screen and with every tap of the key, letters and words and sentences disappeared.

"You're writing?"

"Obviously," he grumbled, as he quickly turned around, lifted the chair, and then slammed it back into place.

"I thought I heard thunder," I said, laughing uncomfortably. "I woke up and had to make sure it wasn't—"

"Clara, I'm trying to fucking work," he snapped, turning to me with an unexpected and undeserved amount of fury, blazing in his eyes. "Can't you see that?"

Frowning at his tone, I looked away and said, "O-kay. I'm sorry. I just—"

"I have a fucking deadline in a month, and I have hardly written a fucking thing in this piece of shit. So, if you could *please* just leave me the hell alone, I'd really appreciate it."

Then, with finality, he dropped into the chair and began to type furiously. Stunned and silent, I watched him for all of three minutes before he stopped writing to grip the strands of his hair and pulled, growling with rage. I thought for a moment that his anger might be directed at me, and I took a few steps back toward the hall, when I realized he no longer seemed to care that I was even there.

"Stupid. It's all fucking stupid. Stupid, stupid, stupid," he chanted, rapping his knuckles against his temple. "It's right there. I have it right there. Why can't I just fucking do it right?"

"August," I said, cautiously walking back toward him with my hands out, palms open. "Honey."

He turned his head to look at me and I was glad to see the anger had vanished, but what had replaced it was a heartbreaking dose of guilt. "Clarabell," he said, standing abruptly and pulling me into his arms. "I'm sorry. I'm sorry, I'm sorry, I'm sorry. I'm just in the middle of this and it's not doing what I want it to do, but God, it's not your fault and I shouldn't take it out on you. I'm so sorry."

"It's okay," I said, my cheek against his chest and my brow furrowed with concern. "It's okay."

***

I was grateful to convince him to come back to bed, and although he seemed to fall asleep without any further issues, I couldn't say the same for myself. Even with his arm wrapped tightly around my waist and his chin nestled comfortably against my shoulder, there was no sleep to be found when I closed my eyes. There was only the sight of his anger and the sound of hatred in his voice. I reminded myself that the outburst had been short lived, and that he hadn't hurt me, but the fact that it had happened at all raised a red flag I wasn't sure should be ignored.

But later on, after I managed to sleep for an hour or two, I asked August about it on our way to Marjie's. He sighed as he tipped his head back to stare into the sun, like the question alone exhausted him, but when he brought his head back down to stare at the sidewalk ahead, he wore an apologetic smile and shame in his eyes.

"I should have told you about my process," he said. "I can be a real dick when I'm writing, and a lot of times, I don't even realize I'm doing it. I should've warned you not to bother me when I'm in the middle of working, and I'm sorry I didn't."

I narrowed my eyes in contemplation. Something Ernest Hemingway had once said came to mind, that the only real key to writing was to sit down at the typewriter and bleed. I wasn't a writer, or an artist at all, really. But I could imagine that, to offer a piece of your soul to paper would be painful. It had to be, and so, it seemed reasonable that such a painful process would make someone angry. The thought made me wonder why anybody would even bother, until I remembered all my books back at home, and then I was grateful to the men and women who sacrificed their blood and soul and guts to give them to me.

"It looked like torture," I admitted, looking back to him and the sloppy crown of curls on his head.

"It is," he agreed, nodding. "It's absolute agony and a lot of times I hate it."

"Then, why bother?" I asked, trying to understand why anybody would want to do something that caused them so much pain.

I was hoping he could offer some insight. A little anecdote to help it all make sense. But he didn't. He just offered me the smallest, saddest little smile and said, "Because I wouldn't know how else to live."

CHAPTER TWENTY-FOUR

The discomfort from witnessing his creative rage the night before dissipated as the day passed. By the time evening had fallen over River Canyon, I found my place back on August's lap, kissing his lips and running my hands through his curls. Every press of his mouth to mine served as a salve, protecting my mind from the anger I'd witnessed in the dark, and with every grind of our hips, all was forgiven.

"Take these off," he muttered, his hands beneath my skirt and the scent of chocolate on his breath.

I was all too eager to comply, climbing off his lap to slide my underwear down my legs and kick them away to lay in a crumpled little heap of sky blue on the bleached wood deck. A seagull called from overhead, and another answered, as I straddled his legs, and when his hands slid along my inner thighs, my hums of satisfaction drowned out the avian chatter above.

"You're still wearing your pants," I said between kisses, my mind spinning with every brush of his thumbs against my naked, sensitive flesh beneath the shroud of my skirt.

"Later," he replied, his voice gruff.

His fingers were soft and uncalloused, the type you'd expect to belong to a man who spent his life on art and not hard labor. But they were skilled and never careless, their precision always impressive. His ministrations intensified and the moans escaping my throat followed suit, as I tipped my head back and closed my eyes.

"August," I whispered, hanging by a thread at the precipice of orgasm. "Oh, my—"

"Oh! Oh, Jesus Christ. Um ..."

Christy's voice joined the blended chorus of calling gulls, pants, and moans, as I nearly fell from August's lap. Quickly standing, I spun on my heel, smoothing my long, gauzy skirt out and hoping it covered anything incriminating, as I watched her clap a hand over her eyes, before hurrying back along the boardwalk to the street.

"Christy, wait! It's okay!" I shouted after her.

"I'm sorry. I should have called. I'll come back—"

I ran after her, leaving August to collect himself. "No, honey. It's okay. We were just—" I swallowed. The girl wasn't a girl at all, and she knew exactly what we'd just been doing. "It's fine. You're fine."

She stopped and turned slowly, facing me with red cheeks and embarrassment. "Are you sure? I don't want to interrupt ... you know." She gestured awkwardly toward the deck and my boyfriend, busy brushing his tangled hair from his eyes.

"I'm sure," I promised.

She blew out a breath and met my eyes with her uncertain gaze. "Okay," she said with her exhale. "Because I really need to talk to someone, and it can't be my mom."

My galloping heart slowed to a hammering crawl as I took in her serious expression and the way her hand gripped tightly to her purse's leather strap. A thousand possibilities instantly raced through my mind, and I had to stop it from jumping to a thousand different conclusions.

"Okay, sweetie," I said, swallowing at my trepidation. "Let's get inside."

***

August slipped out with a firm press of his lips against mine and the promise to call me before he went to bed. Christy continued with her apologies for ruining my night, and as I boiled water for tea, I continued to promise she hadn't ruined anything, while ignoring the heap of burning lust between my legs that had only begun to fade with sulking disappointment.

"Oh, please," my niece replied, doubtful. "You guys were two seconds away from doing it."

"We do *it* plenty," I answered, blushing as I laughed. "Missing one night isn't going to kill us."

"Aunt Clara!" Clearly impressed, Christy's eyes widened, her grin broad. "Good for you!"

"Oh, God," I groaned, waving her praise away. "Stop."

"Seriously," she replied, sitting on the couch and tucking her legs under her bottom. "I told you before and I'll tell you again, he is hot as hell."

Sighing and shaking my head, while my lips betrayed me, twitching toward a smile. "You said you wanted to talk to me about something?" I asked, changing the subject.

A rumble of thunder rolled somewhere in the distance, and my niece turned toward the screen door leading onto the deck. "What the hell is with all this rain?" she muttered, shaking her head and obviously running away from the chat she had initiated. "It's relentless this year. We're gonna need an ark."

"Christy."

Her throat bobbed as she turned back to me, her eyes dark and her mouth pinched in a tight frown. "Um, so I, uh ..." She swallowed again and dropped her gaze to the mug between her hands. "I'm ... pregnant."

Since seeing August, I had hardly consumed a drop of alcohol, and in the time that I'd been with him, I found that I didn't miss it much. But suddenly, in my kitchen, sitting with my niece and listening to another incoming storm, I was desperate for a glass of wine and made a beeline for the cabinet. I could feel her eyes on me as I pulled out a bottle of red and a glass, and with shaking hands, poured, unable to turn around to face her until I took a preparatory sip. Then, with a deep breath, I brought my glass back to the table and sat down beside her, somehow simultaneously ready and unprepared.

"Okay," I said, calm and controlled, despite the frantic beat of my heart. "Do you know who the father is?"

"Aunt Clara, *please*." Christy shook her head and looked away, perturbed by the question.

"Well, I have to ask. I know you've been seeing a few guys—"

"What the hell do you think I am?" she fired at me, defensive and on the verge of tears.

I blinked rapidly, surprised. "Your mom said—"

"I don't know what the hell Mom is telling you, but I'm not out there, sleeping around. I've gone on a couple dates, yeah, but I haven't had sex with anybody since … since Josh." She dropped her watery gaze back to her hands and her lip quivered, before she bit it, fighting back the tears.

"Oh, honey." I reached out, grabbing for her hand and holding it in mine. "Does he know?" She shook her head, unable to look me in the eye, even as she held onto my hand with desperation. "Are you going to tell him?"

"Of course, I'm going to tell him," she said, still defensive in her tone. "I can't just … *hide it* from him. I would never be able to live with myself."

"So, can I assume you're going to—"

"Keep the baby?" she asked, finally bringing her gaze to mine, and I nodded. "Yeah. I mean, I-I've wanted a baby for as long as I can remember, so … if this is how it's gonna happen, then …" She shrugged, and then, the tears began to fall. "I … I just never thought I'd be doing it alone, you know?"

Time warped in that moment and instead of sitting across from my niece, I saw my sister. A teenager, pregnant with another teenager's baby. Two and a half decades later, I could still recall the fear in her eyes and the way her hands shook in her moment of confession. I remembered her reluctance to embark into parenthood, certain she would be doing it all alone, only to find herself forever wrapped in the embrace and support of her family.

"You're not alone," I assured my niece then, as I had once assured my sister, her mother. "No matter what happens, you are never alone. I want you to remember that."

"I know," she said, nodding and wiping at her tear-streaked face. "I know. But you get what I mean."

"I do," I replied. "You're afraid of being a single mom and raising a baby without another parent, I get it. But as long as you have me and your parents and all of your grandparents, you are never, ever, *ever* going to be alone. Okay? We're all going to help you get through this."

Swallowing back a sob, she nodded. "O-okay."

"Now," I said, squeezing her hand in mine, "let's figure out how we're gonna tell your mom."

CHAPTER TWENTY-FIVE

The storm from the night before had left the ground saturated and the air crisp. I was grateful for a reprieve from the humidity, even while I cursed the heels of my sandals as they sank into my sister's yard with ease, like slicing through warmed butter.

"Dammit," I muttered, pulling my foot from the ground with a sickening squelch.

"Nobody told you to wear heels," Marjie reminded me, rolling her eyes in my direction, as we walked together from the shed to her back deck.

"Yeah, well, I didn't think I'd be traipsing through your yard. When was the last time Mark mowed?" I complained, as the dewy blades of grass, still wet with rain, tickled my toes.

"The other day."

"Yeah, right. This is too long to have been cut recently."

She shrugged. "Grass grows fast. Especially with all this rain we've been having."

I grumbled as we walked up the steps and over the wooden deck, then through the back door. Mom's eyes were on us, as if she'd been watching the entire time, her brows raised with hopeful expectation.

"Did you find it?" she asked, her gaze dropping to our empty hands.

"No," Marjie replied, disgruntled. "I told you the other day. That old typewriter is in your basement somewhere."

Mom frowned. "Are you sure? Because I could've sworn I—"

"If it's not in the shed, and it's not in the basement or attic, then it isn't here," my sister interrupted, huffing with agitation, and Mom deflated. "I've looked everywhere, okay? I don't have it."

"Hm," Mom sighed, folding her hands on the table and turned to Dad. "I want to find that thing. August would love it."

Days ago, my mother had remembered my grandfather's old Corona typewriter. She'd thought August might like to have it, and I smiled, touched by my mom's insistence on gifting the old relic to my boyfriend. But it was also an heirloom none of us had seen in at least a decade, and nobody seemed to have a clue of where it might be.

"Mom, it's okay," I assured her. "Don't go crazy trying to find it."

She returned the smile, even as her eyes held determination and stubbornness. "Oh, I know," she said. "I won't go nuts or anything. I just thought he'd like to have it. It would look nice in his office."

"He doesn't have an office," I said, laughing.

"Well, maybe, one day, he will," she insisted, lifting her chin with confidence.

I thought about the spare room across the hall from my bedroom, with a big bay window overlooking my garden in the front yard. When I had bought the house, the realtor had suggested to use it as a nursery, as if I, a single woman, had given the impression I'd ever need one. It was a small room, and all of these years later, I had never found a use for it. So, it had sat there, containing nothing but a few boxes and some pet supplies that I could easily find a home for elsewhere. Now, I envisioned August in front of the window, sitting in a wingback chair and reading his manuscript, while a computer screen glowed from an old library desk in the corner. I smiled at the thought. It wasn't much but I could make it his, if he ever wanted it, and for the first time in my life, I hoped I could one day come home to a man.

The front door of my sister's house opened, abruptly breaking me away from my domestic reverie, and my stomach dropped at the sound of my niece's voice.

"Hey, I'm home!" she called cheerfully, as if nothing had changed. But for me, everything had already changed, and soon, nothing in our family unit would be the same ever again.

Silently, I braced myself for the inevitable turmoil, as Christy entered the room and went around the table, doling out kisses and hugs to us all. When she got to me, her eyes met mine with a firm, steely glare, silently saying, "Let me handle this," and I assured her with a quick nod. There was no way I was leading the way into that conversation, not unless she had asked. It wasn't my place, nor did I want it to be.

Christy then sat beside me and loaded her plate with waffles and handfuls of strawberries and blueberries. She easily roped her mother into a compliment regarding the breakfast spread and for a few quiet moments, it seemed that Marjie didn't suspect a thing. But when Mom asked Christy if she'd like a mimosa, every vertebrae in my spine locked into place, as I waited for the bomb to drop.

"No, thanks, Grandma. I'm fine with water," Christy replied.

Mom's eyes narrowed with immediate suspicion at the uncharacteristic statement. Nora McKinley possessed a number of superpowers and seeing through a lie was one of them. "You're never fine with water," she pointed out. "What's going on?"

Christy glanced at me and I answered with a shrug. My mother turned to Marjie and asked again, "What's going on here?"

"Come on, Nora. Nothing's going on," Dad said. "She just wants water. What's the big deal?"

"No, no," she said, addressing the entire table now with skepticism. "Something's going on here."

Christy's leg bounced uncontrollably beneath the table, brushing against mine with every jittery movement. This wasn't what she had planned, or how she wanted it to go. I listened as she swallowed audibly, her breathing increasing in pace. I reached beneath the table and took her hand, squeezing with assurance that I was here and I had her back, and she took a deep breath.

"Okay, Grandma," she said, swallowing again. "You got me. I, uh … I didn't want to tell you guys like this, but …"

"Christy?" Marjie spoke to her daughter with concern. "Is everything okay?"

"Um, well, I, I don't know," Christy replied with an uneasy smile and a shrug. "I guess it depends on how you look at it."

Mark laid his fork on the table, giving her his full attention. "Christina, what's wrong?"

The room was now completely silent with the weight of Christy's big secret and all eyes were on her. She shifted uncomfortably in her chair, her hand growing sweaty in mine. I could only imagine the chaos happening in her stomach, coalescing with the nausea I knew pregnancy could bring, and I eyed the empty bowl in front of me, once occupied by fruit, ready to grab it, just in case.

"Well, um," she cleared her throat, "i-it looks like I'm pregnant, so, um …"

Her confession hung in the thick, stale air, and I longed to be outside, breathing in the fresh dew leftover from the morning. My eyes flitted around the table, taking in the shock and stupor. Mom and Dad blinked at their granddaughter, eyebrows raised and mouths open. Mark's brow was furrowed as his gaze landed heavily on the table. The twins looked at each other, confusion and concern blending together in the young lines creasing their foreheads. And Marjie, poor Marjie, could only stare at her daughter, caught somewhere between heartbreak and suppressed joy.

"Is anybody gonna say something?" Christy laughed uneasily, tightening her hold on my hand. "'Cause it's getting really uncomfortable in here."

Determined to be the strong man of the household, Mark opened his mouth and released a choppy sound, before shutting it again. Neither of my parents wanted to be the first to speak, and Marjie couldn't move.

It was Lydia who spoke first, hesitant and unsure. "You're ... going to have a baby?" she asked, finally looking at her older sister.

Christy nodded, unable to fight her smile. "Yeah. I am."

"When?" Leah chimed in.

"Um, well, I haven't been to the doctor yet to make sure, but I think, if everything goes according to plan, he or she will be born in, like, eight months or so."

Then, without warning, Marjie stood from the table and hurried from the room. Christy's smile died on impact and she turned to me, fear and sadness in her eyes.

"I'll go talk to her," I said, and as I stood from the table, Christy let go of my hand.

***

I found my sister in her bathroom, sitting on the closed toilet with her head in her hands. She was crying and sobbing into her palms, and without a second thought, I sat on the floor beside her, strappy heels and all.

"She's going to be okay," I assured her quietly. Marjie was silent, apart from her tears, so I continued. "You didn't think you'd be okay, either, but look at you. You did it. She can, too—"

"What are you talking about, Clara?" Marjie spat, dropping her hands to her lap. "I wasn't *okay*."

Swallowing and taking a deep breath, I replied, "Well, no. I know you weren't okay in the way you would've liked."

"Clara, I was a fucking *kid* in *high school*. I got knocked up by an asshole who wanted nothing to do with me. I had to work twice as hard to get myself to graduation and through college, all while taking care of a baby. I wasn't *okay*. I mean, I survived, sure, but I was never okay. I was far from it!" She stood up from the toilet like it was made of fire, hurrying across the room to grip the edges of the vanity.

"But you weren't alone," I pointed out, slightly miffed by her refusal to acknowledge us, her family. The people who never once left her side.

"No," she replied quietly, shaking her head. "I know that, and I never took it for granted. But that doesn't mean it was a good situation. Because it sure as hell wasn't."

I sighed and watched my sister, as her hunched shoulders heaved with every labored, panicked breath. "Marjie," I said. "You can't act like this is the same thing. You haven't even talked to her yet."

"I can't talk to her right now," she replied, her voice barely a whisper.

"Why not? If you just—"

She spun on her heel and shouted, "I didn't want this for her!"

"I know, but—"

"No. You *don't* know. I did everything I could to keep her from following in my footsteps and look where that's got us." She looked off somewhere beyond the bathtub and shook her head. "I, I just can't wrap my head around it."

Without another word, Marjie rushed past me and into her bedroom. I continued to sit on the bathroom floor, with my eyes on the cold tile, and wrestled with my words and what I should say. She wasn't wrong in feeling whatever was going on in her head, but I also knew how difficult it was for Christy to announce the pregnancy in the first place. If there was ever a time for Marjie to be there for her daughter, it was now.

"You know what I think?" I called, planting my hands on the closed toilet seat, and pulling myself up onto heeled feet that had begun to fall asleep. Then, I headed into my sister's bedroom, to find her sitting on her bed, with her knees tucked tightly under her chin. Before she could begin to reply, I said, "I think you're being really self-centered."

Marjie turned to me, her eyes narrowed and angry. "Excuse me?"

With my hands on my hips, I stared her down and said, "That girl came to my house last night and told me about the baby—"

"Wait, she came to you *first*?!"

"—and she told me, the thing she was afraid of most, was telling you, because she knew how upset you would be. But I insisted that it would be fine, because you understand better than anybody else what it's like to be in her position. And now, I'm just sorry I lied to her."

Marjie's eyes softened, and her shoulders slumped forward. "You didn't lie to her," she said quietly.

"Then, why the hell are you up here, instead of reassuring her that she's going to be okay?" Marjie's bottom lip quivered, before she trapped it between her teeth. With a sigh, I sat beside her, wrapping an arm around her shoulders. "You're valid in feeling however you're feeling, Marj, and you'll have plenty of time for that later. But right now though, she needs you more than she needs anybody else."

With a nod, Marjie laid her head on my shoulder for a moment, then said, "You're really good at what you do, you know that?"

I laughed. "Yeah, I'm the best," I said, kissing her temple. "Now, get downstairs and hug your daughter."

CHAPTER TWENTY-SIX

The Sound was calm, and the sky was clear that Sunday evening. While I sat in a dining chair on the deck, August carried a bowl of freshly made cobb salad out from the kitchen. He spooned a helping onto my plate, before he sat beside me and took a sip of water. When he caught my eyes on him and the smile on my face, he smirked and asked what I was smiling about.

"I could get used to this," I said, as I picked up my fork and took a bite.

"What?"

"Being waited on," I replied, laughing. "This is excellent, by the way."

He shrugged and laid a napkin on his lap, as he said, "All I did was throw some stuff in a bowl and mix it up. I'm no gourmet chef."

"Well, maybe it tastes so good because you made it for me." I grinned at him, and he chuckled, shaking his head.

"How's Christy doing?" he asked, before digging into his salad.

The other night, after Christy had stopped by with her unexpected announcement, I'd called August after she had left. Just to tell someone and let him carry the weight of her secret with me. Now, I blew out a heavy breath and wished that I had a glass of wine.

"She's okay, I guess," I replied. "Breakfast was tense."

His eyebrows tipped with sympathy. "Your sister didn't take it well?"

I shook my head. "Not initially. But after I talked to her, she seemed to handle it a little better."

He smiled with a glint of cherished pride in his eyes. "You have a gift."

"Yeah," I grumbled sardonically. "That's me. Always making sure everyone else is okay."

The happiness in his grin wilted a little and his gaze fell back onto his plate, before asking, "So, what's Christy going to do? Has she talked to her boyfriend yet?"

"*Ex*-boyfriend," I corrected pointedly. "And no, she hasn't called him yet. I think she's going to see if he'll meet up with her sometime soon, after she sees the doctor. She's terrified of what he's going to say, but like I told her, it's better to get it over with sooner than later."

214

"Absolutely. And you never know; maybe he'll even be happy about it," August offered, picking up his napkin and wiping his mouth.

I hoped so, and I wished that my hope could be enough, as a pang of foreboding continually struck my gut at the thought of Christy talking to the father of her unborn baby. I didn't want to talk about it anymore, knowing that I'd be talking about the pregnancy plenty in the upcoming months, and I smoothly segued into a conversation about the book he was writing.

I knew it was different than his usual thing—a contemporary revolving heavily around the love between an older woman and a younger man, with a suspenseful twist. I had been intrigued since he'd first mentioned it, and my interest had only grown over the weeks we'd been together. I knew he didn't like talking much about his current projects, but I sat up straighter, hoping he'd be a little more open this time and ready to answer more questions. But August shied away from any further interrogation with his cheeks glowing red in the faded orange glow of the sunset.

"Oh, come on," I urged, scooting to the edge of my seat. "Tell me just a little bit more?"

He shook his head, as his brow furrowed. "I don't work like that," he explained, an unexpected chill in his voice. "I told you that."

"No, I know, but—"

"Clara, stop," he said sharply. "Talking about it takes me out of the storyline and fucks the whole thing up. And it's not like I can even *explain* it to you, anyway. You'd have to read it to fully understand, and it's far away from being remotely close to that point. So, please. Just *stop*."

I swallowed, hurt by the harsh tone he used. "Oh, okay. Sorry I asked."

He groaned, laying a hand over his eyes, and taking a deep breath. "No," he said with a sigh, dropping his hand back down to the table. "Don't *apologize*. I'm just explaining to you how it is. I'm not one of these authors who can just, I don't know, shout about their work from the rooftops. And not for nothing but it's still in such a premature stage, it could turn out completely different by the time it's done. I'd rather you just read the finished product."

Nodding, I replied, "Okay, I'll wait for you to be finished, then." And without another mention of pregnancies or work, we finished our dinner in silence before taking a walk along the shore with Agnes leading the way.

The salty air kissed my skin, bringing along a whispered mist from the water. With a straw fedora perched on his crown, August aimed his smile, serene and jovial, across the Sound, while holding my hand tight and Agnes's leash even tighter. I was convinced that no other life could be as perfect as this. No moment could be as perfect as this one, and I understood how he had been married twice. He was undeniably easy to love, carrying an element of romance everywhere he went, and I knew that, if he asked me to be his wife, I would have said yes. The thought warned my heart and practical mind, with the reminder that I had never felt this way about anybody before him, and alarm bells rang in my head, telling me to slow down.

But I didn't want to.

We headed back to the house, strolling along lazily and stopping every few steps to kiss, each one becoming deeper, harder, and faster, promising sex once we were in bed. Agnes sighed irritably, rolling her eyes up at us whenever we began walking again, and we laughed through our lustful bliss.

After we made love, I fell asleep quickly in his arms to the sound of his heart, beating its sweet promises into my ear. A dream filled my mind, in which August and I were married, and I was happy. We lived together in my little house, where he typed his stories in the room across the hall during the day, and at night, we ate dinner to a soundtrack of seagulls and made love to the water's lullaby. But the reverie the dream brought only lasted for so long, and I was awakened by a loud clatter, coming from somewhere in the house.

"August?" I said with a gasp, sitting up in bed and finding him gone. Immediately, I knew the sound had come from him, and that foreboding I felt earlier for my niece was now aimed directly at him.

My robe was draped over an arm chair by the window, and I grabbed the pink, silky garment and pulled it on, before leaving the bedroom and heading down the hall. August soon came into view, pacing back and forth in the kitchen. The moon shone brightly through the window, and its glow caught onto something in his hand, glinting and gleaming, and when I squinted my eyes to see the knife he was holding, I choked on a gasp.

"So, so, so ... he's going to come up from behind her," he raised his arms, knife held high, "and he's going to ... *grab* her, holding the blade to her throat. But does he kill her now?" He stopped his pacing to think for a moment, tapping the knife's sharp and pointed tip against his temple, then shook his head. "No. No, not yet. He, he's too in love with her, he *thinks* he loves her. He needs to abduct her first. He needs to, to, to ... FUCK! Fucking hell, no!" August slapped the knife down to the kitchen counter, and I flinched at the piercing sound of metal meeting stone. "God-fucking-dammit! That changes the entire fucking thing!"

I watched as he thrust both hands into his disheveled nest of hair and yanked on the strands while grimacing angrily in the moonlight. He turned, eyes closed, groaning and shaking his head, and I just stood there, helplessly wondering what I should do. This wasn't unlike the episode I had seen recently, but it was somehow worse, scarier.

"August?" I asked, my voice timid, as I stepped forward, keeping my eyes on the knife.

He looked at me, chest rising and falling rapidly. His eyes were wild, and his face was twisted into a look of seething rage, as he demanded, "Go back to bed, Clara."

"You woke me up," I admitted quietly, reaching the counter, and pushing the knife out of the way. I didn't think he would hurt me, but I also found I couldn't trust that he wouldn't.

"So, go back to sleep," he growled, enunciating every word from between clenched teeth.

"Why don't you come back to bed with me?" I asked, slowly raising my hands to press them against his bare chest.

"I'm working. I have to work. I have to—"

"But maybe you should try to—"

"I'm not going to sleep, Clara. I *can't* sleep. Not when I can't stop thinking and I have all of this writing to do and my editor needs this back in the next few weeks. There's no time for fucking sleep, so don't even ask. Okay?"

I hesitated, as I kept my hands against his chest and felt the frantic pattering of his heartbeat. I thought about Sylvie and what she might tell me to do. I thought about Phoebe. And then, I said, "August, I think we should go—"

"I'm not going to the *fucking* hospital, Clara, so don't even say it," he interjected angrily, assuming he knew what I was going to say and brushing my hands off his skin. "I just have to write this damn book, and then, I'll be fine. Everything will be fine, okay? So, just go back to sleep, and I'll get back to writing, and everything will be fine."

***

I don't know how I managed to fall asleep, but when I peeled my lids open, beams of sunlight assaulted my exhaustion. The space on the bed beside me radiated with the heat from August's body, and I sighed with relief at

219

the realization that he had, at some point, fallen asleep, too. But when I rolled over to lay my arm across his chest, I found him wide awake and staring at the ceiling, with tears filling his eyes.

"Oh, my God, what's wrong?" I asked, pulling myself up and holding his face in my hands. He shook his head, attempting to brush me off. "No, no, August, what happened? Tell me what happened."

"Nothing," he muttered. "Nothing happened."

"Did you sleep?" I brushed the hair away from his eyes. "God, you look exhausted."

"Just ..." He turned away from my touch. "Clara, please, can you just leave me alone?"

"But I—"

I was cut off by an impatient groan, as he tore away from my persistent hands and got out of bed and left the room. The anxious thrum of my heart filled my ears, as I stared at the open door, watching him shuffle down the hall and toward the kitchen. I wasn't a psychologist, nor did I have a degree in the field, but I had enough experience in my job to know something was wrong. The manic episodes, teetering precariously at the edge of violence, and now this sudden state of depressive behavior.

"August," I said, climbing off the bed and hurrying after him. "Maybe you should come to work with me today."

He stopped on his way to the backdoor and turned around to stare at me with an expression of hurt blanketing his face. "Why? Why do you think I need to do that?"

"Be-because I think you should talk to Dr. Sher—"

"You think I'm crazy?"

"No, no," I said, shaking my head. "Of course not. But I'm just wondering when you last talked to her, and—"

"I don't need to talk to her," he said, his tone unwavering. "I'm just tired. I'm overwhelmed. I have a lot of shit on my plate. Like I said last night, I need to finish this damn book, and then, I'll be fine."

Pulling my lips between my teeth, I fidgeted with my fingers, not knowing what to do, having never been on this side of mental illness, so I just nodded. I wasn't going to argue with him, but as I got ready for work, I made sure to convince him to leave my house and be with his grandmother. Just knowing he wasn't alone made it that much easier to leave.

When I walked into work with Agnes at my side, Sylvie raised a suggestive brow and smirked, as she asked, "Busy morning?"

I laughed without an ounce of humor and mumbled, "Yeah, I wish it was that kind of busy."

Her smile wilted in an instant. "What's wrong?"

"Nothing," I lied, then thought better of it with a sigh of resignation. "Things have just been a little rough with August."

She gnawed on her bottom lip, dodging her gaze toward the nurses, before saying, "Clara, I told you—"

"No, it's not," I sighed, closing my eyes and shaking my head, "it's not that. He's just been a little tense while writing his new book. It's fine."

"Are you sure?" I opened my eyes to find her doubtful stare on me. "You can tell me if things are going on, you know. It's okay to admit that you can't—"

"Really, it's fine," I said in a hurry, while thinking about how scared and concerned I had been this morning.

I headed to Phoebe's room, as I wondered why I had blown Sylvie off. August had raised every red flag right before my eyes, and it had left me terrified for not only my safety but his own as well. Why I didn't say something to her, I didn't quite understand, until I was in Phoebe's room.

"Thanks for picking me up and bringing me here," she muttered, stroking her hand over Agnes's blonde head.

"Of course," I replied.

Before she could say anything else, I said, "Can I ask why you didn't tell your father how you were feeling? I'm sure he would've brought you here."

Phoebe's eyes landed sharply on mine and she shook her head. "Because he would've treated me like I'm crazy, and I'm sick of it," she snapped.

"Don't you think he cares about you?" I countered gently.

"Yeah, maybe, I guess," she said, her face full of disgust. "But he doesn't know how to look at me like I'm not a, a, a psycho or something. It's like, there are grey areas, but all he sees is black and white. Crazy and sane, that's it, and I'm always going to be crazy to him."

"You didn't call Dr. Sherman, though," I mentioned, as my curiosity grew.

"Because she's the doctor."

"And I'm not," I contributed, trying to understand.

Phoebe sighed and raked her fingers through Agnes's fur. "You talk to me like I'm a friend. You never judge me or act like I'm a sick person. That's how everyone else treats me, like I'm sick. And yeah, okay, maybe I am, I *know* I am, but you don't act like that. You just ... you," she blew out a breath, "you *know* I'm different, but it doesn't matter to you, and that's really nice."

I nodded and told her I understood, even as I struggled to fully grasp what she was telling me. But then, as she sat quietly with Agnes, I thought more about what she had said. I allowed it to seep in and settle against my heart and in my bones, and it struck something in me, somewhere deep inside. It resonated, loud and crystal clear, as it occurred to me that maybe that was why I hadn't told Sylvie about the issues August was having. I was afraid of what she might say, the judgments she might make, or the actions she would suggest I take.

I didn't want anybody to treat my boyfriend, the man I loved, like he was crazy or sick ... not even her. No matter how true it might have been.

I just hoped I'd recognize the time when I had no choice but to get him help, if—or when—the moment inevitably came.

CHAPTER TWENTY-SEVEN

"Clara, can I get you anything else?" August's grandmother asked me from across the little, round table in her kitchen.

I shook my head, a grateful smile on my lips, and said, "No, I'm fine. Thank you, though."

"Are you sure?" She stood from the table, using her cane to steady the climb to her feet, as she watched me with hopeful eyes. "I made so much. Maybe you can take some home with you? Do you eat leftovers?"

There was a half-full tray of baked ziti on the table, with another two on the counter. The old woman had made enough food to serve an army of hungry men, and yet none of us—August, Nana, and me—had eaten much at all. August especially, and with a glance in his direction, I noted the downturn of his lips and the layer of scruff coating his jaw, thicker than usual.

I couldn't help but laugh in reply to her question. "I used to live off leftovers, before meeting this guy and finding a reason to cook," I said, reaching out to touch August's arm. "I'd be more than happy to take some off your hands."

"Oh, good," she said with a grateful sigh. "I'll just send you home with a tray, okay?"

I knew I wouldn't eat it all myself, and a call to Marjie and her family would be in order. But I didn't say a word in protest, as Nana wrapped one of the trays in foil and set it aside.

She turned to face the table, holding tight to her cane, and continuously opened and closed her mouth, as if she had every intention to speak but thought better of it with each attempt. Her worried gaze was fixed on August, in his work polo and slacks, and I felt a desperate need to talk to her and hear her opinion regarding his current state. She knew him longer, she knew him better, and I assumed she would know what to do, or at least I hoped so.

I waited for an opportunity to get her alone, and it came easily, just fifteen minutes later, when August announced in a melancholy tone that he needed to change out of his work clothes. He left Nana and me in the kitchen, both of us watching his every move as he left the room. We remained still and quiet, until we heard his footsteps on the treads leading upstairs, then we turned to face each other, both our foreheads crumpled with worry.

"I don't like this," she said in a hushed tone, moving slowly to the table and sitting down beside me.

"Neither do I," I agreed, blowing out a heavy breath. "I was actually hoping you could, um … I don't know, I guess give me some insight on what I should do, if I should get him help, or …" I shrugged helplessly. "Honestly, I don't even know if it's my place to step in and push him."

She sighed, as she nodded and cupped her hands around her mouth. Her eyes closed and her brows pinched together, as another deeper sigh passed through her lips. A sick feeling enveloped my gut, souring the ziti I'd just eaten, as I watched her in this moment of assumed preparation. Something was coming, I could tell, and I wasn't sure I was ready to hear it, or if I ever could be.

"Clara," she said, finally opening her eyes and looking to me, her gaze heavy and weary.

"Yes?"

"What do you know about my family?"

I swallowed and shook my head, not wanting to say the words but knowing I had to. "Um, I know that August's parents passed away, and that you've been raising him since he was a teen—"

"Do you know how his father died?"

"He took his own life," I stated in a whisper, barely nodding.

Nana slowly nodded, as her gaze, now full of mournful sorrow, dropped to the table. "My son had always been … very troubled, and his entire life, I did everything I could to try and keep him from succumbing

226

to the demons living in his head. But shame on me for thinking I could outsmart something as strong as Fate."

My stomach turned violently at the sound of her grief. "You couldn't have known," I said, repeating the line I'd used so many times at the hospital.

"Yes, I could," she stated, looking back to me. "I knew it was coming. I had watched it happen to my husband—"

"Wait," I interjected, disregarding how rude it was of me to interrupt. "Your husband ... so, August's grandfather ... he—"

"Killed himself," she finished for me, her words blunt and sharp. "As did his father and uncle before him. And even though I don't expect the same of August— he's never given me as much reason to worry—I can't deny what's living in his blood."

***

Ernest Hemingway had once said, "*Dying is a very simple thing, and really I know. If I should have died, it would have been very easy for me. Quite the easiest thing I ever did. But the people at home do not realize this. They suffer a thousand times more.*"

In several of his writings, through his characters, he'd stated that this was the reason to not commit suicide, for the people at home. For the children left behind. He had firsthand experience, knowing what it was like to be left behind in such an unthinkable way, after suffering through the tragedy of his father's suicide in 1928.

But nonetheless, in 1961, Ernest Hemingway succumbed to his own lifelong battle with depression and committed suicide. And according to several sources, he had always known he would suffer the same fate of his father.

After learning about the generational curse that had taken the lives of August's father, uncle, and grandfather, I spent the drive back to my house in River Canyon chewing on my bottom lip and battling a torrent of discombobulated emotions. August sat beside me, clueless and in better spirits, flipping through the radio stations and complaining about the state of the music world. I tried to smile and nod my agreement, to engage in conversation and focus on the moment, but the relentless nagging of my fears and worries kept me from finding any semblance of relaxation. I hoped August wouldn't notice, but of course, he did, and he mentioned it when we got back to the little house on the shore.

"What's wrong, Clarabell?" he asked, coming to me with open arms and slipping them around my waist.

The question seemed stupid to me. It was as if he'd forgotten the recent nights and the moments in which I'd fought a war between reason and love.

"I talked to your grandmother tonight," I replied honestly, staring out the kitchen window toward the Sound, with my hands over his.

He nodded against my shoulder. "I figured."

"Why didn't you tell me about your grandfather?" I was afraid the question would insight anger, and I found relief in his sigh against my neck and the kiss he pressed beneath my ear.

"I didn't think it mattered," he answered quietly. "I never met him, so his death didn't impact me all that much, honestly."

"But it impacted your father," I gently pointed out.

"I'm sure it did."

"And your father ..."

"Impacted me," he concluded with a weighted sigh. "I understand your concerns, and I'm sure I don't do much to alleviate them. But you don't have to worry."

In all of my forty-two years, I had never once been in a position quite like this. I had never felt the warmth of a man's arms around me and had it accompanied by the desperate need to keep him there, or the sadness of thinking there could ever be a time where he might not be there at all. I loved August, and I wanted him in my life until the day I died. But that love was now paired with a fear that I never could have anticipated, and maybe that was foolish of me. Maybe I should've been warned by his stay in the hospital and what had brought him there. But would it have changed anything? Would I have found him any less attractive or appealing? There was no way of knowing for sure, and besides, it didn't matter. This was my life now, and it was the pain and worry I'd chosen to carry.

"Are you still on your meds?" I found myself asking without hesitation, my voice wound tightly around the love I felt and the fear that threatened to swallow it whole.

He released my waist and turned away from the window. I looked over my shoulder to see him shaking his head and rapping his knuckles against the counter, and my stomach bottomed out.

"August," I demanded in a tone elevated by desperation.

"Clarabell, come on ..."

"Just tell me you're still taking them!"

His silver speckled eyes lifted to find mine in the kitchen, lit only by a small pendant lamp hanging above the island, and I saw the answer in them before he could even speak.

"Oh, God, August," I murmured with exasperation and disappointment, laying a hand against my forehead.

"I don't need them," he insisted. "I've been fine without them for a few weeks now, and ever since I started seeing you—"

"A few *weeks*?!" Both of my hands thrust into my hair, as I stared at him in a state of disbelief.

"Yes, and like I said, I've been fine."

I shook my head. "I'm not sure I'd say you're *fine*," I fired back.

"Okay, fine. I know that things can get a little out of control when I'm writing," he said, and then, he chuckled, as though his belligerence was somehow something to laugh at. "But I told you, that's just part of my process, and the meds only hurt me. I cannot stand what they do to my head, you cannot even understand what they do to me. I can't focus, I can't do the shit I have to do to get this damn book done."

"So, then we'll talk to Dr. Sherman," I said, walking toward him and pleading, as my hands reached for his. "We'll see what she can do to work something out with your dosage, or maybe there's something different you can try, or—"

"Yes." He nodded, pulling my knuckles up to his lips and kissing gently. "Yes, we can do that, and I swear, we will."

The weight of my fear immediately lifted from my shoulders, as a ragged sigh escaped my lips. I brought my forehead to rest against his chest, as his arms went around my waist again, and I inhaled the scent of his leathery cologne, so grateful, thankful, and relieved.

"I just have to finish this book," he said softly, with his chin resting at the top of my head. "I have to finish it first, and *then*, we'll talk to Dr. Sherman."

Tears bit angrily at the back of my eyes, every sting a warning, as I shook my head and clung to his shirt. "August, please ..."

"Clara, I have it under control, okay? I swear to you, everything's going to be fine."

I didn't believe him. How could I? And what kind of professional would it make me, if I didn't at least try to get him back on the medication I knew he needed?

But then, as his lips found my neck and his whispered voice breathed a thousand promises against my ear and into my heart, I laid the fear and worry I held deep down to rest, just for a little while. We made our way down the hall and to the bedroom, where my legs tangled with his and he moved inside me, rocking my heart back to where it longed to be. The love we made lulled us both to sleep, and I sighed happily within his arms, welcoming dreams of a life I knew we could have, one we would eventually have, and they were good. They always were.

But dreams are only dreams. They always come to an end, and soon after slumber had found me, I was awoken once again by the sound of August's rage, erupting from down the hall.

CHAPTER TWENTY-EIGHT

Two weeks flew by and brought the news that Christy was, in fact, within the first trimester of a viable pregnancy. At the time of her visit to the OB/GYN, they estimated her to be about seven weeks pregnant, and so far, everything was looking as it should. The baby was healthy, and so was she, and despite the initial feelings of dread and anxiety, we were all happy.

What amazed me more was, the feelings of contentedness were still alive and well in my relationship, despite the persistent sense of foreboding that seemed to have set up camp in my heart. My nagging was relentless, with me constantly asking him to see Sylvie or to start taking his medication again, and his stubborn will to stay off of them made me sick with worry. But underneath it all was the honest love I felt for him, and the desperation to be by his side, despite the ugliness that grabbed a hold of him, mostly in front of his computer screen.

Now, he burst through the kitchen door, an excited grin on his face, as he dropped to his knees before me. I couldn't help but smile at the windswept mess of curls on his head, longer now than they were when we'd met, and the beard he'd grown into. His shirt had been shed, and his skin was heavily kissed by the sun. A souvenir of the hours we'd spent on the beach, in the sand and each other's arms.

For a man who had once claimed to hate the summer so much, he sure seemed to love it now.

"It's so good, Clarabell," he said, snaking his arms around my waist and leaning in to press a kiss to my stomach, before laying his head on my lap. "Oh, God, it's so good."

"You read through it already?" I asked, surprised to find myself overcome with relief that not only did he finish the book, but he was happy with it.

"Already?" he barked boisterously, lifting his head with a wider grin than before. He laughed incredulously, lifting his hands to cup my face. "I've been reading it all damn day!"

August pulled me forward, to snag my lips in a deep, sensual kiss. My shoulders softened and my bones melted to nothing, as I slipped into his pleading embrace. It was fascinating, the control his lips had over my body. Within seconds of having his tongue sweep inside my mouth, I was ready to spread my legs on the kitchen floor. But August had other plans, as he chuckled and pulled away, then laughed some more at my expression of obvious disappointment.

"Don't worry," he said, standing and offering his hand to me. "We'll come back to that. But first, I'm taking you out to dinner."

"Oh, you are?" I quipped, as he pulled me from my chair at the kitchen table. "Are we celebrating?"

"We are."

He grinned and wrapped an arm around my waist, pressing his body against mine as he pressed another kiss to my lips. His other hand slid gracefully down the length of my arm, over my hip, and beneath the hem of my skirt, where his fingers skimmed over lace in a tantalizing dance that left my cheeks red and my legs begging to buckle.

"And this," he muttered against my mouth, "will be my dessert."

***

Summer was in full swing on the shore of Connecticut, and at the little seafood bistro on the beach, I watched with a smile as a group of small, laughing children ran toward the welcoming waves, sloshing against the shoreline. The littlest one, a girl in a pink polka-dotted bathing suit, squealed in delight as the water licked her tiny toes, and my smile only grew wider. Maybe even a little sad.

"Do you want kids?" August asked, drawing my attention away from the little girl and her joy.

I cleared my throat and dropped my gaze to the near-empty plate of lobster rolls and shrimp. It was an awkward question, because at this point in life, what did it really matter? Pregnancy could be tough on even the youngest of bodies, and at my age of nearly forty-three, I could only imagine what carrying a baby would do to me.

My silence had dragged on for too long and August smiled apologetically. "I'm sorry if I offended you," he said quietly. "I was just wondering."

"No, it's okay," I replied, my voice raspy. "I just didn't expect you to ask."

He chuckled. "It's a pretty normal question to ask the person you're in a relationship with," he countered with a shrug. "I mean, we should probably know these things about each other, don't you think?"

"I do," I agreed, nodding.

"So, you don't want them?"

A sigh left my lips, as my eyes flitted back toward that little girl in the polka-dot bathing suit. "It's not that," I said, unintentionally injecting a hint of sorrow into my tone. "I just feel like it's a little too late for me."

His brow furrowed with question. "Who says?"

"Medical science," I replied with an incredulous laugh. "Women become more and more high risk as they get older. Thirty-five is considered a geriatric maternal age, never mind forty-two. And if I were to get pregnant right now, I wouldn't be giving birth until I'm forty-fucking-three."

"Hm," he replied with a slow, understanding nod.

"God, and then, by the time that kid graduated high school, I'd be," I screwed my face up into a look of horrified disgust, "God, *sixty-one*." I cringed at the thought. "I know some women give birth later in life, and they're perfectly happy doing it. But I'm not one of them. I would've been happy having a baby earlier in life, but I don't want that for myself now."

August nodded thoughtfully, then laughed. When I asked what was so funny, he said, "I was just thinking, when you're sixty-one, I'll be forty-seven. That's crazy."

The comment caused me to lift my head and lean back in my chair. It served as a reminder of just how much younger he was, and I studied him now. I saw the years between us and shook my head in disbelief of how much it really didn't seem to matter. Not like it had in the beginning, not anymore.

"Does that still bother you?" he asked, as though he could read my mind.

"No," I replied honestly. "I'm just … realizing that I had completely forgotten you were so much younger, until you mentioned it just now."

"I forget, too," he said with a smile. "But then again, it never bothered me in the first place."

A group of older kids, I guessed to be in their teens, ran past our table on the boardwalk. August watched them, smiling at their enthusiastic shouts as they turned and made a beeline for the water. Then, he said in a casual tone, "I don't want kids."

It didn't seem like the type of phrase you should be able to say so easily, as if it were nothing more than a comment about the weather or the shiny apples one

237

found at a farmer's market. But August did, and after he said it, he sat across from me with a natural nonchalance and waited for my reply.

I was surprised to find myself relieved.

"Never?" I asked, watching him studiously as he shook his head. "Why?"

He sniffed a little laugh and lifted one shoulder in a half-hearted shrug. "My bloodline isn't exactly the best to be born into, Clarabell," he replied quietly, spreading his lips in a smile that seemed to hide his shame. "But even more than that, I don't think I'd be a great father. Hell, I don't think I'm all that great of a romantic partner, either, but ..."

"I would disagree with that," I commented with a coy smile.

August laughed at that. "Well, you can't say I'm without my faults."

"No," I nodded, "I guess that's true. But you could say that about anybody."

"Well, in any case, I like my life the way it is. I don't need children to be my legacy," he said, studying the empty shells on his plate. "I have my books and that's all I need. It's all I want, really."

"So, did you ask to make sure I didn't want them, too?"

He shook his head, bringing his eyes to mine. "I asked because if you had wanted them, I would've given them to you. I would've done that, because you are, above everything else, the most important thing in my life, and I want you to be happy with me."

The wind touched my hair with salt and sea, as I reached across the table to cover his hand with mine. He smiled as my fingers blanketed his, and I said, "August, I would never need children to be happy with you."

My empty womb wept at the thought of never knowing what it was like to carry a baby, and I wasn't sure it would ever stop crying. But I meant what I'd said to him, that I didn't want to raise children this late in life, and that I was perfectly content without them. I had a good life, a great one even, and having August in it made it that much better. I was filled to the brim with love, and I would never need a child to feel complete.

He breathed in deep and slow, then nodded, as his eyes dropped to watch his hand envelope mine. Then, he said, "I want you to read my book."

"You're ready for me to see it?"

"I am," he stated confidently. "I think it might be the greatest thing I've ever done, but ..." He pinched his brows and shook his head slowly. "But I never know for sure, you know? One second, I'm thinking I've outdone myself and have written the book that's going to put me on the map. And the next, I'm ready to hurl the fucking thing into a fire. So, I need you to read it, and I need you to be honest with me."

"Oh, God," I laughed, throwing my head back. "You can't put that type of pressure on me. I don't think I can handle it."

"No, no, no," he said, squeezing my hand and pulling my attention back to him. "I need you to do this for me, because if you truly love it, then I'll know it's

239

truly great. And if it's truly and honestly great, then this might be it for me."

I considered what he was saying, while taking in the hope burning brightly in his eyes, and asked, "Do you really think so?"

"I really, really do," he pressed, nodding. "And Clarabell, if it's as good as I think it is, and if it sells as well as I think it will, S&S might offer me another contract, with an even bigger advance. I could quit my shitty job at The Beanery—can you imagine that? I could actually write for a living."

My heart plummeted toward the depths of my gut at the thought of him spending even more of his time writing, and how terrible was that? It was his passion, the greatest love of his life, but it was also his greatest and darkest downfall. I pulled my bottom lip between my teeth at the very thought of him never being on medication again, for the sake of his creativity, and allowing his illness to dig its claws deeper into his brain.

And what, then?

"What?"

I shook my head at the sound of his voice and saw the tinge of hurt that crumpled his forehead. "No, it's … it's nothing," I stammered, forcing a smile.

"No, it's not. What are you thinking?"

"I'm …" I took a deep breath and brushed a tendril of hair from my shoulder, stalling. "I'm, um, I'm just thinking that, um …"

"Do you not think I should write for a living?"

He was hurt, and every word spoken was another jab of a knife, stabbing deep and twisting. His fingers unwrapped from around my hand, and that hurt me.

Blinking and trying to recover from the moment, I pulled my hand back into my lap and said, "No! No, it's not that. It's just, I wanted to make sure that you're still going to talk to Dr. Sherman about—"

"Clara, I *told* you! I'm going to talk to her as soon as I'm done with this book. How many times do I have to tell you that? I'm not lying to you, okay? I promised, and I keep my fucking promises."

My lungs filled with salty air, as I nodded. "Okay," I said, my heart hammering. "Okay, I'm just making sure you didn't forget."

"I didn't forget," he replied softly, and at the sight of his smile, my lungs emptied.

Just like that, the tension was lifted, and everything was good again. August raised his hand and asked our passing waiter for the check, then turned back to me with mischief in his eyes. I asked what that look was for, and he held his hand across the table, in search of mine once again. When my palm molded perfectly to his, he squeezed my fingers with warm reassurance and brought my knuckles to his lips, kissing them one, two, three times, while never taking his eyes away from mine.

Then, in a low, graveled voice, he said, "I think I'm ready for dessert now," just as the waiter returned with the check.

CHAPTER TWENTY-NINE

On Tuesday, Marjie called and asked if I'd like to double date with her and Mark. The invitation was welcomed with open arms, and by the time I got out of work, August was already waiting on my porch, in dress shirt and slacks. But when we arrived at the restaurant, we discovered that Mark had been called into work, leaving Christy in his place. Marjie was quickly apologetic, sorry for making August the only man at the table, but he took it in stride and said he was just glad to be out with beautiful company.

"So, August," Marjie said, "Clara told me she read your manuscript."

From beside me, August dabbed the corners of his mouth with a cloth napkin, before returning it to his lap while nodding. "She did," he replied, unable to contain his grin.

"She said she loved it."

I laid a supportive hand on his thigh beneath the table, as he sat up a little straighter, his face expressing the pride he felt. He nodded and cleared his throat, as he reached for the glass of wine he'd sworn would be a one-off. I had tried to bite my tongue when he'd ordered the drink, knowing he shouldn't have alcohol while taking his meds but also knowing he wasn't on his meds at all. Remembering what he had once said about how he was when he drank, the glass of wine irked me. It left my shoulders tense and my spine rigid, but I took solace in the way he sipped slowly and that he hadn't yet drained the glass in the hour we'd been in the restaurant, so I tried to relax.

"I don't want to brag, but she said it was one of the best things she's *ever* read," he said, reiterating the things I'd told him on Monday night, after taking two days to read through the final, unedited draft. What he left out was the time I'd spent on my knees, continuing the celebration of his achievement with him in my mouth, and I bit my lower lip at the salacious thought.

"It's not bragging if it's true," I said, lifting my hand to stroke the downy hairs at the back of his neck.

Marjie smiled fondly at the two of us, her eyes volleying from left to right, as August found my hand beneath the table and blanketed it with his own. A lull in conversation fell upon the table, and the clatter and clanging of utensils filled the dead air, bouncing off the high ceilings in the restaurant and echoing against the

243

marble floors. August sipped more of his wine, Marjie ate more of her veal parmigiana, and I thought more about those moments in my living room, with his hands in my hair and his length in my throat.

It was nearing late-July, and it amazed me that my passion for our time together had yet to dwindle.

Christy interrupted our drinking, eating, and thinking with an agonized groan, as she dropped into the chair across from me and next to her mother. Her cheeks were flushed, while her forehead was dotted with sweat. She complained that she needed water, addressing the empty glass in front of her, and August promptly handed her the full glass he hadn't yet touched.

"Thank you," she said gratefully, while sipping at the cool drink.

Condensation dripped from the glass and into her hand, and she swiped the moisture across her forehead. Our waitress returned and took one look at Christy, then asked with concern if she was all right.

"She's fine," Marjie said, smiling reassuringly. "She's just pregnant."

"Oh," the waitress replied, sympathy touching her eyes. "Can I get you some crackers, sweetie?"

Christy nodded. "If you have some, that would be great." Then, she raised the now empty glass of water, as she asked, "And can we get some more water, too, please?"

"Of course, honey. I'll be right back," the young woman said, before hurrying for the swinging kitchen door at the back of the dining room.

My niece planted her elbows on the table and cradled her face in her hands. I caught Marjie's eye and saw the sympathy she held there, as she laid her hand against her daughter's shoulder.

"This sucks so much," Christy groaned.

"I know, sweetheart," Marjie said, slowly rubbing her back.

Christy lifted her head and looked at August, then at me, and said, "I'm sorry, guys. I know I'm not great company right now."

August shook his head and smiled reassuringly. "Don't worry about it," he said, as he lifted the wine glass back to his lips. "You have a good reason to be miserable."

"Yeah, I guess," she mumbled with a sigh. "It doesn't help that I finally got in touch with Josh ..."

"Oh, finally!" I exclaimed. For what seemed like weeks now, Christy had been trying to get in touch with her ex-boyfriend and tell him about the pregnancy. I had begun to worry she'd never hear from him at all, or that she would, at some point, give up. "What did he say?"

"He said he still doesn't want a baby," she replied bluntly.

"Oh ... oh, God, honey," I said, pressing my hand to my chest, as if that alone could keep my heart from shattering for my niece. "I was hoping he might change his mind."

She shrugged, like the abandonment wasn't a big deal, while also struggling to control the wriggling of her bottom lip. "I mean, I can't force him to want something he doesn't want," she reasoned weakly. "He made it very clear he didn't want kids, so why should this change anything?"

Marjie shook her head. "It's still his baby," she stated angrily. "It takes two to get pregnant, and it's complete bullshit that he's just going to make you go through this alone, while he gets to, what? Run off and do whatever the hell he wants?"

"I made the decision to keep it, Mom," Christy muttered in defense of the man she had spent years of her life loving. "And he's not demanding I do otherwise."

"But in return, he wants nothing to do with you or his child," Marjie replied in a flat, dangerously serious tone.

"Mom."

Marjie shook her head and looked up toward the vaulted ceiling. "I just can't understand how you can so easily settle for that. And then, you claim that you still, for some reason, love him."

"Can you stop?" Christy begged, laying a hand against her forehead.

"I'm sorry," Marjie said, using the words while there was nothing apologetic about her tone. "I just don't understand it, but I guess I don't have to."

The air was vacuumed from the room, leaving us barren of oxygen and suffocating in the tense dynamic between mother and daughter. August glanced at me through the corner of his eye, silently pleading for me to do or say something to lighten the mood. But I had nothing. I couldn't blame my sister for being upset, and my mouth struggled to contain my own two cents about the matter.

246

This wasn't something I expected from Josh. He had been involved in the family for years, and had always struck me as being a kind, respectful young man with pure and noble intentions. This sudden willingness to abandon the woman carrying his child seemed, to me, uncharacteristic, and I thought about saying as much.

But before I could open my mouth, August cleared his throat.

"I'm sure it's none of my business, and I should probably keep my mouth shut," he began, fiddling with the stem of his now empty wine glass. "But it's my opinion that, a man who abandons his child, isn't a man at all. And if he said those words, that he wants nothing to do with you or this baby, then forcing him to be in your lives would only serve to make you miserable with his resentment."

Marjie's gaze dropped to the table, as the impact of his statement settled in. Then, she nodded, and said, "I know, you're right."

Christy tried to smile, but that lower lip was relentless. A single tear slipped over her cheek and dripped off her chin, and she wiped at her face before the rest could fall.

"That's exactly what I've been thinking," she said. "I just feel like ... like ..."

"Like you're mourning the idea of what you could've had with him?" August offered, and Christy nodded, as her tears won the battle and began to fall. "I get that, and you have to give yourself the time to grieve. But believe me, the sooner you give your heart the permission to go on, the better off you'll be."

247

The sound of my noisy heart resonated through my bones, as August then excused himself from the table, to leave the three of us stuck in a shaken silence. Marjie chewed her lip, while Christy relentlessly wiped at the tears streaking her cheeks.

"He's a good one, Aunt Clara," Christy finally croaked, her gaze meeting mine. "You got really lucky."

I nodded, smiling and lifting my gaze to search for August in the crowded restaurant. "I know it," I replied softly, when I found him amidst the crowd of diners.

My eyes were pinned to the crisp white shirt, covering his slender back, as he carried the empty wine glass to the bar, and the slamming of my heart was met with the plummeting of my stomach. *It's only his second drink*, I told my worried mind, as the bartender refilled his glass. But no matter how many times I repeated the new mantra, I couldn't forget what he had said to me months ago. That he had a very narrow alcohol tolerance, before he became someone else, and I had no idea what that tolerance was. Was it two drinks? Three? What if it was only one, and he was now stepping over that threshold and heading straight toward belligerence?

As he walked back toward me, with a smile on his face and a twinkle in his eye, I tried to return the grin and hold tight to the lucky feeling I'd felt for months. But with the regular episodes of mania and now this anxiety of seeing him with that second glass of wine, I couldn't help but worry that our summer of love was nearing an untimely end.

CHAPTER THIRTY

It truly was an amazing book. A suspenseful, dark, and deeply romantic story about an older woman, desperately and passionately in love with a younger man. Their relationship is good, perfect even, and it seems nothing could possibly go wrong for them. Until her psychotic ex-boyfriend emerges, determined to get her back. Fueled by an obsession to call her his, she finds herself abducted and chained to a bed in his basement. Just when all seems lost, the hero comes to rescue her, killing her infatuated and crazed ex-boyfriend in the process.

I loved it, and it was my favorite of August's work. It was easy to see how much he'd grown since writing *Murder & Mayhem*. Or maybe it was simply that, this time, his creative flow hadn't been obstructed by medication.

Now, the manuscript was with the editor at his publishing company, and August's initial burst of confidence had vanished, making room for anxiety and depression to take residence in his mind. Seeing him stay in bed well into the evening, with the covers pulled haphazardly over his head, I struggled to accept that, just the night before, he was riding a wave of excitement and making passionate love to me until sleep demanded our attention.

"August," I said, kicking off the heels I'd worn to work. "Have you gotten out of bed at all today?" No answer came from beneath the blanket, but I knew he was awake. August snored gently when he slept, and he wasn't snoring now. "Hey." I pulled at the corner of the quilt, but he held on tight. "August, honey, get up. Let's get some dinner, okay? What do you feel like eating?"

Still no response.

I knew he'd been upset; I could tell the moment I woke up to him staring at the ceiling and fighting back tears. But he'd told me that he needed to shower and that he would go to his grandmother's house afterward. Now, seeing that he had lied, I was angry, not at him but myself. I never should have left him. I should have called in sick and stayed, but I didn't. So, what kind of girlfriend did that make me, if he couldn't count on me to be there when he needed me most?

"I'm going to order pizza, okay?" I asked, laying a hand on his covered leg. "I'll be right back, and I'll hang out with you until dinner gets here."

My worried stomach warned against eating, and I had a feeling the pizza would sit, untouched, on the counter until it grew cold, and it was time to put it away. Even still, I left the room to call the local pizza place and put in an order for a large pepperoni pie. Then, I hurried back to the bedroom, where I was relieved to find August sitting up with his back against the headboard.

"Clarabell," he said, as he dropped his head into the palms of his hands.

"Yeah, honey?" I sat beside him, wrapping an arm around his shoulders.

"What if they won't renew my contract? What if ..." He hesitated, as he sighed, then asked, "What if this is it for me?"

The fragility of his heart and his desperation and fear were expressed in every one of those words. It was crushing to witness, the sound of his pain and the sight of his withered, defeated soul. He needed this, that much was apparent, and I wanted it for him. But then, there was the ever-present knowledge that, his creativity was also his greatest downfall, the weightiest burden, pressing on his shoulders and holding him back from treating his illness and getting better.

I was tempted to say something, but I knew better than to bring him down further. So, I kissed his shoulder and rested my head against his tensed arm. "Try not to think about it, okay?" I practically begged. "You already have soon-to-be five books in the world, and that's pretty great, right? Some people never—"

He pulled abruptly from my touch, and through my rejection, I watched him clamber to leave the bed from the other side. "There would be nothing left of me if I couldn't write and publish, Clara," he snapped. "Don't you fucking get that?"

"B-But you could still—"

"What would you do if you were all of a sudden incapable of living your dreams?" he interjected with a shout. "Do you even *have* any, or is this good enough for you? Huh? Because I'm telling you right now, this isn't enough for me."

The reality that the man talking to me right now wasn't well, and that he was burdened by a sickness he couldn't help, was lost beneath the hurt his words had caused, and I sat there on the bed, struggling not to cry.

"The only dream I've ever really had was to find a man like you," I said, almost in a whisper.

The comment seemed to bring pause and made him think, just for a second, as he faltered in his hurry to get out of the room. But he didn't stop or glance in my direction, as he entered the hallway, grumbling something about how I'm never going to understand, how *nobody* is ever going to understand him. And then, the backdoor slammed, and with tears in my eyes, I waited for the pizza to arrive, knowing it would grow cold and be left uneaten.

***

August had left without saying goodbye, and that was fine. We both needed the space to breathe and think, and I hated to admit it, but I was grateful to him for being the one to take the initiative and leave without being asked. But then, as I struggled to fall asleep in a bed that now felt too big, it hurt that he hadn't called to at least say goodnight.

When I eventually woke up, after a night of tossing and turning, I threw on a pair of jeans and the only sneakers I owned. The thought of putting an effort of any kind into my appearance was exhausting, and when I trudged my way into the hospital, Sylvie nearly dropped her iPad at the sight of Agnes and me.

"What happened to *you*?" she asked, slowly placing the device on the nurses' station counter.

"What do you mean?"

"I ... I don't know," she said, tipping her head to study my face. "You just look ... tired, I guess."

I laughed without humor. "So, you're saying I look like crap," I replied dryly.

"Well, I mean—"

"No, it's fine," I said, waving away her impending apology. "I *feel* like crap. I slept like shit last night, but ..." My voice trailed off at the realization that I was teetering dangerously close to admitting that things with August weren't going as smoothly as they were just weeks ago. I quickly shook my head and forced a smile, then said, "I just need a good night's sleep, and I'll be okay. Agnes was a bed hog last night, and I like my space, you know?"

She nodded slowly, as her eyes filled with skepticism. "Yeah. I know what you mean," she replied hesitantly, studying me through a narrowed gaze.

"Anyway," I said, quickly steering the conversation away from problems I wouldn't speak of, "I guess I'll start making the rounds. I'll see you at lunch?"

"Yeah," she replied, nodding and putting on a smile that made me sigh with relief.

With another quick grin at my friend, I steered Agnes in the direction of Patty's room. There I found the old woman sitting on her bed and reading a book—a romance from the looks of the cover. She glanced up from the pages and smiled kindly at the sight of me, as she pulled her reading glasses off, to place them beside her on the bed.

"Hey, Patty!" I exclaimed, hoping I sounded happier than I felt. "How are we today?"

"You know," she said, closing the book and folding her hands over the cover, "it was the strangest thing."

"What was?" I asked, as I let Agnes off the leash.

The dog jumped onto Patty's bed and laid her big, soft head on the woman's lap. She broke out in an instant smile, one far bigger than I'd ever seen her wear before.

"Well," Patty began, smoothing her hands over Agnes's silky ears, "I had a dream last night. About my daughter."

I slowly moved my head in a deep nod. "Ah."

"And she looked ..." She closed her eyes and took a deep breath. "She was so beautiful," she said, keeping her voice soft and light. "And so *happy*."

"What were you doing in the dream?" I asked gently.

Opening her eyes and still wearing her bright smile, she replied, "I was camping. At first, I was alone, but I was still having a nice time and just enjoying nature. But then, I caught a glimpse of someone sitting by the fire, and when I went over to see who it was, there was my girl. She looked up at me, wearing this big grin, and said,

'Hey, Mom!'" Patty quickly brushed a tear away from her cheek before it could fall. "Just like that, like she hasn't been gone since … since she died. And I sat next to her and took her hand," she lifted her hand from Agnes and held it in front of her eyes, turning it over in the air, "and it felt so real, like she was really there."

Emotion built in my throat, hard and heavy, and I swallowed at it repeatedly, before saying, "Maybe she was."

Patty nodded, her eyes flooding. "Oh, she was. That was her, I have no doubt about it," she replied with certainty. "She said to me, 'I'm good now, Mom. I'm better and happy, and I don't want to see you worrying about me anymore. Promise me, you won't worry about me anymore.' So, I promised, and then, when I woke up, I felt … different. Better, I guess."

I smiled and nodded. "Maybe you just needed that closure, of knowing she's fine, wherever she is, to finally feel better."

She nodded as a sob burst through her lips, before she laughed and apologized for her emotional display. She wiped at the tears streaking her cheeks, before leaning down to kiss the top of Agnes's head. The relief she felt was evident in every easy breath she took, and I couldn't help being jealous. What she had needed to find peace seemed so simple in comparison to August now, and what I would've given to wave a magic wand and change things for him. How wonderful it would be if something as simple as a dream could cure his ailments.

Patty looked up at me then, to study my face for the first time since I entered the room.

Tilting her head, she asked, "What's wrong, honey?"

I forced a smile and pushed the thought of August from my mind, and said, "Nothing. I'm just tired."

"No," she replied softly, shaking her head. "There's something else. You're sad about something."

Shifting uncomfortably in my chair, I kept the smile on my face and shrugged. "I'm fine, I promise. I'm just exhausted." That wasn't a lie, I was in desperate need of a strong cup of coffee or a good night's sleep, and I hoped Patty would see the truth in that statement and leave it alone.

Luckily, she did, and we spent the rest of our session discussing her doctor's plan to release her within the week. I listened as Patty mentioned maybe going camping with her husband, and maybe even inviting her grandkids and son-in-law to join them. I responded by assuring her that's exactly what her daughter would've wanted.

But all throughout the conversation, I couldn't shake the pesky little voice in my head, asking when enough would finally be enough. Because all of this—August's disorder and his insistence to not get help—was weighing heavily on me, and it was beginning to show. People were noticing my exhaustion and concern, and shouldn't that be a wakeup call that it was time to intervene and help him, even despite his reluctance to help himself? And if not now, then when? When would my love for him and the worry I carried outweigh the fear of his wrath?

CHAPTER THIRTY-ONE

Outside, the sky was clear, and the water was blue. The deck was swept, and the table was set. Beneath the pergola, a fresh bottle of Prosecco was standing on a table between the two lounge chairs facing the shore, and a beautiful cheesecake from the local bakery waited in the fridge. Standing back, I nodded approvingly at the sight, grateful that the evening weather promised to be beautiful. Then, I glanced at my watch with eager anticipation, as Agnes impatiently thumped her tail against the floorboards beside me, pointing her hungry gaze toward my eyes.

"Okay, okay," I said with a sigh, heading back into the house to get her dinner ready. "Do the rest of you want to eat, too?" I called to the cats, and I was answered by the scurrying of sixteen little feet.

Cans were opened and dishes were filled, and just as I was laying the last plate of cat food onto the floor, the sound of a car door slamming came from the front of the house. I quickly rinsed my hands in the sink, drying them hastily with a hand towel, and hurried to the front door. Pulling it open and stepping out onto the porch, I grinned at the sight of Sylvie, carrying a bucket of fried chicken and a plastic bag.

"I know I offered to bring dinner, and I honestly tried to keep it classy. But I had such a hankering for some comfort food," she explained apologetically, as I took the bag from her hand. "I hope you don't mind."

"You have no idea how badly I need some comfort, too," I laughed, leading the way back into the house.

In all of the years we'd been friends, Sylvie had never once seen my house. Life had always found a way to ruin our intended plans, as it too often does. So now, as she walked through the living room and into the kitchen, I couldn't help but puff with pride, as she complimented me on my taste in style and décor.

"If this job doesn't work out, you could always get into interior design," she complimented, stepping out through the backdoor and onto the deck.

I laughed and nodded, putting the plastic bag down onto the table. "That's not a bad idea," I said. Then, deciding to grab the opportunity and just cut to the chase, I added, "With the way things are going, that might be happening sooner rather than later."

As Sylvie took a seat, she furrowed her brow and asked, "What do you mean?"

Pulling in a deep breath, I sat at the table and opened the plastic bag. As I pulled out the assortment of sides, I plucked at the first topic I could think of, and said, "I told you about Christy and the baby, right?"

"You did," my friend replied, cracking the lids off the mashed potatoes and macaroni and cheese. "And there's been nothing else from her boyfriend?"

"Nope," I answered with a sigh.

"That's so shitty."

"It is," I agreed. "I'm not even worried about Christy, though. She's going to be fine. What bothers me about the whole thing is, we had known Josh for *three* years. That's a pretty long time to get to know someone and the type of person they are. You'd think one of us would've gotten the impression that he was an asshole in that time, you know?"

Sylvie shrugged, before saying, "Sometimes it takes a crisis for someone's true colors to be revealed."

I pursed my lips and nodded thoughtfully. "That's true. And before now, they had never actually dealt with any *real* problems."

"No," she agreed. "And you did say that she broke up with him because he wasn't ready for kids or marriage."

"I know. I just figured he'd step up to the plate, you know? He's a good kid. Or I thought so, anyway."

"Maybe he will," Sylvie offered, grabbing a crispy thigh from the bucket of fried chicken. "There's still time for him to redeem himself. She's only, what? A couple months along at this point?"

"Yeah," I replied, selecting a breast. "That's true. Maybe he'll surprise us. I hope so, anyway. I mean, like I said, she'll be fine. She has us, and she's a strong girl. I just have a hard time believing he wants nothing to do with his baby."

"Everything's going to be fine," she insisted, taking a bite. "And besides, how can you feel depressed or upset about anything when you have this view?" She thrust her hand out toward the water.

"It is pretty great, huh?" I laughed, turning my head to stare out toward the sun, only now beginning to set.

We ate together, chatting easily about everything we could think of. Her kids and husband. My parents and sister. Work and the seemingly never-ending struggle of helping Phoebe. It was comforting, to know we shared the same well-intentioned frustration and desperation to guide the girl to a state of stability. Sylvie understood the things nobody else seemed to. She was a true friend, a good one. So, after dinner, when we moved from the table to the lounge chairs, I made the decision that this was it, the moment in which I'd confess my concerns for August.

"So, um," I said, before taking a preparatory breath, as I poured the wine into our glasses, "can I talk to you about something?"

The unease in my tone left her with an expression of wariness, as she replied, "Of course."

"Can it, um," I hesitated and bit my lip, before continuing, "stay between us?"

She lifted her chin and nodded slowly, eyeing me with newfound concern. "You don't even have to ask."

She took the glass I handed to her, and together, we sipped quietly, with anxiety and uncertainty mingling somewhere between us. In synchronicity, we swallowed and placed our respective glasses on the table with the bottle of wine, and I took another deep breath as she turned to look at me expectantly.

"Okay, um …" My mouth fumbled with the words, hesitating while I began to second-guess the decision to talk to her. It felt like a betrayal, to go behind August's back and discuss the things I had no right to speak to his doctor about. But it was more of a betrayal to say nothing, to let him drown in whatever he was feeling, and with that reminder, I pushed my hesitation aside.

"So, I've been seeing August for a couple of months now," I told her, dropping my gaze to watch my fingers, twisting nervously on my lap.

"Yeah …" Her single-worded reply lilted with a question, and I sighed.

"And, um, I think things have been going pretty good. We work together in a way I didn't think we would," I went on, stalling with unnecessary facts. "We have so much in common, it's crazy."

"That's great," Sylvie replied, her gaze soft. "I'm really happy for you."

"Thanks." I nodded, pursing my lips. "Honestly, he's everything I think I've ever wanted in a man … but—"

"There's a but?"

I groaned and reached for my glass. "Yeah. A pretty big one."

"Clara …" Sylvie sighed, shaking her head, and I wished I hadn't said anything at all. "I told you, younger guys can be—"

I nearly choked on my gulp of wine. "N-no," I sputtered, before swallowing. "That's not the problem at all. *We're* fine. But *he's* not."

Sylvie slumped into her chair with an immediate understanding and said, "Oh."

"I'm worried about him," I confessed. "He needs to talk to you, but I don't know how to convince him to give you a call."

"You've expressed your concerns to him?"

I nodded adamantly. "Of course, but he doesn't see that there's a problem. He thinks I'm overreacting and need to back off, but ... like I said, I'm worried. And I'm frustrated that there isn't more that I can really do for him. I don't even feel right talking to you about it, if I'm being honest."

"I can understand that," Sylvie replied softly. "But do you truly feel he's a danger to himself?"

I stared into the pool of wine, sitting still in my glass, as I considered the question, and then shrugged. "I don't know, it's hard to tell. But, but I guess he could be. I-I don't really know."

"If you can't give me a flat-out no, then I'd say you're doing the right thing by talking—"

"What the hell is going on here?"

My head whipped toward August's accusing tone, to see the anger and betrayal painting the shadows on his face. Sylvie's swallow was audible from beside me, as I hurried to stand in my shock, dropping my wine in the process. The glass shattered against the deck, spraying speckles of crystal and droplets of wine across the wooden planks.

"August," I gasped. "Sylvie ... Dr. Sherman ... just came over to—"

"To talk shit about me?" he interjected sharply, heading up the stairs in a hurry.

"N-no, that's not—"

"Don't fucking *lie* to me!" he shouted, stepping toward me and crunching over bits of glass as he went.

"August, try to calm down," Sylvie said softly, standing up. "Clara and I were having dinner, and only just now did she tell me she's worried about you. Okay? That's all."

"Oh, she's worried about me," he snickered sardonically, shaking his head. Then, turning to me, a hot, angry inferno burning deep within his eyes, he sneered. "Did you tell her to lie to me? Did you tell—"

"Have you been drinking?" I asked the moment the heavy scent of alcohol seared my nostrils.

Shaking his head, he stared me down with disgust. "Oh, so first, you think I'm crazy, and now you're calling me a fucking drunk?"

"I-I didn't say that. I was just asking."

"Oh," he replied, sneering. "Okay, you were just *asking*. Fine, sure, then the answer is yes, yes, I was drinking. Even though it's none of your fucking business."

He stepped closer, invading my space and using his height advantage as a threat. He was drunk and confrontational, and he wasn't well, but I wouldn't allow that to serve as an excuse for his behavior.

"Go lie down, August," I told him in a firm, even tone. "Go to bed and sleep this off."

"Why?" he shouted. "So, you can talk to her about me? You can tell her all about what a fucking psychopath I am and how much I scare you? Or, excuse me, how *worried* you are?"

"I *am* worried about you," I replied, crossing my arms as I fought the urge to cry.

In a flash, he reached for the bottle of Prosecco and threw it down, letting it explode in a burst of liquid and glass. Sylvie and I both flinched at the sound, and then again, when he shouted, "Bullshit, Clara! That's fucking bullshit, and you know it. Because every fucking time you say you're worried, what do you do? You fuck me, and then, it's all better again, isn't it? Because that's all I'm good for, right? Tell me I'm right."

Embarrassment scorched my cheeks, and I looked away from his scorching gaze, as the flimsy truth in his accusation bit at the backs of my eyes. "You need to leave, August. Give me your keys and get out of here."

"Tell me I'm right, Clara. Tell me that's all I'm good for, and we'll go inside and I'll make it better again. Go ahead, and—"

"Give me your keys!" I shouted, thrusting my hand out toward him.

For a moment, I thought he wouldn't listen, as he stared at me with a hateful, anger-fueled challenge burning deep and dark in every line on his face. This wasn't the man I loved. This wasn't even the man I wanted. The person standing before me only slightly resembled August Gordon, and I found nothing remotely attractive or appealing about him in this moment. He was scary and threatening, and while I wouldn't tolerate this type of treatment, I also couldn't predict what lengths he would go to.

But August surprised me by digging the keys out of his pants pocket. With a permanent sneer etched to his face, he dropped them into the puddle of wine and glass at my feet and shook his head.

"Don't act like you give a shit if I live or die, Clarabell," he said in a low, grave tone.

"Don't you dare say that," I managed to reply through gritted teeth. "And don't you dare call me that name. Not when you're like this."

Without another word or look in the doctor's direction, he turned and stormed away, leaving the deck and then the yard. My shoulders sagged with a ragged breath, and Sylvie reached out with a comforting hand. She fed me positive words, saying that it was okay, that everything would be all right, and that I'd made the right call, but I knew it was all a happy lie. She couldn't know that anything would be fine, now or ever again, and nobody on this planet could tell me that what I'd done was right. Especially when, even now, so soon after he'd left, it already felt wrong.

CHAPTER THIRTY-TWO

"Y ou're sure he doesn't want to see me?" I asked Nana, and she shook her head for the third time.

"I'm sorry, honey," she said regrettably. Then, lifting the keys in her hand, she added, "But I'll be sure to give these to him. He'll appreciate it."

I peered around the old woman and into the living room, as make an attempt to catch a glimpse of my boyfriend, but he was nowhere to be seen.

"Can you please just tell me if he's okay?" I asked, all too aware of the anxious gnaw, festering deep in the pit of my stomach.

Nana pressed her lips together and eyed me with a look she seemed to wear comfortably. It was one of sympathy and knowing, and I imagined it was an expression she'd offered every woman August had brought into his life. The thought was unsettling and made me shift awkwardly from foot to foot, suddenly wanting to get out of there, while also desperately wanting to get inside and assure him I was still here.

Nana sighed and shrugged with her feeble shoulders. "It's hard to ever know for sure," she replied honestly. "He came home drunk last night, told me you had upset him and made him find a new way home ..." She offered a weak smile. "Thank you, by the way. He was in no condition to drive."

"There was no way in Hell I was letting him get back into his car," I replied, shaking my head profusely.

She nodded. "He's an ugly drunk."

"I didn't think he was drinking at all," I replied, defeated and sad.

Nana shrugged again. "It's always the same never-ending loop with him. He'll be fine for a while, stay on his meds like he should, and then he finds every reason to stop taking them. Next comes the drinking." She shook her head. "I never seem to know what to do, other than to always give him a place to lay his head."

I glanced at my watch and silently cursed my need to work. Nana caught my frown and reached out to lay a kind, soft hand on my arm. I looked up to meet her gaze and found no relief in her gentle smile.

"Don't feel bad, honey. I'll let him know you came by."

"Will you tell him to please call me?" I practically begged, glancing over my shoulder, to find Agnes's head poking through the open car window. Her tail wagged happily at the sight of me, and I wished to be as carefree as her.

"I will," she promised, and with a defeated sigh, I wished her a good day, hoping it wouldn't be long before I saw his name light up my phone again.

But it never did. Not during work, or after, or even the next day, and the more time that passed, the more irritated I became. I had embarrassed him in front of the doctor and wounded his pride, I understood that, but I hoped he wasn't waiting for an apology because it wasn't coming. He had acted like an asshole, and I deserved an apology far more than him. Still, with every passing moment, I missed him more than the moment before, and I began to wonder when I'd hear from him again.

At work, Sylvie had taken it in stride, brushing the incident off with a casual, "It happens." But my curiosity couldn't help but wonder what was really happening in her head. What was she thinking? What judgments did she have that she would never say? It wasn't any of my business what someone thought of him or me or us, but I couldn't help the anxiety that wrapped around my gut and left me feeling uneasy in the presence of my friend.

Now, as I reheated a lonely dinner of leftover pasta in the microwave, my phone rang from the kitchen table. With the hope that it was August, finally willing to make amends and move forward, I abandoned my pasta, and ran for the phone, only to find that it wasn't my boyfriend.

Sighing, I answered and pressed it to my ear. "Hey, Marj," I grumbled, sulking my way back to my dinner.

"That's exactly the tone I like to hear from you," she replied sardonically. "So happy to get a call from me."

"I'm sorry," I said, huffing with another sigh. "I thought you might be August."

"You still haven't heard from him since—"

"Nope," I interrupted before she could bring up the awkward incident on the deck.

"Jesus," she muttered.

"It's been almost three days," I added, opening the microwave door and pulling out the hot bowl of pasta.

"Are you going to call him?"

"Absolutely not," I said in the heat of the moment, but I knew that wasn't true. If this silence continued for much longer, my concern would have to take over and at least make sure he was okay.

And that moment came the next day, shortly after my visit with Patty.

She'd been getting ready to be released, and was dressed in a lively green dress. She looked more alive than she had in the entirety of our time together, and I was glad. She was a lovely woman who deserved to be happy, and although I knew that the pain of losing her daughter would forever remain, I also believed she was now ready to move on. It was time. But I was also sad to see her go.

Before we'd said our goodbyes, she had asked me if I'd seen August or heard from him at all, to which I said no. Her face was blanketed in concern, and she urged me with a grip of my hand to call him as soon as I got the chance.

"Clara," she had said, moving in close, her eyes stern. "If you truly love that man, and I believe you do, you will call him. You won't push him away. You will not ever, ever, ever give him a reason to believe he's alone. Be mad at him for what he did, talk with him about your issues, but never, ever, ever let him believe he's alone."

Patty's insistence gave me reason to rush from the hospital at the end of the workday and call him as soon as I'd reached my car. I let the phone go to voicemail three times, and with each ignored call, my panic grew. But on the fourth try, he answered, and I immediately released a sigh of relief.

"Oh, thank God," I uttered breathlessly, laying a hand over my forehead. "I was ready to drive over there and make sure—"

"What? That I'm alive?" he asked. There was a hurt in his voice that made me feel sick.

"August ..."

"No, Clara, let me say something," he said, accompanied by a sigh. "I'm sorry about the other night, and I'm sorry I haven't called. I had gotten a call the other day from my publisher, and they, uh ... they don't want to extend my contract. They don't want me. And so—"

"Oh, August," I interjected softly, my heart sinking to the pit of my stomach. "I'm so sorry."

"Yeah. They said they liked the book enough, and they're going to publish it, to uphold their end of the contract. They have to, really. But they don't want to work with me any longer, because, and I quote, I'm too difficult to work with. So, that's the end of that, I guess."

My bottom lip was trapped between my teeth, unsure of what to say. I didn't know August in a professional capacity, outside of our brief stint in the hospital, when we'd first met. I couldn't say what it was like to work with him, but knowing him, knowing the varied layers of his psyche, I could only imagine the interactions he'd had with his publishing house. But my mouth remained shut, not wanting to add insult to injury, and I let him talk.

"But anyway, I went to the bar on Saturday. I shouldn't have, and I know it, but I did, drank a few too many Death in the Afternoons, and then, I took it all out on you. I'm sorry."

"It's—"

"I will say, though," he continued hurriedly, cutting me off. "It did catch me offguard to see Dr. Sherman at your house. I wasn't expecting that. I knew you were friendly with her, but I guess I wasn't aware of *how* friendly, exactly."

Running my hand along the steering wheel, I licked my lips, before asking, "Does that bother you?"

"No," he replied plainly. "Well, not really. You can be friends with whoever you want. I don't want you to think I expect to have that type of control over you or your life. But when I overheard the little bit of your conversation that I did, it pissed me off. It's not the best feeling when you overhear your girlfriend talking to your doctor about the crazy things you're doing."

"I can understand that, and I really am sorry about that," I said, dropping my voice to a whisper, as the shame heated my cheeks in the already warm car. "But you have to understand, I've been so worried about you, and it seems that you're not—"

"I told you, I'm going to talk to her."

271

"Right," I replied, nodding slowly. "You said after the book was done. But it *is* done, and you still haven't—"

"Clarabell," he cut in with an exhausted sigh. "I don't have the energy to talk about this right now, okay? All I want to do is come over and have dinner. Then, I want to lay in your bed and make up for the past few days. Can I do that, please? Are you busy?"

There was more to be said, *so* much more, and my gut told me to push forward with the conversation. It was obvious he was trying to distract me with food and sex and all of the other things that made up the good parts of our relationship. I knew I shouldn't have given in so easily. But I also missed him, and after days of silence between us, I felt I needed those things just as much as he did.

So, with a sigh, I agreed and hung up, with a silent promise to come back to this conversation, sooner rather than later.

***

It was the best sex we'd had, since that first time months ago. The days apart had only served to build the energy between us. Then, afterward, desperate to catch my breath and steady my heart, I clutched to his chest and pressed my forehead to his shoulder.

"My God," I muttered, raking my fingers through his chest hair, damp with sweat. "I might be getting too old for this."

272

August's chuckle rasped against his throat, as his fingertips ran the length of my trembling arm. "No, you're not," he replied, satisfaction and pride in his voice. "You're perfect."

"Compliments won't make me ready for round two any faster," I said, rolling to my side and laying my cheek against his beating heart.

"I know that," he said, kissing the top of my head. "I'm just telling you the truth. You're perfect. You're the most perfect woman in the world for me, and I know I don't deserve you."

My smile grew to painful lengths as I closed my eyes and wrapped my arm around his waist. "You do, though. I wouldn't be with you otherwise, and you know that. I'm too picky to stay committed to someone I didn't want to be with."

"Or maybe you just pity me."

The love that we had made, the love that continued to course through my bones and veins, wasn't enough to quell the sudden dose of discomfort and foreboding I felt with that small, simple comment. My eyes snapped open to stare ahead toward the wall, while my mouth flopped open, unsure of what to say in response. My brain struggled to grasp how he could even think that, even when I already knew the answer.

"August, you know—"

"I know," he said with a chuckle, squeezing my shoulder. "I'm just kidding, Clarabell. You know I know you love me."

"Do you, though?" I couldn't help but ask, because all of sudden, I wasn't too sure.

"Stop," he replied gently, pressing a kiss to the top of my head. "You know the answer to that. And for good measure, I love you, too. More than you can ever know."

He grew quiet then, and soon, he began to snore softly into the dark room. With my head on his chest and his steady heartbeat beneath my ear, I tried to drift toward sleep, too. My body was exhausted, as was my troubled mind, and I knew a good rest was often the best medicine for such ailments. Yet, I was restless and completely unable to coax my psyche to shut down long enough to doze off. My nerves were too on edge, fully expecting to wake up to another tirade in the kitchen and the anxiety of witnessing his rage. He needed me to be strong, but how could I be, when I wasn't even sure I was strong enough to protect myself from him?

In the sleepless hours I laid awake, I couldn't help but wonder how a relationship was meant to survive such a tumultuous trial. Patty's words played on repeat in my head, telling me over and over and over again not to give up on him, and that was the last thing I wanted to do. But somehow, a commitment to him also seemed like a betrayal to myself, and how could a relationship like that ever be healthy?

I sighed into the darkness and rolled away from August's body. I didn't want to give up on him, of course I didn't. But I also didn't trust that he wasn't giving up on himself. I knew I couldn't allow my love for him to find that acceptable. This constant state of anxiety or the fear of his unpredictability and what his next move would be. Loving him shouldn't have meant hurting me, and I was in pain every day.

Imagine how he feels. Tears filled my eyes at the thought, and at the knowledge of what I knew I had to do.

CHAPTER THIRTY-THREE

"Clarabell, come back to bed," August groaned from behind me, as I headed for my closet, in search of something to wear to work.

"I have to go," I told him, my tone groggy from the lack of sleep. "I'm already late."

"Take the day off," he begged, flopping forward in bed and reaching out to grip my bare side.

"I can't," I replied brusquely, brushing him away and stepping into the closet, as I rummaged through the rows of dresses and sighed with aggravation. Nothing felt right. Not my clothes, or my life.

I heard August climb off the bed, and then, he stood in the closet's entryway. Now, cloaked in his shadow, my stomach flipped with guilt and anxiety. God, this wasn't how I wanted to do this. Not now, not when we were both stripped down to nothing, naked and vulnerable. I needed to be guarded, protected from his potential wrath and the shattering of our hearts combined.

"Clara," he said.

"What?" My voice was breathless, as my hands flipped through the rows of dresses and my eyes struggled to focus on their fabrics and patterns.

"What's wrong?"

"Nothing," I lied. "I'm just late for work, and I need to get going."

"Something's wrong," he accurately assessed, stepping in closer to press his naked body to mine.

The strength of his erection pressed against my back, and I closed my eyes, determined to fight the urge to relent and fall back into bed. But then, one of his hands cupped my breast, while the other slid smoothly around my waist and between my legs. Once again, I was a willing participant to his expert ministrations, damn him, and my head tipped back with the simultaneous escape of my whispered sigh. His lips touched my neck in an endless stream of kisses, and with every plunge and stroke of his long, deft fingers, I asked myself that old question: could this be enough? Could I happily and naively brush away my concern and fear in exchange for the most glorious sex I'd ever had? Was I that shallow, that horny and desperate? *Yes*, I wanted to say, as he nudged my legs apart and eased my body forward, to bend at the waist and accept his rigid length of flesh and steel.

"Yes," I did say, from reflex alone, letting my head fall forward and reaching out to grip the wooden dowel holding my collection of vintage dresses and tops.

"I knew this is what you needed," he muttered, stroking my back and feeding my hungry body with every inch of his. "I always know how to take care of you."

If he had kept his stupid mouth shut, I might have forgotten last night's revelation. I might have been seduced into a stupor of sated bliss and went through my day with the reminder of our morning causing another ache of longing between my legs.

But he didn't.

Swallowing the remainder of my lust, I pulled away from him and turned around to leave the closet. But August mistook my actions for a change in position and grasped my face in his hands, pressing a hard, bruising kiss to my lips. Groaning through a blend of want and aggravation, I pushed at his chest, urging him to back off and leave me alone. And he did, with a look of confusion and rejection blanketing his beautiful face.

"What—"

Before he could say anything else, I pushed past him and headed back into the bedroom, unreasonably wondering if it would be at all acceptable to walk into work naked. August was close on my heels, as I moved to the dresser and pulled a drawer out in search of something to throw on in a hurry.

"What the hell is going on?" he demanded.

"You *don't* take care of me, August," I said, as I grabbed a pair of shorts and a t-shirt. "You can't even take care of yourself. How the hell do you expect me to believe you could take care of *me*?"

"What are you—"

"You know *exactly* what I'm talking about," I interrupted, pulling on the shorts without bothering to find a pair of underwear. "I know you don't ever plan on talking to the doctor, and I know you have no intentions whatsoever of getting better."

"You have no idea what I plan on doing!" he shouted, now angry and snarling with disgust.

Glaring up at him as I clasped my bra, I rolled my eyes. "August, if you were going to, you would have done it already. You are so full of excuses, and I'm not saying they're not valid. But you aren't even willing to try and find a solution to this problem and—"

"I don't have a fucking problem! You're the only one who thinks I—"

"I'm not the only one," I said gently, after pulling my shirt over my head.

His eyes bore through me with paranoid speculation, probably wondering who the hell I could possibly be referring to, but he didn't ask. He only studied me, with his pulse trembling at the base of his throat and his naked chest rising and falling in rapid succession. Unable to face him this way, and knowing where this moment would take us, I turned away and scooped my sneakers from off the floor, then hurried out and down the hallway.

I made it to the living room without his footsteps heading toward me. But then, as I sat on the couch, there they were, and I wished they weren't.

"Clarabell," he said, his tone softer than before.

Glancing up at him, I saw the acute pain in his eyes. I knew I was hurting him, and my heart was aching for us both. But none of that mattered when I knew this is what had to be done. And maybe it wasn't the right choice to make. Maybe it was foolish and reckless. But at this point, who could say what was right, anyway?

"This is the end, isn't it?" he asked when he realized I wasn't going to speak, and I tore my eyes away from him, to stare at the red Persian rug at my feet, and my head bobbed with a hesitant nod. "But I love you," he added, a new desperation in his voice.

"I love you, too," I replied quietly, jamming my foot into a shoe. "But I need time. I need ..." Pinching my eyes shut, I laid a hand against my forehead. "I need to *think*."

"If you love me, what the hell do you need to think about?"

Looking back to him with an insistent plea in my gaze, I replied, "If I can handle watching you go through this."

His tensed shoulders loosened as realization seeped in. He narrowed his eyes and leveled me with a steely glare, as he replied, "My mother never left my father. She always knew how he'd end up, and she never left."

"What are you saying?" I asked, with the other shoe hanging limp in my hand.

But he didn't answer the question. He only continued prattling on. "And she found him. Did you know that? Did you know *she* found his body?"

"Why are you telling me this?" I raised my voice, desperate for him to hear me and answer my damn question. "Are you—"

He interrupted me with a short, bitter, angry laugh. "No, Clara, I'm not *planning* on killing myself, if that's what you're asking. But then again," he chuckled, "I don't think my dad planned on it either. Or my grandfather, for that matter."

He continued to laugh at my expense, but there was nothing funny to be found in this conversation. I stood up, my shoe still hanging from my hand, and jabbed a finger at his chest.

"This isn't funny!" I shouted at him, tears welling in my eyes.

"I'm sorry," he said, taking a deep breath and controlling his laughter. "I'm just saying, my mom and Nana both knew what they were getting into, but they didn't leave. They didn't need time to *think*. They loved them enough to stay, so what does it say about your love for me?"

Pulling my lips between my teeth, I allowed the tears to slip over my cheeks and onto the floor at my feet, one shoe on and one shoe off. Shrugging, I looked away, fighting my tongue to regain enough control to speak.

"M-maybe they loved them more, or-or maybe they were just too fucking afraid of what would happen if they left," I stammered quietly, looking off toward my shelves and missing the days when the hardest choice I had to make was what old book I'd reread that night. "Maybe I'm just a bad person, I don't fucking know."

"But you're not a bad person, I know you're not," he replied gently. "I *know* you love me, and I love you, and that's why I can't let you go. I love you too fucking much to let you go, Clara. I—"

"August," I interrupted with a plea, painfully aware of my exhaustion. "Please, please, if you love me so much, then please love yourself enough to get better. *Please*."

***

The clock said I was nearly two hours late for work, but I didn't care, as I left the elevator with Agnes at my heels. We headed toward the nurses' station, where I found a note from Sylvie, saying she would see me at lunch. The letter felt a little like being called to the principal's office, as if my friend already knew I had asked August for time apart and had made him leave my house. The shame I felt made me question how confident I truly was in my decision to split up for a while, and maybe a better person wouldn't have done it. Maybe his mother and grandmother truly were better than me in that regard. But wasn't he better off without me, then? Wasn't he better off finding someone more like them, more understanding and strong, who would love him enough to even potentially watch him destroy himself?

Knowing better than to bring my problems to work, I shoved them aside, stuffed Sylvie's note into my pocket, and headed down the hall to see Phoebe, hoping she was in brighter spirits than she had been the past few times I'd seen her. Ever since that night when I'd brought her back to the hospital, she'd struggled to find any semblance of joy. But they say that when you're at your lowest, the only way to go is up, and I was hopeful that, with time, care, and patience, there would be some improvement.

Now, as I turned into her room, my heart soared at the sight of her welcoming smile.

"Hey!" she exclaimed, beaming and outstretching her hands to lure Agnes onto her bed. "Come here, Ag!"

Dropping my bag at the side of her bed and sitting, I smiled and said, "Hey, Phoebs. How are you today?"

"Uh-*mazing*," she enunciated, wrapping her arms around Agnes's neck and kissing the top of her head.

In spite of the morning I'd had, my grin stretched to astronomical lengths. "I cannot tell you how happy I am to hear that."

She nodded enthusiastically. "My dad and I had our very first therapy session today, and it went *so* well."

Taken aback, I blinked and hurried to find my voice, before saying, "I didn't know you two were going into therapy together." It had been a suggestion, yes, but I hadn't known they were committed to the idea.

Phoebe shied away a little, her cheeks flushed and her smile shrunk. "Yeah, well … I had thought about it for a while, after you had said something, and we decided to give it a shot," she explained. "And it went really, really well. Like, I know we're not fixed. We have a long way to go. But … I don't think I'm mad at him anymore."

"Oh, Phoebs," I said, reaching out to rest a hand on her knee. "I'm so happy to hear that, honey. That's great."

She stroked Agnes's ears and the dog smiled in reply. "Yeah. We, um … we talked a lot about my mom and how shitty she actually is. Like, I know I never told you, but she left when I was like, really little. I think I've seen her a couple times since then, but I barely remember

283

it, and ... I dunno. She always told my dad I was the reason she left, and I guess 'cause of that, I've always just wanted her to want me, like the way she wants my sister. Because she always liked Tay, you know? I told you that, right?"

"You did," I replied softly, still unable to understand how a mother could accept one of her children and not the other.

"'Cause the thing is, Tay is easy to deal with, but I'm ... I dunno, not, I guess." Then, she surprised me with a laugh, looking up at me with apology in her eyes. "I mean, I guess you know that already."

"You're not so bad, Phoebs," I said softly, offering a small, fond smile.

"No, no, no," she chanted, nodding. "But I *am* bad. I'm a handful, I always have been, and my mom didn't want me because of that. And it took me forever to understand that, if she didn't want me, then I shouldn't want her. But you know who *does* want me? My dad. My dad has always wanted me, he has always loved me, and ..." The girl's voice broke and her bottom lip trembled. I clutched her knee and stroked my thumb over the knobby bone. "I took that for g-granted, and I told him I was sorry."

"What did he say?" I asked, my voice barely above a whisper.

She wiped at her face and offered a weak smile. "H-he said that even if I never love-loved him back, he would a-always love me, no matter what," she replied. "He said that's wh-what unconditional love is, to love someone always, always, always. No matter what, no matter who they are or, or what they do."

My morning with August bombarded my mind and crashed against my heart in a whirlwind of guilt and pain, but I wouldn't allow it to disrupt the moment with Phoebe. I was happy for her, truly, and I smiled, squeezing her knee again.

"You're so lucky to have him, Phoebs," I said, while my stupid, mouthy brain whispered, *August is better off without you.* "I'm glad that it's working out."

Her watery gaze met mine, as she replied, "We never would've been doing this if it wasn't for you, Clara. You … you helped us so much, you have no idea."

My teeth bit hard against my lips and tongue, as they begged to tell her I was incapable of truly helping anybody. I was a lady with a sweet dog, that's all, and the extent of my help was minimal. How could I possibly believe I helped anybody when I was unable to convince my own boyfriend to seek the help he desperately needed? How could I believe her when I could hardly handle one summer with a man suffering the same ailment that I once claimed to have patience for? I was a liar, a good one, and my tongue longed for nothing more than to tell the poor girl I'd tricked her into believing something that simply wasn't true.

But all I said was, "Oh, come on. I'm not that great. I just—"

"No," Phoebe stated firmly, shaking her head. "You don't get it. You saved my life, and you saved my relationship with my dad. That's all you."

"Oh, stop," I muttered, shaking my head and gently rolling my eyes, feigning sarcasm, while hoping she couldn't see just how serious I really was.

But Phoebe was adamant. She took my hand from her knee and squeezed her fingers around my palm. She held my gaze with a firm grasp, shaking her head, while a fresh batch of tears began to stream from her eyes. Then, she said, "I don't care if you never really believe how much you mean to me, but I'm telling you anyway. You *saved* me. I would be dead if it weren't for you, I mean that, and if you won't own the hell out of that, then I will. But I really, really wish you would."

CHAPTER THIRTY-FOUR

That week, I tried to convince myself that I'd done the right thing regarding August, with constant reminders that he was sick and burdened with a generational curse that he couldn't seem to break away from. Not to mention I had only been with him for a couple of months with zero obligation to stay. It seemed reasonable, especially when I took into consideration that I'd left men in the past for pettier reasons than these and without any inkling of guilt holding me back.

But August was different. He always had been.

The men in my past had never met my ridiculous standards. They had been fun for a time, good in bed and easy to look at, but the potential for a long-term commitment had never been there. Never once had I considered marriage a possibility. But with August, I could envision our wedding day. I could see a long, happy life with him at my side, and if I couldn't have that, I knew that any man in my future would be compared to him and only him, in the way that every man before him was compared to James Dean and Gregory Peck. Yes, he was troubled, and yes, there would always be the possibility that his illness could bring our life together to an abrupt and painful halt. But is any relationship truly without its faults and heartbreaking possibilities?

I knew the answer to those questions, and I couldn't help but feel like a fool. Nothing could ever prepare me for what his troubles could theoretically bring, but even without that looming over us, tragedy has a way of finding you, anyway. Love wasn't supposed to give up during the hard stuff, love wasn't supposed to leave. So, by Friday, I decided I'd had enough of missing his voice and, with determination, I drove to his grandmother's house with Agnes in tow.

Because while she helped others to be strong, she helped me just as much.

Running up the steps to the buttery yellow door, I knocked loudly and the sound blended seamlessly with distant thunder. It had been such a rainy summer, one that had kept me inside more than on my beloved beach, and my hair hadn't been kissed by the sunlight nearly as much as I'd preferred. But I had barely noticed when I'd had August in my arms and bed, where our conversations and love kept me up at night.

When I realized nobody was answering the door, I banged my fist against the wood harder, louder. Still, there was no response, and after only a few minutes of waiting, I was beginning to get worried.

"August!" I shouted upward, to where I knew his bedroom was. But the window was dark, all of them were, and I didn't like that. Not at all. "August?!"

A sick, agonizing ache needled at my stomach, and I wondered if I should call the police. It was a little after eight o'clock at night, it was possible they were sleeping, but I needed to be sure. I wouldn't be able to leave without being absolutely certain they were fine, even if they never wanted to speak to me again. So, I pulled out my phone and found the number for the local authorities, when finally, a light from inside illuminated the yellow door's window.

"Oh, thank God," I mumbled, breathing a sigh of relief, as the door was pulled open to reveal Nana Gordon, wearing a pink, flowered robe and slippers to match.

"Clara," she greeted me, offering a small, kind smile that left my heart just a little lighter. She wouldn't be smiling if something catastrophic had happened in my absence. "It's nice to see you, honey."

"I'm so sorry if I woke you up," I said hurriedly. "But I really need to talk to August."

Nana smiled again, this time with a little more apology creasing the deep lines around her eyes, and my heart already began to sink. "I understand," she began, before sighing, "but I don't think I'll be able to convince him to come down from his room. He's …" She pressed her thin, wrinkled lips together, then continued, "He's not

289

okay. This whole thing, with the publishing house and—
"

"And me," I interjected softly, my tone laced with guilt, and she nodded once in agreement. "I never wanted to hurt him. I just—"

"I would never believe you'd mean to hurt him, honey," she replied, gentle and far too sweet. "But that doesn't—"

"I needed time, I needed to know for sure that I wanted this, but now, I know that I do," I said, unsure of why I was even talking at all. Nana didn't seem like the one who needed convincing. "I really do. And I just need him to know that I changed my mind. Can you please tell him that I changed my mind?"

The rain began to sprinkle down from above, with an accompanying rumble of low, growling thunder, and it wouldn't be long before I was drenched beneath the angry sky. But I didn't care. I wouldn't leave until I received the promise that August's grandmother would pass my message along, and luckily, I didn't have to wait for long.

Nana smiled reassuringly and nodded. "I will tell him. I can't guarantee anything will come of it, but—"

"That's okay," I hurried to say, as the rain fell harder and the drops got bigger. "All I ask is that he knows. And where we go from there ..." I shrugged, my shoulders heavy. "We'll see, I guess."

After wishing her a good night, and throwing in another apology for good measure, I turned to walk back to my car in the middle of a downpour. Agnes waiting inside, her snout poking through the open window, and I smiled at her, glad that I at least wasn't going home alone. I was glad to have my house, animals, and the waves, all awaiting my arrival. It was a life I always found to be satisfactory, and I'd always been content. Nothing had changed about that since meeting August and knowing what it was like to be with him. Except now, I *was* aware, with a sharp, agonizing pain ailing my heart, of what I was missing. Of what I'd been missing all along, and I wasn't sure how I could ever move on from that, if I never heard from him again. I wanted to barrel through the front door of Nana's house. I wanted to run up the stairs and to August's room, to demand that he speak to me and take me back, no matter how stupid and selfish I'd been. I was only human, and humans make mistakes; I was willing to own up to that now, just as long as he'd take me back. Yet still, I walked, with my head held high and my hair getting soaked in the rain, because as much as I needed time, I could respect that he'd need time, too.

"There isn't any harm in hoping," Nana called after me, bringing my feet to a halt and turning me around on my heel. Her smile was bright, a beam of sunlight between the battering raindrops. "In fact, I find that hoping can be the most powerful thing of all."

I offered her a smile of my own and a nod, unable to hide the sadness in my heart as my bottom lip quivered at the sound of her sentimental words. Then, I got into my car and left, knowing I'd never stop hoping. Hoping for him, hoping for our future, hoping for happiness and my personal Hemingway.

That's what I'd always known to do, after all, and I was good at it.

CHAPTER THIRTY-FIVE

"Isn't it a beauty?" Mom asked, standing back to admire the old, black Corona typewriter she'd finally found in her garage. She had polished it to a shining finish, and it gleamed beneath the wrought iron chandelier in Marjie's dining room. I ran my fingers over the keys, appreciating the solid craftsmanship and knowing August would've, too.

"It is very nice, Mom," I said, injecting every bit of the melancholy I felt into my voice, and Mom wrapped an arm around my shoulders.

"He'll call," she assured me, and I smiled, the way I had for the past few days since showing up at Nana's house in a rainstorm. But it had already been a few days, I reminded myself. If there was any chance of him calling me, I would've expected him to do so by now, and so, I was convinced I would never hear from him again.

With every passing day, I'd forced my mind closer to accepting that I had screwed up. I carried my faults willingly, while also knowing that not every flaw in our relationship fell into my corner.

From the beginning, I'd had my doubts about our potential as a couple. I had known who he was, and I'd had my suspicions of it lasting beyond the summer. And now, as the end of summer rapidly approached, even I had a hard time believing how right I'd been. But August had been persuasive and made me trust our chances of being more than a fling. He made me fall in love, too hard and too fast, just as he had implied I would. That was his fault. He knew what would happen, and he'd let it happen, anyway.

But still, I'd been a willing participant, and I'd enjoyed almost every second of it.

I just wish I'd kept my heart a little more guarded. Just a little. Only to keep this pain from penetrating so deep, and breaking my spirit with every minute that ticked me further away from him.

"Aunt Clara, just think," Christy said, coming into the dining room with her hand laid over her growing belly. "Soon, you'll have a new little baby around to take your mind off how shitty this feels."

I laughed. "We can only hope," I replied, offering a weak smile in her direction.

"Well, it's working for me," she said, aiming her adoring grin toward her stomach. "Otherwise, I'd be down at the bar, crying over Josh and getting drunk on martinis."

"What are you talking about?" I barked with an incredulous laugh. "You *do* cry over Josh."

Wearing a cheeky smirk, she poked my shoulder with a slender finger. "Yes, but do you see me down at the bar, getting drunk on martinis?" I rolled my eyes in response, and she exclaimed, "See! This baby is already doing some good."

As much as I joked, she was right; the baby *was* doing a lot of good.

Marjie had quickly emerged from her disdain toward the pregnancy and barreled straight into doting grandmother mode. The baby didn't even have a name or a gender yet, but Marjie had already begun to buy furniture for the guest room she was turning into a nursery. Nobody could talk about the little jellybean in Christy's belly without wearing a grin, and we spent much of our time together discussing potential names and placing bets on what the gender would be. Mark was hoping for a boy, desperate to have some testosterone around the house, while my sister and mother prayed for a little princess. However, Christy and I were in agreement—as long as the baby was healthy, nothing else truly mattered.

But like every other happy moment, it ran away to make room for another sad thought about my failed love life.

"So, do you want to take this home with you?" Mom asked.

I glanced at her hand, seeing that it was gestured toward the typewriter, and wiped my palm over my cheek as I sighed. "I don't know," I replied. "I don't really know where I'd even put it."

"I think it would look lovely on your bookshelf, personally."

Marjie nodded her agreement. "It would."

"I don't know," I repeated defiantly in a grumbled voice.

They were right; it would fit in well on my bookshelf. The antique Corona was similar to the one used by Hemingway himself, and I could see it sitting proudly beside *The Old Man and the Sea*. But I couldn't will myself to want a thing that was meant for August. It didn't belong on my shelf, it belonged in his future office at the front of my seaside cottage, and the thought that it would never know its rightful place broke my heart a little more.

"What do we want to do for dinner?" I asked the women in my life, changing the subject. I didn't want to think about August anymore.

Christy didn't allow for anybody to claim they didn't know. She slapped her hands against the dining room table and said, "Oh, my God, I am *dying* for Chinese food."

Marjie laughed and laid a hand against her daughter's shoulder. "Well, I guess that settles that. I'll go grab the menu," she said, before turning to enter the kitchen.

"Chinese sounds—" My phone cut me off with a melodic chime, coming from my pocket. Without another word, I pulled it out, unsure of what to expect, and then, without a second thought, I answered, my voice a breathless burst. "Oh, my God, August?!"

"Clara ..."

Ignoring the inquisitive glances from my mother and niece and their mouthed questions of what was going on, as if I knew, I hurried from the dining room and onto Marjie's back deck. The mosquitos were in attack mode, jabbing me the moment I stepped outside, but I couldn't care about that. Not right now. Not when I finally had him on the phone and was finally hearing his voice for the first time in almost two weeks.

"August, I'm so sorry. I am so, *so* sorry for telling you I needed time. I was such an idiot, and I—"

"Clara, I-I don't know what to do," he interrupted. He didn't sound like himself. This voice, it belonged to someone weak and shriveled, a shadow of who he was. My heart began to hammer loudly in my chest, while my lungs questioned how they were supposed to breathe.

"What do you mean?" I asked, standing still and frozen, in the middle of the deck. A mosquito landed on my shoulder and promptly jabbed me with its stinger, but I didn't smack it away.

"I don't ... I don't think I-I can do this anymore."

"Do what?" He groaned in response, like I had some nerve asking, and I asked, "What can't you do anymore?"

"*This*!" he shouted, his voice now shrill and breaking. "I am so, so, so sick of pretending like I can win this battle against my own stupid fucking head. It was arrogant of me to think I could be better than my own father. I want to be, I really, really, really do, but I'm not. I'm just not, and maybe it's time to just ... accept it."

Turning slowly on the spot, I looked through the French doors, peering through the panes between the white trim and clutching the gauzy fabric of my dress against my chest, as I allowed his words to hit home, and they hit hard.

"August," I finally said, forcing my tone to maintain its composure, "you *are* better."

"Oh, God, Clara. Don't try to save me now, okay? Don't. Just don't. You were right, I don't love myself enough to get better. But I do love myself enough to let go of the fantasy that I can *be* better." He sounded so fragile, so exhausted and broken, and I knew I had to hurry, if I had any hope of saving his life.

Throwing the door open and ignoring the concerned voices of my sister, mother, and niece as I grabbed my purse and ran through to the front door, I said, "I'm on my way over, okay?"

"Don't," he demanded. "Don't try to stop me. I didn't call you for that."

I climbed into my car, as I asked, "Then, why did you call me?" I slid the key into the ignition and peeled away from the curb, hoping my questions could buy me some time. "If you were going to kill yourself anyway, why give me the opportunity to talk you out of it?"

"Because I wanted your voice to be my last memory," he replied simply, so matter of fact. "I love you, Clarabell. More than anything in this world, I love you, and I wish I could've been the man you deserve."

"But you *are*," I insisted, holding tight to the wheel, while barely slowing down for a stop sign. "I have waited a long, long time for someone like you to walk into my life, and I've had enough time away from you now to know that I am never letting you go again. Do you understand me? I am *never* letting go, and maybe if I hold on tight enough, you won't—"

I narrowed my eyes as I turned onto the highway. Could I still hear him breathe on the other end? Was he still there? I listened intently, keeping my eyes on the road, and heard nothing. My heart sped up toward a blinding panic, and I shouted, "August? August, you're still there, right?"

When I didn't receive a response, I glanced quickly at the phone's screen, only to find it blank.

He had hung up.

***

"August!" I screamed, beating my flattened palms against the yellow door. "Nana! Please open the door!"

The woman was old and didn't move very quickly. On most days, I had all the patience in the world for the elderly and was forgiving of the things they couldn't help. But today wasn't one of those days.

"Goddammit!" I screamed louder, pounding the wood, before peering through the adjacent window. The curtains were closed, and I couldn't see much, but there was a faint shadow of movement. So, I screamed again, "Nana! *Please*!"

A brief moment of relief washed over me as the lock was turned and the door was opened, to reveal Nana and her frown.

"Clara," she greeted, her voice flat and unwelcoming. I couldn't blame her. I was making a scene, and I could only imagine what the neighbors were thinking of the crazy woman, beating on the buttery yellow door. But I didn't have time to apologize or feign a friendlier greeting.

I pushed past her and ignored her confused, bewildered commentary, as I ran up the stairs and began to open each of the doors, peering into a bathroom and what was clearly Nana's bedroom, until I finally spotted August. My heart dropped immediately at the sight of him holding the three bottles of prescription pills, while my brain cautiously rejoiced.

He hadn't taken them yet, and he wasn't dead.

I had made it in time.

His head turned to pin me with his darkened gaze. Every one of his silver sparkles had dulled, clouded by despair, and I hurried to him, dropping to my knees with a loud, painful *thunk* on the hardwood floor and taking his face in my hands.

"Please, please, please, *please* don't leave me," I begged him, digging my fingertips into his bearded skin. "If you can't love yourself, then let me love you enough for both of us. *Please.*"

I thought he would protest, as he stared at me, still gripping those pill bottles and staring with a complete lack of emotion. I thought he would insist I leave him alone and let him die. But then, the walls of his exterior combusted with a sob, and the tears fell in an endless stream from his eyes. His head fell against my shoulder, as he dropped the bottles to the floor, then his arms flew around me to hold on tight, as if my appearance alone was enough to bring him strength.

"Let me take you to the hospital," I said, running my fingers through his knotted curls.

"Oh, G-God, no," he sobbed, shaking his head against my shoulder.

"Please, August," I whispered, kissing his temple. "If you can't do it for you, then do it for me. Please."

He groaned, helpless and desperate, then nodded. "Fine, I'll go. I'll do it for you. Because you came."

"Of course, I came," I said, allowing myself that moment of relief. "Remember? I promised you, if I ever got that call, I'd answer. I'll always answer. *Always*."

CHAPTER THIRTY-SIX

Walking into St. Mary's the following Monday was surreal, knowing that August was also there, in a room on the very floor I rode the elevator to. I could imagine him, in his sweatpants, t-shirt, and socks. Looking much like the way he had when I'd first met him. As I stepped out onto the cold linoleum floor, I thought about that time, months ago now, before the first date and sex and love. Would I have done it all again, knowing what I know now, I wondered? Would I have even walked into that coffee shop with my sister and niece, knowing that, by some stroke of luck, he'd be there?

Yes, I answered silently with a gentle bob of my head, as I approached the nurse's station. *I'd do it all, no matter what the outcome was or how bad it hurt.*

"Hey," Sylvie greeted me, wearing a tight-lipped smile. She clutched her iPad to her chest, carrying herself with a stiffness I wasn't used to.

"Hi," I replied, offering a forced grin as an attempt to lighten the heavy mood. "How—"

"You know you can't ask me how he is," she replied softly, cutting me off before I could barely take a breath.

Taken aback, I blinked and shook my head, diverting my eyes to the dog at my feet. "I wasn't—I know I—"

"I'm sorry," she quickly interjected again, loosening her arms and laying a hand over her eyes. "I know you know. This is just ... you know, it's..."

"Weird," I finished, and she nodded apologetically. "I know it is. I don't even know how to handle myself right now. I feel like I shouldn't even be here at all, but I can't not do my job."

We sighed heavily in unison, and for a moment, I was grateful that we were in this strange place of discomfort and confusion together. Lines had been crossed between the realms of black and white, and now this place we found ourselves in was too uncertain, too grey, and I didn't like it.

And still, I'd do it all again and again and again and again, just to know him and his heart.

"There's no reason you can't be here," Sylvie finally said. "You just can't see him. Unless you really feel you can't handle being here, in which case I'd completely understand."

If Phoebe hadn't been there, just a few doors away, I knew I would've been more inclined to leave. There was no doubt in my mind of that. But I wasn't selfish enough to leave my friend because of my personal problems, so I brushed Sylvie's concern away and went about my day with my head held high.

But that didn't make it any easier to walk past August's room.

***

"Clara," Phoebe said, standing up to greet me. She had never done that before. "You look so sad!"

"Sad?" I forced a laugh. "I'm not sad!"

She wrapped me in a tight hug and said, "You don't need to hide it from me. We're friends."

Agnes pushed her flank against Phoebe's leg, urging her to stop with the nonsense and give her some attention. I pushed another laugh from my lips and shook my head, encouraging an end to the hug. Phoebe dropped to her knees to offer her hellos to Ag, as I turned away to hide my watering eyes and find my chair.

"I'm fine," I lied. "How are you doing?"

"I'm doing great," she said from behind me. "Dad and I had another therapy session the other day. Dr. Sherman says we're doing really, really good."

"I'm so happy for you guys," I said, sitting down. "I hope this is the beginning of a new life for both of you."

She nodded and led Agnes to her bed, where they both hopped on and snuggled together. "Me, too. Dad told me today that you're a miracle worker, because like, without you, this never would've happened."

I still wasn't convinced of that, but I smiled anyway and said, "If something I did could help you guys, then I'm glad."

"And if you could make us better, then you can definitely make August better, too."

It was inappropriate for her to mention my relationship with him, and I wasn't going to entertain the topic. So, I shifted uncomfortably on my chair and picked at an invisible wrinkle on my top, trying to keep her from seeing my discomfort while knowing I was failing miserably.

"So, um," I began, trying to change the subject, but Phoebe was faster.

"I know you won't talk about it," she said quietly. "It's fine, I get it. But I just thought it might be nice to hear." She shrugged with one shoulder, offering the smallest of smiles, and I smiled back.

"Thanks, Phoebs," I said quietly. "It is."

I hadn't lied. It *was* lovely to hear and puffed my heart up with the tiniest shred of hope. But that sliver of good served as nothing more than a whisper in a windstorm, and it was gone before I stepped out in the hallway and walked past August's room. The room where I knew he sat, looking much like he had when we first met, and I feared I'd never see him again. I feared that he'd never want to hear my voice, that it was somehow too correlated with bad memories. All of it felt like a battle I was destined to lose, when all I wanted was to win.

***

305

The days that followed were filled with an uncomfortable uncertainty that left me questioning what I was supposed to do. It had been a week since I dropped him off at the hospital, and I knew he was being assessed and treated in whatever way the doctors saw fit. But I couldn't help but feel as though I was trapped in some sort of permanent purgatory of not knowing where to go or what to do while I waited.

One night, exactly a week after I'd banged on her door, the thought crossed my mind to call August's grandmother. A bundle of nerves grew rapidly in my gut, as a barrage of questions filled my head. What if she didn't want to hear from me? What if she didn't even have answers and the conversation was filled with nothing but awkward, unnecessary chit chat about things neither of us cared about?

But what if she was alone and tired of the silence, too? A silence not even the waves could remedy.

"Hello?" she answered.

"Hi, Nana," I replied, my tone immediately giving away my anxiety. "It's, it's Clara."

"Oh, hi, dear. How are you?" The casual inflection of her voice furrowed my brow with a sudden onset irritation. How could she act so nonchalant at a time so critical and worrisome?

"I'm, uh … I'm okay, I guess," I said, before shaking my head and pushing away my own false indifference. "No, actually, I'm not okay. I'm … I'm sorry for calling, but I was just wondering if you—"

"Heard anything from August?"

My shoulders sagged a little at her interruption, as I nodded to the bedroom window ahead of me. "Yeah."

"No," she replied simply.

Closing my eyes to the picturesque view of the Long Island Sound and releasing a held breath, I uttered a just-as-simple, "Oh."

"But," she went on, "I called Dr. Sherman and asked if he's improved at all, and she says he's been doing a little better these past couple of days."

Tears filled my eyes, grateful for the update, while knowing she was under no obligation to give me one. Then, I said, "Oh, I'm so happy to hear that. Thank you for letting me know."

Silence lingered between our phone lines, and I wasn't sure if I should hang up and leave her alone. Should I just let us both wallow in our shared yet separate troubles and concerns? It was getting late, and she'd probably want to get to bed, if she was finding any sleep at all these days—I know I wasn't.

I opened my eyes, to stare out toward the never-ending expanse of dark water, and opened my mouth to wish her a good night, as good as it could be. But she spoke first.

"It's a roller coaster, Clara," Nana said with a sigh, weighed down by a lifetime of sorrow and exhaustion. "And it's never easy. Ever."

The thought that she had buried both her husband and son due to mental illness was never far from my mind, and right now, it sat heavily against my heart. "I can only imagine what you've been through," I replied, not knowing what else I could say.

"It was different with August's father," she went on. "I didn't see it coming with my husband, but with my son … I hated that I had almost expected it. And maybe it was just my heart's attempt at preparing itself to break again, but I had known that it would happen. It was just this deep, horrible, nauseating feeling I'd always had. But I prayed that it wouldn't, I prayed so hard." She sighed into the phone. "Obviously, my prayers went unanswered."

A sick, gnawing ache filled my gut as she spoke. I was about to lay a hand over my eyes, to shield my view of the horizon once again, but Bumby ran into my bedroom, batting at a toy mouse. Agnes groaned at the abrupt intrusion and rose from the bed, to jump down and leave the room. The mischievous cat ran in a chaotic spiral around the floor, until he reached my feet, where he stopped and looked up, straight into my eyes.

"I'm saying this, Clara, because I don't get that feeling with August. I honestly don't, and I never have," Nana continued, as Bumby's stare remained fixed to my eyes. "Who can say what the future holds, but I have never had that sort of … horrific premonition with him, and maybe that makes me a fool. But … I just don't think so."

"I wish that made me feel better," I admitted, and then, I gasped as the cat jumped into my lap.

He had never done that before and had never taken a second to show any sort of affection. Now, coupled with the nature of the conversation, tears flooded my eyes as he nudged his velvety soft nose against my fingers.

"Like I said, it's a roller coaster, and it always will be," she replied with an empathetic sigh. "The highs and lows are unpredictable, and what comes next is never guaranteed, but the love always is. And I truly, truly hope that it's enough for the two of you to make this work and stick it out. Because while I don't have any sort of feeling about August succumbing to this illness, I do have one about his love for you."

Bumby's little head fit perfectly into my palm, and I swore I saw him smile as my fingers massaged the scruff at the back of his neck. His purr began as a low, gentle rumble, and then escalated quickly to rival a semitruck's engine. Tears fled my eyes and dripped onto his back, but I was smiling—how could I not?

"It's enough," I told Nana, scratching behind Bumby's ears. "It's more than enough."

CHAPTER THIRTY-SEVEN

It had been a little more than two weeks since I'd seen or heard from August, and although I was committed to waiting for him, I couldn't deny the worry of never hearing from him again. Nights were spent craving the sound of his voice, the taste of his skin, and the touch of his smooth, careful fingers, while the days moved by slowly with the necessities of life carrying me along. It was a cruel existence, and it seemed to me that only Nana understood exactly what I was going through. We'd grown close over the weeks since August was admitted, regularly calling each other with updates or just to chat whenever the worries of the night drove us closer to insanity. I liked her a lot, and it was some consolation to know she liked me, too.

The restaurant I was now entering felt too packed with happy couples, and my gaze kept drifting toward their tables, feasting greedily and enviously on their slight touches and lingering eye contact. I was jealous and painfully aware of how much I missed my boyfriend, and I desperately needed my family to distract me.

"Aunt Clara!" I heard Christy's voice over the volume of chatter and clattering utensils, and I turned in the direction of her voice, to find her standing some feet away. She waved her arm above the head of an oblivious woman. "Over here!"

I made my way to her and found everybody else was already with her. I greeted them all with a genuine smile and warm hugs, because this wasn't just a normal family dinner. This was an announcement and a celebration, and I couldn't wait to hear the news.

"So, how did your appointment go?" I asked Christy, wrapping an arm around hers.

"Good," she said coyly, as the maître d' escorted our family to the table.

"Everything okay? Baby's healthy?"

"Everything's perfect," Christy clarified, her cheeks rosy and rounded with contagious joy.

The table was situated in the smaller of the restaurant's two party rooms. My father had insisted on renting it out instead of reserving a table in the dining room. While at the time, we had all thought he was crazy for spending the money on a private room, I was now grateful. It was worth it to hear the news without the added distraction of nosy strangers and lingering waitstaff.

When we were all seated and had made our selections from the menu, nobody could wait any longer. I had enough to wait on these days, and the last thing I needed was to bite my nails with anticipation over the sex of Christy's baby. So, with an eager grab of her arm, I gave her the nudge to just tell us already.

"Oh, um, they couldn't tell," she said regrettably.

"What?" Marjie gasped from the other side of her daughter, as every one of our faces fell with shock and disappointment. "You're *kidding*!"

Christy laughed, the pink in her cheeks deepening just a little. "Yeah, I am. I'm sorry."

"Don't do that to us," Dad scolded with a playful toss of his straw wrapper in her direction. "I'm not renting this room out again."

We sat at the edge of our seats, as Christy reached into her bag to pull out the latest sonogram picture. Then, with a deep, quivering breath, she passed the black and white photograph to her mother first and said, "That's your grandson."

As Marjie took the picture from Christy, her eyes widened, glinting with excitement and adoration, and exclaimed, "It's a boy?!"

"Yep," Christy said, already brushing the tears from her eyes. "I'm having a baby boy. Can you believe that?"

Mom tittered with giddy laughter. "Oh, my God, nobody in our family has ever had a son! Do we even know what to do with a boy?!" She looked between my father and Mark, who was peering over his wife's shoulder at the picture of the tiny baby in his stepdaughter's belly. "You guys are finally getting some more testosterone around here!"

"It's about time," Dad grumbled, his eyes full of pride.

I remained quiet, as the picture made the rounds. My heart felt so full, too full to remain comfortably in my chest, and my eyes brimmed with the happiest tears I'd ever cried before. The reality that our family was growing settled in again, as fresh as when I first learned of Christy's pregnancy. Except now, there was no worry, trepidation, or fear. There was only exuberance and excitement to meet my great-nephew, and the desperation for August to be there, too. To share this moment, holding my hand and being a part of it all, and I prayed for his strength, so that he could be one day.

"Have you thought of any names yet?" Mark asked, just as the picture was passed into my hands.

"Um, well, kind of," Christy answered, looking over my shoulder to smile adoringly at her baby boy. "It's kind of boring, but I really like the name Michael."

The first and second sonogram pictures I'd seen, I could hardly make out what I was looking at. But now, I could clearly make out the shape of his head, the little buds of his arms and legs, and I brushed my thumb over what was obviously his tiny nose.

"I like it," I agreed, nodding. "Michael is a good, strong name."

"Hey, is someone's phone ringing?" Mark asked. The room fell silent, and sure enough, there was the telltale buzz of a phone's vibrating tone. He pulled his phone out and checked the screen, then shook his head. "It's not mine."

In unison, except for the twins, we all took a peek at our respective phones, and when my glowing screen met my curious eyes, I nearly dropped the sonogram picture from my shaking fingers.

"Oh, my God," I blurted at the sight of August's name. "I-I need to take this," I hurriedly added, as I stood from the table and laid the picture of baby Michael in front of Christy.

"Hello? August?" I answered, narrowly avoiding bumping into a waiter, carrying a tray of drinks into my family's party room.

The distinct sound of someone taking a deep breath came through the speaker, and then ...

"Clarabell."

My name was released on a relieved exhale, whispered and pained, and at the sound of his voice, I slumped against a wall beside the door leading to the restaurant's kitchen. My eyelids slammed shut, holding back the tears, as I clapped a hand over my trembling lips.

After two long weeks and some days of waiting to receive this call, I hadn't found the time to practice what my reaction would be when I finally heard from him again. But I'm not sure I could've predicted the pounding of my racing, frantic heart, or the tears that squeezed between my pinched lids. Then, the sob that escaped my open lips from behind my hand. I found so much relief in the sound of my full name, more than I ever thought possible, and I wished I could more easily find my voice.

"Clara? Are you there?"

I cleared my throat, knowing I needed to say something, anything, and nodded. "Y-yeah, I'm here," I croaked, as I mustered the strength to hurry toward the women's room. "I'm ... God, I'm just so happy to hear your voice." I laughed, not knowing what else to do with all of these emotions flooding my veins, as I ran inside, ducking into a stall and locking the door.

"I know," he answered quietly, regret woven into his words. "I should've called sooner."

"When were you discharged?" I asked. Surely I would have noticed if he hadn't been at the hospital.

"About a week ago."

"A *week*?" The betrayal was quick to hit my heart, as I turned to face the toilet and pressed my back against the stall door. "You've been home for a whole *week*? But Nana said--"

"I told her not to say anything," he quickly interjected. "I'm sorry about that. And I know I should've called, but I wanted to ... I don't know, clear my head."

With a deep and cleansing exhale, I released the betrayal I felt and encouraged compassion instead. "Right. Of course, I under—"

"Clara, stop doing that, okay?"

Narrowing my eyes, I asked, "Stop doing what?"

"Stop talking yourself out of feeling however you feel," he said, exasperated. "I have my reasons for not calling you sooner, and they are, *I* think, valid, and I would hope you'd accept them for what they are. But you're also allowed to feel hurt that I didn't call you sooner. You're allowed to feel upset that you haven't heard from me in weeks. You're allowed to feel whatever the hell it is you're feeling, because your emotions are just as valid as my reasons for not talking to you sooner. You don't need to shut them out, and I'm sorry for ever making you feel as though you had to."

A strange, fluttery laugh escaped my throat and burst past my trembling lips, as I said, "I don't think I know how to do that."

"Well, I've been working on a lot of things lately, self-love and that sort of thing, so maybe I can help you a little with that," he said. "If you'd like."

Pulling my lower lip between my teeth, I took the moment of quiet to look back on my life. Forty-two years of focusing on others more than myself, and whenever I had allowed moments of reflection or summers of selfish love, I'd pushed them all away the second they became too much, or too real. My emotions had never felt important, my needs never felt warranted, and so, I had shoved them onto backburner. Until August. Until I'd decided that this was important enough to hold onto. For him, yes, but also for me. I had learned so much in such a short period of time, but there was always room for improvement.

"That would be nice," I replied.

"Great." There was a smile in his voice, and then, he cleared his throat. "Anyway, I know this is very short notice, and I don't know what you have going on right now, but if you're free this evening, I'd really like to see you. It's been a long two weeks, and I don't think I can wait another second to make up for lost time."

My grin was unstoppable. My cheeks burned hot and my body shivered at the delicious thought of being with him again, finally. But then, just as quickly, came the disappointment of remembering where I was and who was waiting for me at the table.

"I can't tonight," I said regrettably. "I'm out with my family. We're, we're celebrating ..."

"Celebrating?"

"Yeah, um ... Christy ..." I blew out a breath, releasing what remained of my excitement and anticipation. "Christy found out the sex of the baby today. She's having a boy."

"Seriously?" he exclaimed, just as excited as I'd hoped he'd be.

"Yeah," I replied with an affectionate smile. "She's going to name him Michael, I think."

"That's a great name," he said, and I nodded and quietly said back, "It is," only to kill the momentum of our conversation with those two little words. A discomfort hung heavily in the air between our phone lines, and I tugged at the pendant around my neck, certain it was trying to choke me. There were things to say, so many things that shouldn't be said over the phone, and small talk felt impersonal and inadequate. But not knowing when I'd be able to see him again left my heart jittering anxiously with impatience, and I tugged at the necklace again.

"Okay, well, I'll let you get back to them," August finally said.

"Okay."

"But call me when you're done with dinner, okay? Don't rush on my account, but … maybe I can see you after?"

With a contented sigh, I unlocked the stall door and caught a glimpse of the smiling woman in the mirror. She looked happier than she had in weeks, and I was glad to see her again.

"I will," I replied, and then, headed back to the table.

***

The sidewalk was slick with rain, as I headed toward the bookstore. It was well after closing, and the front window was dark, but August assured me it'd be fine.

Walking up to the brick-faced building, I remembered that first date, just a few months in the past. It was hard to wrap my head around the copious amount of changes my life had faced since that night. Falling in love. Christy's unexpected pregnancy. Phoebe's progress with her father. The inability to see a life without this man who wasn't without demons but left me yearning to stand by his side while we took them into battle.

I was always meant to love him. I couldn't remember if I knew it then, on the day we first met and he was listening to Perry Como, but it all seemed so obvious now. I couldn't wait to see him again, and even though I knew he was here, just beyond these bricks, time seemed to crawl at an excruciating pace. Seconds turned to hours as I tried the door to find it locked, and I groaned, reaching into my bag to dig out my phone. But before I could dial his number, a text came through.

August: Come around back.

He never texted, and I considered replying to tease him about it. But I was too excited, too eager, and I ran as fast as my heels could take me in the rain.

The bookstore's back door led to a musty storage room of boxes, books, and dust covered antiquities that I would've admired, had it not been so dark and dingy. Beneath my breath, I cursed him for making this so difficult and made a mental note to give him grief, when I heard the faintest tinkling of piano keys the closer I got to an open door.

The store was dark, illuminated only by a few spotlights of recessed lighting, but I didn't have far to walk before I came upon the baby grand piano. There, I found August, hunched over the keys, his fingers dancing with dexterous skill. I only listened intently to a few notes before recognizing Elvis Presley's "Can't Help Falling in Love," and I approached slowly, while begging my tears to remain at bay.

"The first time you snuck up on me like that, I couldn't tell you were there." He spoke while continuing to play, and I laughed softly, not wanting to overpower his song. "But now, I can feel you there before my ears, nose, or eyes can give you away. My soul knows yours too well now, I guess."

I sat beside him on the bench and pressed my arm to his, to revel in the comfort of having him there. Then, I turned to look at him and his closely cropped beard, much neater now than when I'd driven him to the hospital, and his curls that now rested at the tops of his ears and not below them, as they had been that night. His gaze was stolen from the keys for the briefest of moments, lifting to glance into mine, and there I saw his silver stars, sparkling in the fathomless depths of brown. The power of his spirit was burning bright, the way it had when we'd first met, and my soul held tight to his, grateful for whatever had made him better and brought him back to me.

"I missed you so much," I couldn't help but say, and he looked away as his lips curled into a smile.

"I missed me, too," he replied. "But I missed you more."

The books encircling the piano spied on me, as I lowered my temple to his shoulder, whispering their stories, questions, and accusations as he finished the song. My lips moved in time, silently singing along and asking him to take my hand and my whole life, too, and I hoped his soul knew mine well enough to listen.

Then, when it was over, his hands stilled, and the store and all its literary inhabitants fell into an eerie quiet. My heart thundered inside its cage, and August breathed, his shoulder lifting with every push and pull of his lungs.

"Clarabell," he finally said. "I'm sorry."

Lifting my head at the sound of his rough, raw voice, I asked, "For what?"

"For ..." He shrugged halfheartedly. "Being an ass, Not listening to your concerns, not ... caring enough about them or you or myself ..." He shrugged again, then turned to me. "For everything, I guess."

I shook my head, wishing he wouldn't apologize for something he had no control over. "You can't help—"

"I knew what I was doing when I went off my meds, and I was a selfish prick for doing that to you. So, whether you want to accept it or not, I am offering my apology, because it really is the least that I can do."

I lowered my gaze to his hands, still frozen against the keys. I grabbed one, held it tight within my grasp, and said, "I forgive you."

The sigh that pushed through his lips was laced so heavily in relief, I thought he might float away and out of my reach, as his head fell back and he said, "Thank you."

Then, he told me he was back on medication, a different prescription this time and one that didn't suffocate his creativity. He spoke of the new drug with a gratitude I knew was directed toward Dr. Sherman, and I wanted to hug my friend for bringing him back to me in every aspect of his being.

"What about your publisher? Have you spoken to them at all?" I asked.

He shook his head. "They've made their decision, and that's fine. I'll keep writing, because it's what I do, and hope for the best. But if nothing comes of it, I will learn to be happy with what I've done already."

"You know, you could always self-publish," I suggested, and he nodded.

"Maybe. But before I think about that, I need to work on me." His eyes met mine as he smiled. "Someone told me recently that I need to learn to love myself, and I realized she was right. So, in the meantime," he gestured out toward the bookstore, "I work here now."

"Since when?" I asked.

"Well, the guy who owns it had told me a while back that if I ever needed a job to let him know. I never told you, but before you took me to St. Mary's, I had quit my job at the coffee shop. So, when I got out, I really needed a new job. So, I came in and asked if the offer was still on the table." Then, he grinned and lifted a shoulder in a shrug. "I figure, if I can't publish my own work right now, working with others who do, is the next best thing. Plus," he patted the glossy, black top of the piano, "now, I can play whenever I want."

Then, just like that, his smile wilted, and he sighed. I braced my heart for whatever came next, half expecting him to tell me he couldn't find a place for me in his life when he was working hard on himself. And I would have respected that, I would have accepted it, and I would have left ... but I didn't want to. What I wanted, more than anything, was to pull him into my arms and hold on tight until there wasn't a doubt in either of our minds that this was infinitely it for us both.

But the ball was in his court, and I waited.

"Clara," he said, his voice low and rumbling from deep in his chest. "I don't know what other plans you have for tonight, but—"

"I was going to take a bath and go to bed," I interrupted, my heart racing as he looked up and into my eyes with a hunger I recognized and knew well.

"Then, if it isn't too presumptuous of me, I'd like to invite myself to join you," he said, moving his hand from mine, to rest against my thigh.

I leaned into him, plummeting into the heat of his gaze, and drowned in the promise I found there for a thousand more summers and every season in between. He brushed his lips against mine, squeezing my thigh with urgent, desperate fingers, and every nerve I had unraveled and disappeared until there was nothing left but a confidence in this love.

Then, before kissing him back in a far less gentle way, knowing it was unlikely we'd make it to the bath anytime soon, I wrapped my arms around his neck and whispered, "I hope you do."

EPILOGUE

The sun caressed my skin and touched my hair, as I laid near the beach's edge. The blanket was soft against my belly, and I sighed, closing my eyes and resting my head on my folded arms. It was the perfect day—hot and sunny, with the gentlest of breezes coming off the water and waves. It was the type of day where you scrap your To-Do list and decide to instead read a book or sunbathe on the shore, which is exactly what I had done. Not August, though. Because, as much as he loved me, he hadn't yet developed a love for the summer. So, while I was browning my Winter-pale skin, my husband was sitting in his office, across the hall from our bedroom. Typing away on his laptop.

In the year since we had met, I had watched him change. With Doctor Sylvie Sherman's recommendation, he had changed medications, lowered the dosage, and discovered coping methods he'd been previously unaware of. He made sure to attend their bi-weekly therapy sessions, and all of that combined seemed to encourage his metamorphosis. The result was a man in control of his mind and actions, capable of creating without losing himself in the process.

It was only when he believed in his ability to be better, that he proposed to me. Then, a week later, in the River Canyon Town Hall lobby, we were married by the mayor. Marjie had asked why we had rushed things, instead of taking our time planning a wedding. But, as I'd explained to her, I had waited long enough for a man like him, and August wasn't one to wait at all.

My phone buzzed beside me, stealing my mind away from the memory of our small, impromptu wedding. I glanced at the screen to find that Christy had texted me. Smiling, I opened the message to see a picture of my great-nephew, Michael—Mikey for short.

"Look at him," I cooed to nobody but the gulls. He was only a couple months old, but he was already so different than he'd been when he was first born. Smiling, close to sitting up, and beginning to recognize the people he knew best. It was incredible to watch him grow, and just as beautiful to witness Christy's transformation into motherhood.

No longer one to prefer text over voice, I dialed her number and only had to wait a few seconds before she answered.

"Hey, Aunt Clara," she said, a smile in her voice. "I take it you saw the picture I sent."

"I did!" I exclaimed. "I can't stand how cute he is. It's too much."

"Right?" she replied with a laugh. "It's amazing I get anything done."

Since finding out she was pregnant, Christy had actually "done" quite a bit. Apart from trudging through the pregnancy and adjusting to the idea of being a single mom, she'd gotten a secretary job at Town Hall and moved into her parents' basement. My sister and her husband had decided to turn their basement into an apartment of sorts for their daughter and grandson, at least until she was able to get herself into a position to find her own place. It wasn't unlike what my parents had done for Marjie, when she had found herself pregnant at sixteen, and I marveled at the devotion the members of my family held for each other. It was a special and rare thing, and I knew I was blessed to play a part.

"You do a lot," I assured my niece, closing my eyes to the sun's bright rays.

"I think I do too much," she laughed. "Did Mom tell you I'm going back to work in a couple weeks?"

"She did."

"Like, on one hand, I'm excited to be getting out of the house," she replied with a sigh. "But on the other, I'm going to miss Mikey so much."

"I know, honey. It'll be good for you, though. You know, just to see other people. You have to be so sick of looking at your mom's face," I teased gently, while knowing my sister and her daughter could never be sick of each other.

"Oh, trust me, I am," she played along. "But really, it's not so bad."

Then, there was a pause to the conversation, and a heavier breeze lifted off the water and curled the edges of my blanket. It was getting late, and the sun was starting to set. Soon, I'd have to cook dinner and drag August away from his writing long enough to eat, and I smiled at the thought. Even though we lived together, and I saw him every single day, I found I missed him during days like these, when he spent more time at the keyboard than he did with me.

"Aunt Clara, I gotta go," Christy said. "My food just got here."

"God, you and that app," I mumbled, laughing and rolling my eyes.

"Hey, if it weren't for this app, I'd never remember to eat," she fired back playfully. "And I'd never talk to anybody but people in this family."

"It's so weird that you're friends with your food delivery guy," I jabbed with another laugh.

Christy exaggerated a gasp. "You leave Kev alone," she exclaimed with a laugh. "For real, I'm hanging up now. I don't want cold tacos. Love you!"

"Love you, too, honey," I said, laughing as I hung up the phone.

***

"So, how's the new book coming along?" I asked, looking at August over the brim of my glass of water.

He glared at me, with every one of those silver stars glinting in his eyes. "You know I'm never going to answer that," he replied, chuckling as he shook his head.

"I'm not asking what it's *about*," I muttered, rolling my eyes. "I'm asking how it's *going*."

"Oh, well, in that case," he said, leaning back in his chair, "I think it might actually be the best thing I've ever written."

As I lowered my glass to the table, I exclaimed, "Seriously?"

He nodded. "I've honestly never written with this much clarity before. Absolutely nothing is blocking my creativity, and that's just ..." He shook his head with bewilderment and gratitude. "It's amazing. There's no other way to describe how *good* I feel."

Since beginning his new treatment plan with Dr. Sherman, August had kept his writing to a minimum. The inspiration to sit behind the screen of his computer hadn't struck in a long time. Until a few weeks ago, when in the middle of the night, he sprang out of bed and ran across the hall, into his office. For a moment, I'd been worried, thinking that his late-night, volatile writing stints of the past were back with a vengeance. But I heard nothing but the clacking of keys, and then, a couple hours later, he was back in bed with a smile on his face. It was a relief for both of us, to now trust in his ability to write without losing control. I hoped we always could.

"I've been thinking ... I might actually publish this one," August said, in a nearly hesitant way.

"Really?" I asked, surprised. "Are you going to talk to your agent, or—"

"No, no," he replied, shaking his head. "I actually think I might try my hand at self-publishing."

Slowly, I began to nod, as I remembered the suggestion Sylvie had made not too long ago, during one of their therapy sessions. "I think that's a great idea."

"So do I," he replied. "I think it could do me a lot of good to not have a deadline looming over my head, you know? I can write at my own speed, publish whenever I'm ready ..." He pulled in a deep breath, then smiled reflectively. "I feel good about it."

Intertwining my fingers with his, I returned the smile and replied, "I feel good about a lot of things right now."

August pulled my hand to his lips and kissed my knuckles, before saying, "So do I, Clarabell. So do I."

THE END

For more from Kelsey Kingsley, please visit her
website at:

http://www.kelseykingsley.com

ACKNOWLEDGMENTS

First, thank you, Ernest Hemingway, for providing me with the inspiration to write this book in the first place.

Next, thank you to my husband, Danny, for always supporting my need to talk to my imaginary friends. And thank you to our son, Jude, for being a good boy for Daddy and his aunts and grandma while I write (and thank you to them for always being there to watch him).

Thank you to Jess for being the best editor I could ask for. I lucked out with that one.

Thank you to my beta readers. I was certain this book was garbage until they read it. My confidence would be nothing without them.

Thank you to Murphy Rae for this STELLAR cover. My God. She took my vision and brought it to life, like a freakin' magician.

Thank you to my author pals for the constant encouragement. I'm surrounded by some fantastic talent, and I am blessed to be welcomed into their world.

Lastly, thank you, Dear Reader. My dreams never would've come true without you, and although I know I must sound like I'm beating a dead horse, I can never thank you enough for what you do. Thank you, thank you, thank you, thank you.

ABOUT THE AUTHOR

Kelsey Kingsley is a legally blind gal living in New York with her husband, her son, and a black-and-white cat named Ethel. She really loves doughnuts, tea, and Edgar Allan Poe.

She believes there is a song for every situation.

She has a potty mouth and doesn't eat cheese.

Other Books by Kelsey Kingsley

Holly Freakin' Hughes

Daisies & Devin

The Life We Wanted

Tell Me Goodnight

Forget the Stars

Warrior Blue

The Life We Have

Where We Went Wrong

Scars & Silver Linings

A Circle of Crows

Hoping for Hemingway

The Kinney Brothers Series
One Night to Fall (Kinney Brothers #1)

To Fall for Winter (Kinney Brothers #2)

Last Chance to Fall (Kinney Brothers #3)

Hope to Fall (Kinney Brothers #4)